OutCast

THE UN-MAGICIAN

OUTCAST

THE UN-MAGICIAN

CHRISTOPHER GOLDEN & THOMAS E. SNIEGOSKI

SCHOLASTIC INC.

New York Toronto London Auckland Sydney
Mexico City New Delhi Hong Kong Buenos A

No part of this publication may be reproduced, stored in a retrieval system, or transmitted in any form or by any means, electronic, mechanical, photocopying, recording, or otherwise, without written permission of the publisher. For information regarding permission, write to Aladdin Paperbacks, Simon & Schuster Children's Publishing Division, 1230 Avenue of the Americas, New York, NY 10020.

ISBN 0-439-74622-1

12 11 10 9 8 7 6 5 4 3 2   5 6 7 8 9 10/0

Printed in the U.S.A.   40

First Scholastic printing, February 2005

Designed by Debra Sfetsios
The text of this book was set in Bembo.

For Nicholas, Daniel, and Lily
—C. G.

For Harry and Hugo, the gods of beer, bacon, and good times
—T. S.

Our eternal gratitude to Connie and LeeAnne, for putting up with us. To Mulder, for puppy love. Special thanks to Lisa Clancy, without whom this series would not have gotten off the ground, and to Samantha Schutz, for imagination and enthusiasm. Thanks also to Mom and Dad Sniegoski, Dave Kraus, David Carroll, Paul Griffin, Bob and Pat, Flo and Jon, and Tim Cole and the usual lunatics. To Mom and Peter, Jose Nieto, Bob Tomko, Amber Benson, Rick Hautala, Allie Costa, Peter Donaldson, and Ashleigh Bergh.

OutCast

THE UN-MAGICIAN

CHAPTER ONE

The city of Arcanum was in mourning. Black bunting unfurled from open windows, and the flags of every magical guild had been lowered to half-mast. The ghostfire that burned inside the city's spherical street lanterns had been altered in hue; once golden, it was now scarlet, and would remain so for one full week. Many shops and offices were closed, and thousands of the city's mages had turned out to observe the funeral pyre that raged in the center of Temple Square—all to witness the ritual burning, all to mark the passing of Argus Cade.

In that grieving city, very few others were out and about this night, and those who were gave no notice to the ornate silver carriage that swept through the streets. It floated silently along, crimson lantern light splashing upon its surface, taking the twists and turns of its route with a deftness that revealed the skill of its driver. The silver vehicle whispered through the city several feet above the cobblestones. The carriage doors were emblazoned with a lion about to pounce, the family crest of its occupant. At each of the four corners of the carriage was an image of a silver dragon curled in a mysterious repose.

Perched upon the carriage's high seat was a man draped in deep blue robes, a heavy veil covering his face. His hands were held out in front of him and from his fingertips tendrils of crackling cobalt energy sparked toward the ground far below, fingers of cerulean fire investigating the road ahead of the carriage. He was a navigation mage, just as his father had been, two generations spent perfecting the sorcery of transportation. It was a worthy endeavor. Honest work for an honest man.

Inside the vehicle was Leander Maddox, the man whose family crest adorned its doors. The carriage made the slightest of hums—generated by the navigator's magic—but it was little more than white noise to him. Leander was lost in thought, adrift in the aching sadness left behind in the wake of the death of his mentor and greatest friend. He forced himself to focus on the task that lay before him.

As Argus Cade's apprentice, it fell to him to close down the old sorcerer's residence and to collect whatever papers or journals he might have left behind.

"Argus," Leander whispered to himself, raising a massive hand and covering his face with it. A sigh escaped him and he shuddered, settling more deeply into the velvet seat within the carriage.

The loss pained him deeply. Argus Cade had been the greatest sorcerer of his generation, a master of the magical sciences, an adviser to kings and prime ministers, but to Leander all of those things paled beside the man's kindness and courage. He had been more than a mentor. He had been an example.

Leander had lost his own father as a boy, and Argus had always given him the guidance he would have wished for from a father. And in the midst of the political games and power struggles of the Parliament of Mages, Argus had never compromised his beliefs, never allied himself with anyone who did not share them, and never kept silent to avoid controversy. He was his own man, and had earned great respect for that position.

Leander glanced out the window at the street lanterns, scarlet ghostlights throwing red shadows on the nearby homes and shops as the carriage climbed through the winding street that led up into August Hill, the most exclusive neighborhood in Arcanum. How often as a young man had he trod the cobblestones and steps of this hill on his way to Argus's home? Still each doorway, each sign hanging outside the window of a pub, was familiar.

The navigator slowed the carriage as the street twisted once more, rising up toward the pinnacle of August Hill, where homes hung alongside the ground itself, magic woven into every bit of architecture to keep them aloft. Lower down, the buildings were constructed upon the ground, but as the terrain became steeper, the houses were merely anchored to the earth, jutting out at level angles from the side of the hill.

The sadness in his heart made Leander close his eyes again. He had been here only three nights past . . . the very night that Argus had died. With his eyes closed he could not stop his mind from slipping back in time, from reliving again those tragic final hours of a great man. Argus had been in his bed, the lamps burning low, a gloom settling upon his chamber. He had always been thin, but Argus had become almost skeletal. His long, hooked nose even more prominent than usual, jutted from his sallow, weathered face.

From time to time Argus would open his eyes and there would be a light in them, a spark, and he would laugh and reminisce about the days when he had first met Leander. As a professor at the University of Saint Germain, Argus had taken the burly, leonine man under his wing, and when they were seen together, other mages would remark on what an odd pair they made.

In later years, well after the death of Argus's beloved wife, Norah, the mage had grown withdrawn, keeping his own counsel, and allowing only Leander into his private thoughts. Other than his household servants, the outside world saw Argus only rarely, though he made his opinions known to Parliament and to the heads of the guilds often enough. Leander was a professor at the university himself, now, in the very chair Argus had once held. He had been the great sorcerer's student, his apprentice, and his only real friend.

Leander felt blessed to have had Argus Cade in his life.

But there were things other than grief haunting him now, though all of them connected to Argus's death. Not all of the old mage's ramblings had been sensible, not all of them accompanied by that spark in his eyes. Indeed, some of the things he had said as his spirit was slipping away, as his body and mind were failing him, had confounded Leander greatly.

The hum of the carriage grew louder and the world outside its windows darker, with only the faintest hint of red hues. There were only a few homes this high upon August Hill and, this far from the ground, it required great effort and magical skill for the navigator to carry them here.

Leander barely noticed. His thoughts had been in turmoil ever since Argus's death, but in among that jumble there was something more subtle that was bothering him. Though it was nonsense, it haunted him more with each passing hour.

In his rambling Argus had said things that were . . . simply impossible. The ravings of a fevered brain.

They *had* to be.

Several times Argus had seemed to be on the verge of sleep, eyelids fluttering, only to have his eyes snap open and stare into the dim bedchamber and to whisper, as if afraid someone would hear:

"The boy. I must see to the boy."

At the end, when every breath came in a rattling rasp and seemed likely to be his last, the old sorcerer had let his head loll to one side and, spying Leander, had thrust out a hand and clutched his arm with a ferocious, preternatural strength.

In that moment, though he had tried to deny it to himself,

Leander had seen utter clarity in Argus's eyes. Total focus.

"Timothy," the old man had rasped. "I have kept him well hidden these years, but the secret must be revealed now. To you, Leander, and only to you. You must promise to look after him. 'Pon this one thing more than any other, I must have your vow."

Despite the clarity he saw in Argus's eyes, Leander had told himself that it must be the nearness of death talking. Norah Cade had died while giving birth to their only child, Timothy, and the trauma of his entrance into the world had been too much for the infant; Timothy himself had died within an hour of his mother. It seemed to Leander that Argus had woven an intricate fantasy for himself in which the boy had lived.

Argus had been dying, and all Leander had wanted was to comfort him. The aged mage had asked for his vow, and to give him solace Leander had agreed, promising that he would look after Timothy as if the boy were his very own son.

One final, rattling breath had been Argus's only response, and then the sorcerer had succumbed to the one enemy magic could never overcome. Death had whispered through Argus Cade's bedchamber. The old man's eyes were dull, his chest still, and the light in the room, even in the world itself, had diminished.

In the rush of details that followed, the many things necessary to prepare a suitable memorial, Leander had pushed his grief aside. It lingered, though, a hollow ache in his chest and the pit of his stomach, and Argus's final words also lingered, echoing, coming back again and again.

Impossible, Leander thought.

Yet it was with a certain dread curiosity that he glanced now through the window as the carriage drew up in front of the Cade estate. The house was enormous. It had been shaped and reshaped many times upon the whim of its master. Gables jutted from the roof and vine-covered latticework spilled down the sides, dangling below. Only the southernmost side, where the house faced the peak of August Hill, was anchored to the ground. Otherwise it sprang from the hill at an angle that seemed, in comparison to the level homes in most areas of the city, to be a spectacle of strange geometry.

The navigator moored the carriage at the base of the grand staircase at the front of the house.

"Shall I wait for you, Master Maddox?" the navigator called down to him.

Leander pushed open the door and stepped out over the sheer drop down August Hill, onto the staircase that lay in the shadow of Cade mansion. He glanced up at the navigator's veiled face.

"Please do, Caiaphas. I do not know how long I shall be. However, if you need to rest, be at ease."

"Thank you, sir."

With that, he left the navigator and began the trek up the marble steps in front of the house. Far below, Leander could see the city, the golden lights that gleamed within the homes and the scarlet ghostfire of the street lanterns. An orange glow flickered at the center of Arcanum, and it warmed him to see that the remains of Argus's funeral pyre still burned. It was as though the old mage had not gone yet, not completely. There was still a tether that connected Leander to his dead mentor, for another hour yet. Another hour.

He waved his hand in front of Argus's door and a flicker of violet light danced between his fingers, a spell that was a key. As far as Leander knew, he was the only person alive who had the spell-key to the Cade estate. He steeled himself for the task ahead of him, arranging the dead man's papers, sorting what should go to the university for posterity from what ought to remain secret and known only to Leander. There was research Leander would continue on Argus's behalf, but there were other things as well, things no one else should ever discover. That was the nature of magic.

The door swung open. The house had been empty since its master's death, all of the servants dismissed and everything left precisely as it had been.

Leander passed a hand over the Alhazred dragon insignia upon the wall and the lamps blazed to life. The foyer of the great house was bathed in a warm glow that revealed the portraits upon the walls, the wooden gryphons that sat atop the posts at the base of the stairs, and the elegant Morrigish carpet that ran along the corridor ahead as well as up the circular staircase that wound through the heart of the house.

Inside, Leander brushed his fingers thoughtfully through his thick beard. There was nothing for him to do but begin the work he had come for. He crossed the foyer and started up the stairs.

Vertigo made him grasp the handrail tightly as he went up and up, around in circles; this staircase always seemed far longer to him than it actually was. If he chanced a look down, his vision would swim, for the foyer seemed so far below.

Leander paused and shook his head, chuckling softly to himself. Argus had been fond of conjure-architecture, and it was just like him to build a staircase that would touch the senses, that would inspire thoughts of grandeur and magnificence. The young mage took another step and focused upward.

A flutter of black wings slapped the air and talons swung down toward his face.

"Caw! Caw!" screamed the raven as it glided past him, circling back around and then soaring upward. A moment later it came to roost half a dozen steps from where Leander now crouched with his hands up in defense. His heart was pounding in his chest and violet light sparked from his fingers, but now Leander drew a long breath and let it out slowly.

"Accursed bird," the young mage muttered. "You vex me, Edgar. Truly you do."

There were other words, other curses, that might have flowed from him then, but instead Leander paused and stared at the rook. Slowly he shook his head. This was not right. Not possible. Many mages had animal familiars, companions whom magic had made far wiser than the average beast. The wizards of old had begun this tradition and some kept it up even to this day.

This rook with silken black feathers and glittering ebon eyes had been Argus Cade's familiar. But in all the lore Leander had read, and in all of his experience, a familiar was supposed to die with its master or mistress. Yet Edgar was not dead. The rook perched upon the curving stairs ahead, gleaming shadow eyes locked upon Leander himself, as though the bird thought him an intruder.

"Out of the way, Edgar," Leander muttered. "I've no idea how you survive, but I am here at your master's behest to carry out his final wishes."

"Caw!" cried the rook. And it cocked its head to cast him a withering glare. "Final wishes?" Then it shook its wings out, feathers ruffling. "You doubt him. You should not."

A chill raced through his bones and images of Argus's final hour flashed in his mind. Nothing was as it should have been. Edgar's presence, Argus's strange ravings. Before Leander could demand an explanation, the rook cried out again and took flight, soaring higher and higher up through the tunnel made by the circular stairwell. Leander called after him, but Edgar only cawed and then began to glide round and round under the high ceiling at the top of the house, like a carrion hunter awaiting the weakening of its prey.

Leander climbed the remainder of the stairs at a furious pace, questions and suspicions, wonder and impossibility filling his mind. When he at last reached the top, Edgar circled his head.

"What do you mean, rook?" he demanded. "Tell me what you mean."

"Tell you? Caw! I'll show you!" the bird replied, and with a single beat of his wings, Edgar began to guide him.

The rook led him along one hallway after another, through doors he had never seen, and around corners that appeared to be solid walls until one looked at them from a certain angle. The entire place echoed with the whimsy of a conjure-architect. Argus's fancy once again. There were halls without windows, and corridors with windows that showed impossible views, yet had no doors.

At last the bird led him into a short, narrow, featureless hall without portrait, mirror, or tapestry. The only adornment in this particular corridor was a single door, sheathed in black fire and scarlet mist, barred by glittering green razor wire and blue ice.

The sight of it took Leander's breath away. In all his years with Argus he had never seen this door, and now that he had, his imagination ran rampant with curiosity at what it might hide. "What in all the worlds is this?"

"Enter!" said the rook.

Leander could not help himself. He laughed. "Idiot bird. You say it as if it is the simplest thing in the world. Even the greatest sorcerer, even the wizards of old, could spend a lifetime deciphering the spells used to bar this door."

Edgar glided to the ground. When he had alighted, he hopped several steps nearer the churning magics that blocked the door. Then he tilted his head again and gazed at Leander.

"Caw! True, true!" said the rook. "But the wizards of old would not have the key! Only you! Caw! Only you have the key!"

Holding his breath, Leander stepped forward and waved his

hand in front of the door. Sparks of violet danced from his fingers and all of the magics that barred the door evaporated in an instant, leaving only wisps of black flame and the chill of ice in the air. Leander's breath fogged as he gasped in amazement.

The door sprang open, spilling bright light into the corridor.

The rook's wings fluttered again as he took flight. With Edgar just ahead of him, Leander went through the door.

The white sun shone warmly down upon the Island of Patience, painting the sky a golden yellow that stretched far out across the ocean. In every direction was beauty and desolation, the sky above, the ocean below. The wind whispered through the tall Yaquis trees, their long fronds drooping down to hide the fat, juicy fruit that dangled beneath their branches. The surf washed upon the shores of Patience, and its hushed voice filled the air as if in response to the wind.

On a rocky stretch of the small island's shore, a tumble of enormous stones had been arranged into a promontory by time and the ocean's whim. At the end of that jetty a boy sat upon his favorite stone and basked in the white sunlight. His body had a rich brown hue, like the skin of the Yaquis fruit, and he held in his hand a long pole carved from a branch of that very same tree, chosen for its flexibility. From the hanging leaves of the gnarled Horax trees, further inland, he had made a strong twine. The boy had a mind for such things and had created a spool upon which to wind the twine and a crank with which to turn the spool.

He had created this device, this fishing pole, at the age of six. It made the catching of fish far easier than wading the surf with a spear. In truth, he enjoyed fishing now, and why not? The warm stones beneath, the yellow sky above, the emerald ocean crashing against the rocks . . . and when the fish were ready to be caught and eaten, they would let him know by tugging upon the bone hook at the end of his line.

Tranquility.

It was called the Island of Patience, after all. Though he himself had given it that name.

On this fine day, however, that tranquility was interrupted.

"Caw! Caw, caw!"

The boy's eyes went wide and he laughed happily as he launched himself up from the rocks. He nearly forgot all about his fishing pole, then paused to quickly crank the spool, reeling in the hook and the shattered shellfish he had used as bait. He could easily build a new one, but better to take care now. With the hook reeled in, he put the pole over his shoulder and leaped from stone to stone, deftly navigating the treacherous rocks of the promontory until he reached the shore.

"Caw! Caw!" came the cry of the rook once more. The boy saw it ahead, circling high in the air.

"Edgar!" the boy called excitedly.

But in his heart, that was not the word he shouted. In his heart he shouted, *Father!* For the arrival of the rook meant that his father had come to visit him again. It had been so long—months, by the boy's reckoning—that he had begun to despair of ever seeing his father again.

The rocky coast gave way to beach, a broad expanse of red-hued sand that flew up behind his feet as he sprinted along the shoreline, eyes searching for the door. Then he saw it and his heart leaped. As always, the ornate door and its elegant frame had appeared where no door could possibly have been, hanging in the air above the red sand, just a few feet from the surf.

The door hung open.

The boy's steps began to falter.

The rook cried again and fluttered to land atop the door

frame, perching there and gazing at the boy as he slowed his approach. The figure that had just emerged from the door and now stood upon the beach, just as out of place in that peaceful spot as the door itself, was not his father. This man wore a heavy, deep green cloak with the hood thrown back. He was startlingly tall and broad shouldered, with a thick beard and a dark mane of hair falling around his face in such a way that he reminded the boy of an image his father had conjured once during a lesson. The stranger reminded the boy of a lion.

Yet he was not a stranger, not really. For though the face was unfamiliar to him, the boy had been given his description.

His pace slowed. The boy walked carefully toward the man, his fishing pole slung across his shoulder. The man gazed at him with wide, astonished eyes, just as he gazed at everything else around him. The rook looked on, quietly observant.

"You're Leander Maddox," the boy said, barely able to hear the rasp of his own voice above the surf.

"I am," the massive visitor agreed with a nod.

The boy hung his head, gaze fixed upon his browned feet in the red-hued sand.

"Then my father is dead."

CHAPTER TWO

"Timothy?" **Leander** stared incredulously at the boy, raising his voice to be heard over the rush of the surf crashing down upon the beach.

The dark-skinned youth looked up from his sandy feet with tears in his large eyes. "Yes."

From his perch atop the mystical doorway, Edgar cawed loudly, mournfully, and then the rook glided down to alight upon the boy's bare shoulder. "I'm sorry, kid," the bird said, managing to convey his sympathy with both his eyes and his tone.

"Then it's true?" the boy asked, gazing at Edgar, who seemed markedly different now that he was in Timothy's presence. "My father *is* dead?"

The rook bobbed up and down upon the boy's shoulder before answering. "Caw! I hate to be the one to tell you, but yes. He's gone, Tim."

A warm, moist breeze blew off the water and Leander was again struck by the enormity of the deception that had just been revealed to him.

"Timothy," he said again, striding across the thick sand, away from the open door that would return him to the real world and normalcy. He stared at this boy, this extraordinary, impossible boy. "You're alive," he proclaimed, feeling like a simpleton, but unable to overcome his astonishment.

The rook fluttered his wings, feathers beating the air. "The kid's just learned that his father has passed. How about a little sympathy?" Edgar berated him.

Leander had never heard Argus Cade's familiar speak in such a manner and found it to be a bit disconcerting. He wondered if this new facility with language—albeit coarse language—was a result of his presence on the island, or some aftereffect of Argus's death. *Or perhaps,* he thought, *Edgar always had such an abrasive personality, and it was yet another thing hidden from me.* Not that it mattered, for the rook was right. In his shock, Leander had been deeply insensitive to the boy's feelings.

"My deepest condolences, Timothy," Leander offered, bowing his head in apology. "Please excuse me. I *am* truly sorry for your loss. It's only that I am overwhelmed, you see, by the shock of finding you here—alive."

The boy appeared to be in relatively good health. He was fit and alert, well muscled for a child of his age, and his sun-darkened skin gleamed. Leander had already noticed the pole Timothy held over his shoulder and wondered at its purpose.

"My father warned me that you would react this way at first," Timothy said. His gaze had drifted to the ocean, his sadness terrible to see. Now, though, he raised his eyes and studied Leander's face. "He told me that if anything happened to him, you would come, and that I was to explain to you why I'm here."

"That can wait, Tim," Edgar suggested. "Take some time for yourself. You have the right to mourn as we all did."

The boy smiled sadly and reached up to gently stroke the rook's head. "That's all right, Edgar. My father prepared me for this. He told me Leander wasn't the most patient of mages. He shouldn't have to wait for this mystery to be explained to him."

The bird glared at Leander from the boy's shoulder. "Do what you have to," he said begrudgingly.

Leander felt a tremor of guilt go through him—the boy ought to be given time to mourn—but at the same time he could barely contain his curiosity. He had to know why his friend and mentor would strand his only child this way, abandon him, away from the world.

"Why, Timothy?" the mage asked, stooping to gaze into the boy's eyes. "Why this charade—why did your father want the world to think you were dead?"

Timothy lowered himself down onto the red sand, as if the weight of his knowledge had finally proved too much, crushing him to the ground. Edgar fluttered from his shoulder to land beside him, as though to stand sentry over the boy. The bird began to pace.

"Because I was born different," Timothy said, running his fingers through the dark red granules. He did not look up, and Leander thought he seemed almost ashamed.

"Different, my boy?" The mage dropped to one knee in the sand and put a comforting hand on his shoulder. "Different how?"

Timothy let the red sand sift through his fingers as he contemplated his answer.

"Timothy?" Leander prodded.

"I can't do things like everybody else can," he said, finally lifting his gaze. Another balmy breeze from the ocean ruffled his dark, curly hair and he squinted to keep the sand from his eyes. "I can't do magic," he said. The revelation seemed to sap the strength from his body and he again returned his shamefaced gaze to the rose-hued beach.

Leander frowned, bewildered. "You are unskilled at the art? Not as adept as your father? But surely that's no reason to—"

Edgar fluttered his wings in annoyance. "Listen to what the kid is saying, Leander," the bird squawked. "He can't *do* magic."

The mage looked from the bird to the boy. Timothy almost seemed to have gotten smaller, as if he was withdrawing into himself.

"I can't say it any simpler than that," the boy explained. "My father told me that the world runs on magic, that it's in every-thing, and it connects everyone in a circuit of sorcerous power. But not me. I'm not part of that circuit. There's no sorcery in me. I've no magical ability at all."

Leander was so astounded that he could only stare. These words Timothy spoke with simplicity were words of horror or some morbid jest. To be entirely without magic was tantamount to being without a heartbeat or being unable to breathe. But it was true. Of course it was true. For Argus Cade to have hidden his son away like this—at least now it had begun to make a certain bizarre sort of sense.

"I . . . I'm sorry for staring, Timothy. It's just . . . I've never heard of such a thing," he blurted out, again feeling ashamed by his lack of sensitivity. "That's utterly incredible."

"Hukk! Hukk!" Edgar cried. "Now you see? That's why Master Argus opened the door, why he created an annex here. It's a pocket dimension, but adjoining our own. Simple sorcery for one as skilled as he was."

"Was . . . ?" Timothy whispered, becoming increasingly agi-tated, digging his fingers deeper into the red sand beneath him.

"He was safe here," the rook explained. "Protected."

Questions flowed so fast and furiously through Leander's fevered thoughts that the mage almost uttered a spell of tran-quility to calm himself. Timothy appeared visibly upset, and Leander reached a comforting hand toward the youth. "There now," he began, but the boy scrambled to his feet before he could be touched.

"I'm sorry," Timothy said, a firmness to his voice. "But I think I *do* need some time alone." He turned and strode toward the emerald ocean.

"Yes, of course," Leander called after him, his own heart

aching as he tried to make sense of it all. Argus Cade had meant the world to him and now had passed from it, yet here was his son. A boy whose care had been placed in Leander's hands. "Take all the time you need."

An unpleasant sound came from somewhere deep down in Edgar's throat. "Got a bad feeling about this," he squawked ominously as he watched the boy wade into the ocean waves. "Got a bad feeling."

Leander was not certain precisely how long he simply stood there upon the shore of this tropical island in an alternate dimension, numbed by the enormity of the secret that had just been revealed to him. The warm breeze off the water ruffled his green robes and the strong, sweet scent of blossoming fruit trees made him entertain the idea that this was all some sort of dream. Or a spell, perhaps. A spell of enchantment could have caused him to imagine all of this.

He turned toward the ocean, watching the waves roll in upon the shore. In the distance, a small, dark-skinned boy looked tiny and frail amid the vastness of the sea. *This isn't a dream,* he thought, feeling the pangs of sadness. Nor was it a spell.

Leander turned away from the sad scene of a boy in mourning to gaze about the land on which he stood. It didn't appear to be a very large island, but more than sufficient for one young habitant. This might be a pocket dimension, but it was clear to him that it shared many features with the world of his birth, and he wondered how far the island was from the closest large land mass, and whether or not other sentient beings dwelled upon this world.

The beach ringed a lush jungle, an abundance of Yaquis trees waving their fronds in the tranquil winds as if to entice him closer. His stomach gurgled with anticipation—he had always enjoyed the exotic taste of the Yaquis fruit—and Leander realized that he had not eaten a meal in over a day's time, distracted as he had been by business and grief and now, by the incredible.

Further along the shore and slightly inland, Leander spied an encampment he presumed must be the boy's quarters. He shielded his eyes from the sun, squinting to make out more details of the place. Amid a particularly thick grouping of ancient Yaquis, a large rectangular structure had been constructed above the beach, suspended from the trees. A thick band of smoke trailed up from the roof into the yellow sky. There was another, larger structure below. Timothy certainly had adequate shelter in case the elements should change their mood from pleasant to foul.

As he began to gather his thoughts, Leander's mood started to change. The thought of the young boy, here in this place, all alone, filled him with sadness and great concern. No matter the reason for it, he felt an unwelcome anger toward Argus Cade growing within him. His mentor might have told him what had happened, what he planned. And Leander would have advised against it. Surely the world was not so cruel that it would harm a boy so helpless.

Then another thought, a darker thought, entered his mind. He wondered if perhaps Argus had hidden Timothy not out of protective instinct, but out of shame. The idea troubled him profoundly.

"Don't think badly of him," Edgar said, flapping his wings and flying several feet nearer before dropping back onto the beach. The familiar hopped toward him across the thick, red sand. "I can see it in your face, what you're thinking. But Master Argus loved the boy. All he wanted was to keep him safe. This island is a lonely place, but in a way, it's paradise. No one can harm Tim here, and he has learned how to fend for himself, how to survive, how to create what he needs from the world around him. He's brilliant, just like his father."

Leander averted his gaze from the rook, brow furrowed. Argus Cade had been the finest man he had ever known. "I don't know, Edgar," he said, voice a rasp. "Keeping a child cloistered away, albeit one as severely handicapped as Timothy . . . I am having a difficult time convincing myself that there wasn't another way. A better way."

The mage paused and glanced up at the bird. "And you, rook. You're far more talkative and far more knowledgeable than I ever realized. Are there any more secrets you'd care to share with me?"

The bird hobbled closer using short flaps of his ebony wings to help him across the landscape. "Let's make one thing perfectly clear," he croaked. "I know you don't like me—I could always sense it—and the truth is, I really don't care for you all that much. You're a pompous, humorless ass. But like you, I made a promise to Argus Cade before he died."

Leander was taken aback by the bird's candor, but after a moment he nodded. Edgar was right on each count. A flash of memory went through Leander's mind then as he recalled once more the expression on Argus's face as he breathed his last, and the request Argus had made. "He asked me to look after Timothy when he was no longer able."

"Exactly," Edgar said. "Me as his familiar and you as his guardian."

Leander nodded, something from all this business suddenly making sense. "That explains why you didn't die with the passing of your master. He bequeathed you to the child. Is that also why your . . . demeanor has changed so much? A reflection of the boy's youth rather than your former master's dignity?"

The rook ruffled its feathers. "You figured that out all by yourself, did you?" he cackled. "I can see why you were one of Argus's top students."

The mage ignored this jibe and turned his attention back to the subject of their discussion; the boy standing alone in the green sea. In the world into which he was born, Timothy Cade would be a freak, unable to complete the simplest of tasks, from turning on a light to preparing a meal. If he was utterly devoid of magic, he would not be able to learn as other children did, and the ordinary pleasures of youth, like playing with spells of transmutation or levitation, would be denied him.

But he was your son, Argus, Leander thought. *Your son. To hide him away from the world, and hide the world away from him . . .* The mage still did not understand.

Edgar cawed loudly and took flight, soaring overhead in a long, arcing circle. Leander glanced out to sea and saw that the boy was returning, trudging across the sand, away from the hungry pull of the waves. The white orb of this dimension's sun had begun its descent, giving the sand an even darker hue.

"Remember," Edgar said cautiously. "We're sworn to look after his best interests."

Leander did not respond aloud as he watched the stricken youth approach. *His best interests.* He let the words reverberate through his thoughts. *And what exactly does that entail?*

"You know, Timothy, we don't have to do this right away," Leander ventured. "If you need more time—"

The boy reached down to pick up the strange branch he had dropped earlier. "No, I'm okay," he said, slinging it over his bare shoulder. "I just needed to say good-bye to my father." There was a weight to his words, and he glanced out across the ocean. Then he stood straighter and met Leander's gaze. "He said that I should show you Patience. That I should show you all I've done here—all that I've made."

The boy began walking toward the structures that Leander had noticed in the distance earlier.

"Made?" Leander asked, following the boy up the beach as Edgar glided above their heads on the warm currents of air.

"I make things," the boy explained. He held out the pole fashioned from the branch of a tree as an example. "Like this."

"And what exactly have you got there?" the mage asked curiously.

"It's my pole for catching fish," he said proudly. "I made it when I was six."

Timothy demonstrated the strange fishing pole, turning a crank that unwound a line of twine with a piece of curved bone tied to its end. "You put bait for the fish on the bone hook and lower it into the water. When the fish are ready to be caught, they eat the food and tug upon the twine." He pretended that he had caught something in the sand. "I use the crank to pull the fish out of the water."

Leander had never seen anything like it and yet the simple logic of it was wonderful. "Clever," he said appreciatively.

From ahead of them Edgar cawed loudly. He had already reached the structures, and now Leander and Timothy hurried to catch up with him, quickly coming to the building Leander had presumed to be the boy's living quarters. Its walls were gray metal and wooden beams, and its roof was composed of row upon row of secured Yaquis fronds. A ladder rose up through the roof and climbed to a door set into the bottom of the second structure, which was cradled in the trees above. Plumes of smoke issued up from the back of both the ground-level and tree-level structures.

"Did your father make these buildings?"

Timothy paused outside the door and shrugged. "He helped with the framing, based upon my design. But I did the rest of it myself."

"It must have taken a great deal of time."

Timothy leaned the pole against the outer wall of the building. "Yes. But things take as long as they take. It isn't as though I have other appointments to keep," he said as he approached the closed door, also made from the grayish metal.

If this had been any home in the many districts of Arcanum, the boy would have simply waved his hand in front of a mystical eye and the door would have swung wide, welcoming him. Leander narrowed his eyes to observe carefully as the boy lifted a latch, placed his palm against the door and pushed it open with his own power.

"This is my workshop," Timothy said proudly, beckoning him to step inside. With a heavy flap of powerful wings, Edgar flew in over their heads, barely able to find room to alight upon a table that was littered with unusual debris. "This is where I make the things I picture in my head."

To say that Leander was awestruck would have been an understatement. He cast a quick glance about the room, but that would simply not do, and so he began again, slowly surveying his surroundings. Everywhere he looked there was something that aroused curiosity. He saw stacks of wood of all sizes and shapes, some from the tree of the abundant Yaquis, and others of a finer cut, probably brought over from the world outside.

There were large blocks of stone, as well as stacked bars and thin sheets of the same dark metal that made up the workshop's four walls. All around the large chamber were worktables covered in tools at whose function Leander could only guess, and the strangest-looking contraptions that the mage surmised were Timothy's inventions in various stages of completion.

"Caw, caw!" Edgar cried, hopping about at the edge of a worktable. "Never seen anything like it, have you? Go on, admit it."

The rook was correct. There was something crude and primitive about the workshop, as though the corpse of the world had been flayed open to reveal its inner workings, and yet there was something breathtakingly beautiful about it as well.

"Your familiar is proud of you, Timothy," Leander said. "And I'm sure your father must have been as well. This is . . . it's truly fascinating."

The mage continued to glance around, constantly discovering something that he hadn't noticed the first time. At the rear of the chamber, he could see into another room where large rocks blazed white-hot in a stone-and-metal enclosure. Leander gathered that this furnace was the source for the plumes of smoke or steam he had seen from outside. *Hungry Fire,* he thought. *Without access to the ghostfire, the boy bends Hungry Fire to his purpose.*

"Back there's where I do most of my work with the metal," Timothy said, apparently amused by his guest's response to his workshop.

Leander gazed around at the mostly incomprehensible contents of the main chamber. "You just think of these things?" he asked the boy as he picked up what looked like an attempt to fashion a bird's skeleton from pieces of wood. "You just imagined this—and you built it?"

The boy carefully took the wooden item from the mage's hands, careful not to damage the delicate construction. "I've come to believe that most things that can be done with magic can be duplicated mechanically."

Leander watched with interest as Timothy manipulated a tiny lever of the skeleton's framework and the wings on the device began to flap up and down. "This is just my model," the boy explained, placing it down on the worktable for Edgar to see. "If things test out, I'll build a much bigger version and be able to fly just as well as Edgar here."

The bird flapped his wings in agitation, apparently as startled by the boy's declaration as Leander was.

"And have you always had this gift?" Leander asked.

Timothy shrugged shyly. "My father encouraged me a lot. He brought me all the things I needed to create and survive here." A pall seemed to fall over the boy, dispersing his excitement, as he was reminded that his father would never again visit the Island of Patience.

"I think about what I want to do, and eventually a picture of the things I need to accomplish it forms in my head—then I build it," he said matter-of-factly. He absently straightened some of the items on a nearby workstation.

Absolutely wondrous, Leander thought. Denied the gift of magic, another ability had arisen in the boy to compensate; his very own, special kind of magic had developed.

Leander wanted to inquire about more of the inventions and models in the workshop, but he was interrupted by the sound of a door rattling open at the back of the building. The thing that emerged from that open door startled him into silence, amazing him more than all the wonders around him combined. It came into the room pushing a wheeled cart loaded high with gleaming pieces of dark stone. Leander could only stare at the man-that-was-not-a-man. It was shaped like a man but made of a metal the color of coin. Smoke—*no, steam*—escaped with a hiss from a cylindrical opening connected to the side of its square head. Its round eyes shone brightly as its gaze fell upon them.

"Oh, Timothy, you're back," it said pleasantly, its voice echoing as if from inside a well. "I stumbled upon a lovely vein of heatstone quite by accident while foraging some mannaroot for supper." It wheeled the cart farther into the room, its metal feet clomping heavily upon the wood floor, and placed its load near the door leading into the furnace chamber. "I see you've brought home some company."

Leander stared at Timothy Cade in shock. "In Alhazred's name, what is that?"

"That's Sheridan," Timothy said, watching as the metal man began to unload its cart. "I made him, too."

"And what a fabulous job he did," Sheridan said, executing a small bow as another hissing blast of steam jetted from the side of his head.

"And he's also a very good friend," Timothy said with a chuckle. The boy presented his company to the machine. "This is Leander Maddox, Sheridan, a very dear friend of my father's," he said. "And, of course, you know Edgar."

"Pleased to make your acquaintance, Mr. Maddox," Sheridan said with another slight bow. "And it's always good to see you here, Edgar."

The rook squawked. "I missed you too, handsome."

"Did Master Argus accompany you on this visit?" the mechanism asked cheerily.

Leander dropped his gaze, hesitant, and neither Timothy nor Edgar leaped into the silence with an explanation. But that somber quiet was enough for the metal man to glean some understanding. "Oh, dear." Sheridan's red eyes dimmed. "How horribly sad," he said with a shake of his blocky head.

The room remained uncomfortably silent.

"You made—him?" Leander asked, hoping to lift the oppressive pall.

The boy hopped up on one of the tables. "He was very hard to build, probably my most difficult creation," he answered. "I still haven't got all the bugs out of him just yet, have I, Sheridan?"

The machine held out its arms and wiggled three segmented fingers and a thumb on each hand. "My hands still seem to get a bit stiff when it's going to rain," he said thoughtfully, "but other than that, I get by just fine."

Leander chuckled heartily, a low rumbling laugh deep in his chest as he shook his head in disbelief. "I'm not sure how many more surprises I can stand in one day," he said. The welcome sound of his laughter proved contagious, for Timothy chuckled as well.

Their laughter trailed off and the uncomfortable silence returned until Leander's stomach suddenly rumbled.

"Oh, my," the mage said, embarrassed, laying a hand upon his growling belly. "Please excuse me."

"What've you got, Dire Wolves under that robe?" Edgar asked, flying up from the table to land again upon the boy's shoulder. "Shouldn't really be teasing the mage," the bird chided himself in a whisper that everyone could hear. "I'm hungry too. Is there anything to eat?"

There was no glass in the windows of the workshop, though Leander did not doubt that had he desired to do so, Timothy could have found a way to create a translucent material that would take the place of the transparency spell magicians used. Given the island's tropical climate, the windows were simply open, though there were shutters that Leander imagined the boy closed in case of high winds or a severe rainstorm. Now, however, at the mention of food, Timothy glanced out a window and noticed that the sun had set and the island was peaceful in twilight.

"How rude of me," the boy said, hopping down from his seat on the table. "It's way past suppertime. Please forgive me. My father is the only guest I've ever had, and he never failed to remind me when it was time for a meal."

The boy strode across the workshop to a crank that jutted from the wall. It was very similar in design to the one on his pole, but larger and made of metal. Timothy turned the crank and gazed upward at an opening in the ceiling, from which a ladder began to descend. When he had lowered it fully, he gestured up the ladder toward the opening. "Follow me upstairs and I'll see if I can't put supper together." And the boy started to climb.

"Very nice meeting you, Master Maddox," Sheridan said with a wave of his hand. "I've some tidying up to do in the workshop, but hopefully I will see you again before you depart." A blast of steam shot from the side of his head in a whistling blast as he hefted the cart of stone and wheeled it farther into the back of the workshop.

"It was a pleasure to meet you as well," Leander said, still in awe of the mechanical man. Then he began to climb the ladder from the workshop up to Timothy's dwelling. It was certainly an evening of surprises, and the mage could only wonder what marvels were yet to come.

Edgar fluttered through the opening first and Leander followed, squeezing his large form through the narrow hole into the boy's living quarters. It was quaint, furnished with simple, practical pieces of dark wood. A large black pot hung over a fire in a hearth, and a delicious aroma that made his mouth water filled the air. Yes, it was similar to a dwelling back home, but looking carefully, he could see the things that made this place different. Yaquis fronds covered the walls, and a peek out the windows showed a strange world, where an ice-blue moon was surrounded by four smaller moons, all of them hanging weightlessly in the night sky above an undulating alien sea.

"Welcome to my home," Timothy said, a warm smile on his sun-darkened features. Despite his grief, he seemed to be enjoying this rare contact with an outsider.

How lonely it must have been for him to grow up here, with only rare visits from his father, and a metal man for company, Leander thought. His earlier thoughts persisted. No matter how he had worked to transform the island, Patience was not truly Timothy's home.

"Something sure smells tasty," Edgar croaked, perching atop the back of a chair beside a small dining table. The rook flapped his wings in anticipation, ruffling the thick black feathers around his neck.

The boy beamed, turning toward the pot that bubbled in the hearth. "It looks like Ivar started cooking before we even got to the workshop, so we shouldn't have to wait too long before we eat."

The boy's mention of an unfamiliar name snagged Leander's attention. "Ivar?" he asked. "Who—"

A round vegetable, with skin very like the color of the ocean outside, suddenly seemed to float up into the air from a woven basket at the base of the hearth. It hovered, then dropped into the steaming pot with a splash.

Leander's mind raced. *Is there magic at work here after all?* He could see nothing but a slight shimmer in the air before the stone fireplace.

"He's not used to company either," Timothy said, directing his stare toward the same shimmering spot. "It's okay, Ivar," he said. "You know Edgar. And Master Maddox—Leander—is a friend. They came because my father is . . ."

The air in front of the hearth seemed to thicken, growing darker as something began to materialize. *No, not materialize,* the mage determined. The man had been there all along; it was just that Leander had been unable to see him.

"Ivar is an Asura," Timothy said quietly, glancing at Leander.

Leander looked at the boy askance. "Surely not. They're extinct, the Asura. Savages. The last of the tribe died out half a century ago or more."

Timothy chuckled softly. "Well, he looks fairly healthy to me. I don't know the whole story, but Ivar was living here long before I arrived. My father brought him here, just as he brought me. Ivar looked after me when I was a baby. He and Sheridan are the best friends I have." He looked away from Ivar and a sad smile crept across his face. "The only friends I have, really, now that my father is gone."

Leander was sensitive to the boy's sadness, yet he could not help staring in amazement at the Asura warrior. The savage tribe was not extinct after all; there still lived at least one last warrior. Here was another thing Argus Cade had kept from him, and Leander had to wonder what else his mentor had failed to mention.

According to what he knew of them, the Asura were an ancient race, much more in tune with the natural order of things than the supernatural. The tales told of fierce warriors and great hunters, who had resisted overreliance upon magic and been ostracized as primitives, as savages. When more "civilized" peoples tried to take their homelands, the Asura had fought back and been destroyed.

Ivar leaned over the bubbling pot, stirring the contents with a large wooden spoon. His skin was fair, a pale white, but at a moment's notice its color could change, allowing him to blend with his surroundings. It was a unique talent that had made the Asura such expert hunters.

"All who are present now were friends of the Arguscade," the Asura said in a voice like the rumble of a distant storm. "This meal we shall consume in his honor. The pleasure we receive from it shall be bestowed upon him in the great lands beyond this."

Ivar turned his pale features to all that were present to see if they were in agreement with what he had proposed. Leander had seen only portraitures of the ancient people and was taken by the Asura's strange but fascinating appearance. Ivar was short and powerfully built, pale, almost translucent, with not a trace of hair upon his body. Leander had read that strange patterns demonstrating an Asura's mood could appear on the skin, but currently Ivar's flesh was unblemished. His eyes were dark, penetrating, and his cheekbones high and pointed. He was dressed only in breeches made from dried animal skin.

Everyone agreed that the meal would be eaten in Argus's honor, and in a matter of minutes, they were dining upon a stew of exotic vegetables and fish, the bounty of Patience.

"I usually prefer my meat raw," Edgar said, plucking a chunk from the bowl that had been set down before him in the center of the table. Timothy's familiar tossed the fish back in his throat and gulped it down. "But this isn't bad at all. My compliments to the chef."

Ivar, sitting cross-legged upon the floor, bowed his bald head as he received the familiar's praise.

Seated across from Timothy, in one of the two chairs, Leander watched from the corner of his eye as the boy ate his meal. Though they had met only hours ago, the mage found that he was already quite fond of the youth. There was so much about him that reminded the mage of the boy's father: the way Timothy moved, the way he held his head when he talked. It was like having part of his old friend still around, and the thought of him hidden away in this place was cause for concern.

They finished their hearty meal and cleaned up. Then Ivar excused himself to return to his own dwelling and commune with the spirits of his ancestors, as was the custom of his people. It was peaceful and calm upon the island of Patience, but Leander found himself growing restless, his mind tormented by the frustration he felt with Timothy's banishment.

Edgar dozed, perched atop the back of Timothy's chair, and the boy eagerly showed the mage countless drawings of inventions he had not yet found time to build. When Timothy finished describing a contraption that would allow him to breathe beneath the water, Leander took the opportunity to ask the lad a question that had been on his mind since walking through the secret door in the Cade mansion and finding himself on the sands of Patience.

"Are you happy here, Timothy?"

The question froze the boy. This young man, this un-magician, blinked and then glanced over at Leander. "Of course I'm happy. The island is beauty and peace and my friends are here. And I . . ." Timothy stopped. He might have been pondering the question for the very first time. His brow furrowed and he placed the latest drawing back on the pile.

"I suppose I never really thought about it much," he answered. "This is all I've ever known, so I would guess that I'm happy—aren't I?"

Leander reached across the table and placed a comforting hand on the boy's shoulder. "I cannot answer that for you, Timothy," he said. "But if it was me, just the knowledge that there was something more than this—something beyond Patience—would make me at least curious to explore, both the world and my place in it."

Timothy lowered his head sadly. "Then I guess I'll never really be able to answer your question. I'll never know if I'm happy or not; Patience is all that I'm allowed to know."

"Do you truly believe that?" Leander asked.

The boy looked up, his eyes glassy with emotion. "I can never leave Patience," he said, voice cracking. "It would be too dangerous. I could not survive."

"Ah, but are you certain of that?" Leander asked. "It would be difficult, I've no doubt, but with my help, I'm confident that you would manage."

The mage felt some small doubt, knowing that what he suggested was quite against the wishes of his late mentor. But what he had vowed was to watch over Timothy as if the boy were his own, and if that was the case, then he knew he was doing the right thing. Argus Cade may have been one of the most powerful mages in the world, and the closest friend that he had ever known, but the old man had been wrong in banishing his son, no matter his reasons. Timothy never should have been hidden away, and Leander wanted to rectify his mentor's error.

"Let me take you from this place to the world beyond, the world of your birth," Leander said, grinning and smoothing down his beard. "I will show you there is more to a world than Patience."

Timothy leaped out of his chair, startling Edgar from his nap. His pulse raced, his skin prickling with sensations of heat and cold that had nothing to do with the weather and everything to do with the fear and excitement that began to combat each other in his heart.

"That's impossible!" Timothy said, staring at Leander's face, searching the massive mage's eyes for the truth.

"Caw!" the rook crowed, flapping his wings in surprise. "What's going on?" he asked.

Timothy scratched at the back of his head, breathing evenly, forcing himself to calm down. He began to pace the floor as Leander looked on, eyes sparkling amid all that hair. The boy stopped short and gazed at the mage sitting at the table. "Can I leave Patience?" he asked, and the question felt strange upon his lips.

"All you need do is follow me back through the door on the sand."

Edgar flapped his wings insistently and cawed loudly enough

to forestall any further conversation until he was given their attention. "What's going on? What did I miss? Who's following who?"

Timothy turned to look imploringly at the bird. "You heard him, Edgar. My father said I could never leave—that it wasn't safe. He said that there were people in government and in the guilds who might wish me harm."

The bird's feathers ruffled. "Well, that is what he said, but—"

"Preposterous!" Leander dismissed those words with the wave of one of his massive hands. "Your condition would be looked upon as a handicap and be treated as such. You have nothing to fear from the world outside."

Timothy was terrified, and as he slowly walked to his window, gazing out at the only world he had ever known, he imagined for the very first time that he might step beyond it.

"Just a moment," Edgar cawed from his perch. "Maybe we're moving too quickly."

"Nonsense," Leander boomed. "The boy has been banished long enough."

Properly chagrined, the bird cocked his head pensively. "Well, maybe some day trips to start." Edgar glanced at Timothy. "You won't even know if you're going to like it back there. It's quite different from your little island, let me tell you."

Timothy turned from the window, tremors of excitement unlike anything he had ever known coursing through his body. *This is what it must feel like to have magic inside you,* he thought. And then he spoke the four words that would change his life forever.

"I want to go."

CHAPTER THREE

It was the oddest sensation, stepping through that door on the beach and into a shadowy corridor. How many times had he hugged his father good-bye and watched him step through this very same door, only to have the door disappear from the sand as though it had never been there at all? Magic. That was magic.

Timothy's heart felt as though it might explode, and he held his breath until his chest hurt, just gazing around at his surroundings. Edgar had led the way, cawing loudly, excitedly, and Leander had followed next. Now the rook sat upon the shoulder of the red-maned sorcerer and watched expectantly as Timothy took several steps farther into his father's house.

"My father's house," he whispered, unconsciously putting voice to his thoughts.

"*Your* house now," Leander told him, a warm rumble in his voice and a twinkle of approval in his eye. "Welcome to the city of Arcanum, Timothy Cade. The city of your birth."

The boy froze. Ivar slipped silently past him, blending with the shadows so that he was barely visible, a chameleon, investigating the corridor ahead, sniffing the air. The aged warrior was on guard for anything that might threaten his friends. A moment later Timothy heard the clanking of metal as Sheridan entered this world, also for the first time. They had all passed through now, and suddenly the island of Patience seemed dreadfully far away.

"Hukk! Hukk!" cried Edgar, black wings fluttering as he perched on Leander's shoulder. "You all right, Tim?"

Timothy forced himself to take a breath. He nodded slowly. "I think so."

But that was a lie. He was not all right. Not at all. Though he had sometimes been lonely on the island, Timothy had rarely been afraid. Now fear spread through him with a rush of heat in his veins, as though he had been stung by a cloudfish, its venom infecting him instantly. But that sort of infection was not deadly. In truth it passed quickly enough. And this . . . this fear . . . he wondered if it would ever pass.

How many times had his father explained to him why he had to live alone? Dozens. Hundreds. Here, he was helpless, crippled. Here, he was in peril. People would not understand, his father had told him. And what people did not understand, they often mocked, and sometimes tried to destroy. *An abomination,* his father had said. People would think Timothy was an abomination. And though his father had never hinted anything of the kind, the boy had always sensed that, in a way, Argus agreed.

The corridor was dimly lit by globular lanterns that hung at intervals along its length. It took him a moment to realize that they were not secured to the wall and instead floated in the air. The walls were of a dark wood, with intricate designs branded above each door and on the frames. The floorboards were lighter in color and had a sheen that reflected the flickering lantern light.

A tremor went through him, but this time Timothy did not think what he was feeling was fear. A tiny smile creased the corners of his mouth and he stepped toward the wall. He felt the others all watching him as he gazed curiously up at the gleaming globe.

"How does it work?" he asked.

Leander did not answer at first, so Timothy turned to look at him. The big man ran a hand over his beard, smoothing its tangles, and shrugged. "I don't think I can answer that question. It's magic, Timothy. Everything in this world is magic. The lamps can be lit by command or by simply waving your hand beneath them. They sense your desire for light."

Timothy grunted in acceptance and gazed at the globe again. No oil. No actual fire. No anchor to attach it to the wall. His father had told him much of magic, but many things had been hard to imagine without firsthand knowledge. Magic, he knew, had no mechanism.

Tentatively he waved his hand beneath the globe. It continued to shine.

"It's true, then," Leander observed.

The boy did not even acknowledge his statement. Of course it was true. His father had removed him from his home, hidden him away all of these years . . . he would never have done this unless he was certain. But Leander also seemed certain. Images of his father, whose kind eyes had always seemed out of place in the midst of such stern features, floated into the boy's mind.

Timothy's chin drooped slightly. He missed his father.

With a quiet hiss of steam, Sheridan placed a hand upon his shoulder. Timothy smiled and nodded. The metal man always seemed to know when Timothy was sad or lonely.

Taking a deep breath, the boy looked at the globe again, then he started along the corridor. Edgar took flight, wings beating the air only long enough for him to move from Leander's shoulder to Timothy's. The boy glanced up at the rook and smiled, and though the usually loquacious bird said nothing, Timothy thought there was something in his bearing that approximated a smile in return. At least, as much as a bird could be said to have any facial expression at all.

Of course, Edgar was no ordinary bird.

With a courteous nod, Leander moved out of the way, and

Timothy began to explore, moving down the corridor. There were places where the woodwork was intricate, where images had been seemingly carved into the wood—but of course they would not have been carved, but drawn there with magic. It was so difficult for him to imagine, for Timothy loved to do things with his hands, to create, to feel the texture and the workings of things beneath his touch.

He stopped when he arrived at a door. Upon its wooden surface there danced a swirl of color, violets and greens that flitted together like seabirds courting. With a raised eyebrow, he shot an inquisitive glance at Leander.

"Ah, yes. You think it a symbol," Leander noted. "Often there are such symbols on doors or around them, indicating what might lie beyond. Other times you might find symbols and colors that indicate the presence of a barrier spell. This is merely decoration, however. It is—"

"Art?" Timothy asked.

Leander nodded appreciatively. "Yes. In a manner of speaking, it is art."

The door had no visible latch or handle. Tentatively Timothy reached out and laid his hand upon it. The wood was warm to touch. The swirling colors of the art misted around his wrist.

"You won't be able to—," Leander began.

Timothy pushed and the door swung open. On the other side was a chamber swathed in near darkness. Only the illumination from the hall shed any light upon its contents, which included a rack of yellowed scrolls of varying lengths and thicknesses.

"Caw!" Edgar cried, rustling wings and resettling his talons on the boy's shoulder. "Well, that's interesting."

"What is?" Timothy asked.

When he turned to glance at Leander again he found the mage staring at him. Timothy shifted uncomfortably. Sheridan's joints creaked slightly as he bent to peer into the darkened room. Beyond him, Ivar was only partially visible, his eyes darting about in search of any potential threat, hand on the pommel of a knife he wore in a scabbard at his waist.

Neither of his friends from the island seemed shocked the way Leander did. The mage shook his head in apparent disbelief, and then a low, humorless laugh escaped his lips.

"It seems we may have to rethink what it means that you are bereft of magic," Leander said thoughtfully. At Timothy's puzzled expression, he nodded toward the door. "Close that."

Timothy did as he had instructed, pulling the door toward him and letting it swing back into place with a click. Leander motioned to Ivar.

"Come, my friend. Your turn. Open this door, please."

The warrior emerged from the darkness, his body gaining definition as he came closer to the others, as though it was more difficult to remain unseen up close. The black tribal markings on his face and arms changed even as Timothy watched him, some fading, some stretching until they looked almost like claw marks upon his flesh, others swirling into strange symbols.

Ivar glanced wordlessly at Timothy and then cautiously reached out for the door. He flattened his palm on the wood, fingers splayed, and pushed.

Nothing happened.

Ivar glanced at Timothy, the tribal marks receding, fading from his skin. The marks came and went. The boy had asked Ivar about them several times, but the warrior was the last of his kind and the marks were personal to him. He did not like to discuss their purpose or significance.

"I don't understand," Timothy said, glancing at Leander.

The mage loomed forward and waved a hand in front of the door, which swung open instantly.

"Doors are ensorcelled to admit only those their master or mistress would welcome. This door does not recognize Ivar. It would not open for him. If it had recognized you, it would have opened of its own accord the moment you reached out toward it."

Timothy frowned. "But it did open for me." He shook his head, gesturing toward the edge of the door. "This is silly, Leander. Look at it. There isn't even a lock or bolt to keep it closed. Anyone should be able to push it open."

Leander stroked his beard again. "Not anyone, young Master Timothy. Not Ivar. Nor I, myself, if the door did not know me. You have no magic of your own, we knew that much. But it seems there's more to it than that. If the door will open for you, it can only mean that the enchantment fused into the wood cannot sense your presence. I . . . well, I've honestly never seen anything like it."

A spark ignited within Timothy in that moment. All his life, in those times when he allowed himself to think of himself in relation to his father's world, he had known what he was. *A freak. An abomination. Useless.* Yet as he turned to look back at the door there was the tiniest glimmer of wonder inside him as he considered the idea that it might not be so terrible being a freak.

The spark was extinguished a moment later, buried beneath years of darker expectations.

Still, as Timothy glanced around at his friends once more—and at the magic door and the levitating lanterns—a wave of relief washed through him. He had been prepared to retreat immediately to Patience, had felt the fear bubbling up inside him. Yet suddenly the fear had been dispelled, and he saw before him only possibility.

A grin spread across his features. The island was his home, but this mansion held within its walls his entire history, his father's legacy. Timothy had no intention of staying permanently, but he wanted to explore. He glanced at the walls, at the doors, and thought how simple it would be to rig oil lamps to light the place.

Ivar slid into the shadows. Sheridan watched Timothy expectantly, a tiny wisp of steam curling up from the spout on the side of his head, his eyes glowing brightly.

The rook cawed, and Timothy glanced to his left, eye to eye with the bird.

"You're too quiet, kid. Talk to me. Whaddayathink?" Edgar asked.

Timothy's gaze shifted to Leander, then to Ivar, and came to rest on Sheridan. "I want to see it," he said, feeling a prickle of excitement rush through him. "I want to see everything."

He started down the corridor again, much more swiftly this time, noting the presence of every door and every bit of art adorning any surface. There was a window at the far end but he never reached it. The hallway turned and Timothy followed, and soon enough he was practically running. Edgar cawed and took flight, soaring along above him, then turning back to circle his head.

Timothy wanted to look in every room, to catalog in his mind everything he could learn about his father, about magic, about this world. Transforming this house so that a boy without any trace of sorcerous power could live here would be a fantastic undertaking.

Yet, in a way, it thrilled him, for it would be his greatest project ever.

Around another turn in the warren of corridors, he found himself at the top of a set of circular stairs that wound down into the heart of the house. Ivar was beside him, silently keeping pace without effort. Sheridan clanked along the floorboards, trying to keep sight of them, steam hissing from his metal skull. Leander strode quickly along, watching them all with an expression of wonder.

Though there was much to explore, Timothy had a greater priority. The very first thing he wanted to see lay below. He started down the stairs, quickly descending toward the ground floor, gazing around at the grand chandeliers that glowed with magical incandescence and down the hallways of the floors that he passed. When he reached the foyer, he looked up and saw the others coming down as well. Leander seemed to be moving much more slowly.

The burly mage leaned over the rail of the circular stair and gazed down at him.

"Timothy? How did you get down all of these stairs so quickly?"

The question puzzled the boy, and he frowned as he watched Leander continue slowly downward, still only halfway to the ground floor. Even Sheridan had made his way nearer the bottom of the stairs, gyros whirring and steam spitting.

"There aren't that many stairs," Timothy said. "Why are you moving so slowly? Are you all right?"

Leander paused on the steps and squinted down at Timothy as if trying to focus his vision. The big man swayed from side to side ever so slightly. Then he craned his head around, peering in every direction and at last gazing upward at the massive central crystal chandelier. At length his attention returned to Timothy.

"I knew there was an enchantment on the stairs, but I never understood why," Leander said. He tsked loudly and shook his head and a small chuckle escaped his lips. "There's a glamour cast on the stairs. Argus must not have thought visitors would find it grand enough, so he . . . altered their perception."

Timothy had no idea what the mage was talking about, but

already the conversation was slipping away from him. The rhythm of his heart increased and his chest was tight with excitement and, yes, a little bit of fear. He had not banished it completely. Holding his breath, the hair rising on the back of his neck, a warm prickling running over his skin, Timothy turned toward the massive front door.

Above him, Edgar cawed loudly, fluttered to a landing, and rested atop a large statue—a stone representation of a creature Timothy had never seen in all the scrolls his father had brought him.

"Careful, kid," the rook warned.

Timothy stepped toward the front door, reached for it . . . and then took a step back as the wiry form of Ivar emerged from invisibility beside him. The warrior crouched slightly, so that his face would be level with the boy's.

"You are certain this is wise?" Ivar asked.

With a deep breath, Timothy shook his head. "No. Not certain at all. But I'm not going to let that stop me."

For a long moment the warrior gazed at Timothy, golden eyes gleaming with their own inner light. Then, slowly, Ivar nodded and stepped aside, gesturing toward the door. Timothy reached for it, laid his hand upon the thick, dark, deeply grained wood.

And he pushed.

The door swung wide.

Timothy felt his mouth opening, jaw dropping, but it was as if his entire body was behaving of its own volition. A whistle of breath escaped his throat, the tiniest sound.

He saw it all: The broad, stone steps in front of the mansion ended in nothingness. Some kind of conveyance, a vehicle of sorts, floated in the air at the bottom of the steps. If he walked off the bottom stair he would plunge into a nighttime abyss that would tumble him down and down for hundreds of feet before he at last collided with the face of the mountain cliff upon which the mansion had been built. Timothy whipped his head to the side and noted the place where the corner of the house was rooted—anchored—to the mountainside, and wondered if that was to keep the structure from falling or from floating away. There was magic in every inch of architecture here.

The night sky was painted with swaths of milky luminescence, and beyond that veil was a sky filled with stars and ghostly orbs that must have been moons or nearby planets. Timothy tore his gaze from the heavens and cast it downward, beyond the stairs, beyond the base of the mountain, to the pale, glittering rainbow of lights that flitted about the sprawling landscape of the city below.

Arcanum.

Home? he wondered.

It was breathtaking. All of it. But he was not ready to step off into the abyss just yet. Timothy Cade reached out and closed the door, then turned to look back into his father's house. He stood in the foyer with his friends around him. Ivar was crouched by the door, on guard as always. Edgar was perched atop Sheridan's shoulder, black eyes gleaming. Leander had only just reached the bottom of the circular stairs. He wore an expectant gaze.

Timothy smiled. "I think I'll start small."

One week later, on a beautiful morning when migrating birds filled the blue sky above Arcanum with song, Leander returned to the Cade estate under very different circumstances. The world still mourned the passing of Argus Cade, the Parliament still recalled his memory at every session, and even the most hideous of magical guilds professed to honor his name. None of them were aware of the extraordinary events that had transpired that night when Leander Maddox had first attempted to deal with the aftermath of Argus Cade's death, to collect his research and fulfill his final wishes.

The world did not yet know about Timothy Cade.

Leander had spent every night since at that home at the peak of August Hill, and during the day he stayed every hour he could be spared from his duties at the University of Saint Germain. Along with the savage Ivar and the mechanical man, whose every word and motion still astounded Leander, Timothy had traveled back and forth to the Island of Patience many times during that long week to gather supplies from his workshop. Timothy saw everything as a challenge, as a puzzle to be solved, and he was quickly adapting the house to deal with his magical handicap.

Extraordinary boy, Leander thought now.

Upon his high seat, the navigation mage had his fingers splayed before him, reins of cobalt energy guiding and lifting the carriage. Behind his veil, Caiaphas was silent, though Leander knew the man must be exhausted from a week of journeying up and down the sheer face of August Hill. He made a mental note to reward Caiaphas in the next wage cycle.

Leander leaned over to gaze out the window of the carriage, his eyes riveted upon the peak of the mountain, upon the turret he could barely see, jutting from those dizzying heights even far-ther up toward the heavens. A cold ache filled his heart, and for a moment, Leander closed his eyes. These past days had been filled with such wonder and excitement that there were times he could forget his grief at the passing of his friend and mentor. Then he would see something of Argus in Timothy's face, or think of the old mage in a quiet moment, and his sadness would return.

"His passing is a loss to all of us," rasped a voice beside Leander, a voice as deep and cold as the ocean.

A kind of peace settled upon Leander's heart, and he nodded once, then turned to gaze at his passenger. Lord Nicodemus was ancient, far older even than Argus had been, yet there was a vitality to him that belied his age. His fine hair was silver, as was the mustache that hung down far below his chin, and his eyes were the pale translucent blue of the deepest ice. Upon the seat beside him sat the gray, hairless feline, Alastor, Nicodemus's familiar. Not all mages had familiars, and one look at the purring, hideous creature on the seat reminded Leander why he had chosen against one.

"Yes, of course, my lord," he replied. He wanted to say more, to explain that while Nicodemus was speaking about Argus's talent, his skills as a mage, that he himself missed the man, not the magician. That Argus had been his friend. But he knew that Nicodemus was offering his condolences, in a way, and so he said nothing more.

For several moments they sat together in silence as the navigation mage guided the carriage up August Hill. Leander knew it was an honor to have Nicodemus with him. The man was Grandmaster of the Order of Alhazred, the guild to which Argus had belonged, and of which Leander was still a member. Nicodemus was among the most powerful men in the Parliament of Mages, respected both as a diplomat and a sorcerer.

The world was divided in two ways: into nations and into guilds. Arcanum was the capital city of the nation of Sunderlund, yet the concept of nations had come to mean less and less over the ages as the guilds began to spread across the world. Every country was populated by members of a variety of guilds, and it was truly the Parliament of Mages that ruled, not any sovereign, national government.

Leander had in his own carriage this beautiful, sunny day one of the most powerful men in the world.

Lord Nicodemus shifted upon the plush seat, either uncomfortable or impatient. Leander glanced at him and his anxiety grew. The Grandmaster had agreed to accompany him to the Cade estate in Leander's carriage to avoid drawing unwanted attention. When Leander had told him about the boy, Nicodemus had agreed that the decision to bring him into this world was appropriate, but he had warned Leander that if everything he said was true, Argus Cade might well have been correct in his concern for his son.

If, Leander thought now. Nicodemus wanted to meet the boy for himself. And why not, since despite his handicap, the boy was a member of the Order of Alhazred by birth. Nicodemus would want to see the progeny of Argus Cade for himself, to witness the truth of his . . . affliction.

The navigator guided the carriage to the front steps of the Cade estate and held it there, floating in the air. It seemed to Leander that the carriage was steadier than usual, and he wondered if Caiaphas was making an extra effort because of his venerable passenger.

Leander stepped out of the carriage and held the door for Nicodemus, who scooped the cat up from the seat and carried it in his arms as he exited the conveyance with greater ease than his age should have allowed. Like one of the Wizards of Old, Nicodemus seemed impervious to age. Leander could never hope to have even a sliver of his power, but he was more than satisfied with his research and his teaching. It was a comfort, though, to have a grandmaster as powerful as Nicodemus leading his guild.

"You may tie off, Caiaphas," Leander told the navigation mage.

Caiaphas nodded, but even veiled by the heavy blue fabric that hid his face, he did not gaze long upon his employer or upon the Cade estate, as if whatever Leander might be up to inside was not for his eyes.

Together the two Alhazred mages went up the stone steps. Leander passed a hand in front of the door and it swung inward. The moment they stepped inside, Nicodemus paused and looked around the foyer, with a chuckle and a gleam in his eye. He dropped Alastor, and the cat immediately raced across the foyer and began to investigate the house. Nicodemus stroked his long mustache.

Leander waved the door closed behind them, blotting out the sun and the wind. At first glance the foyer looked no different than it had when Argus was still alive, but he knew that it would take the Grandmaster only a moment to notice the subtle difference.

"What is . . . ?" Nicodemus began, a frown deepening the lines upon his wizened face. "These lights. What are they?"

Nicodemus strode across the foyer toward a tall wooden stand, upon which had been mounted a fluted glass instrument. Inside the glass, fire burned, but it was not fire as they knew it, not ghostfire.

"They are called oil lamps, my lord," Leander told him.

Nicodemus glanced around, his gaze taking in the other oil lamps in the foyer, two of which had been fastened to the wall. Another was set upon a table beneath a mirror, and yet one other had been clamped to the head of one of the gryphon finials at the bottom of the spiral steps.

"But these are . . . the flames within are Hungry Fire, the destructive blaze!" the Grandmaster said, astonished.

"Indeed." Leander nodded proudly, as though Timothy were his own son. "The boy is clever. He has tamed Hungry Fire, put it to work for him in the same way sorcery uses ghostfire. Wait until you see the kitchen. He has made the most changes there.

Unable to use a magical oven, he has created his own cooking appliance, including a mechanical stove. The bath is another marvel. I opened a waterflow for him, and the boy used metal tubes and other accoutrements to build his own shower."

Nicodemus blinked several times, obviously working to compose himself. "And he did all of this in a single week?"

"Less than a week. A matter of days. Most of the materials he took from his own workshop. Some were already constructed."

Leander had more to say, but he did not get the chance. A clatter of metal echoed through the foyer from the corridor to the left of the staircase, and a moment later Sheridan emerged. The mechanical man's head swiveled with a whir, his red eyes brightened their glow, and he hurried toward them.

"Ah, gentlemen," Sheridan said in his crackling voice, executing a courtly bow. "I thought I heard you enter. Master Maddox, welcome home. And I presume this other gentleman is Lord Nicodemus? It is an honor, sir."

Leander smiled thinly, hoping his beard would hide the expression. He had spent some time teaching Sheridan manners. He was an attentive student, a fast learner.

For a long moment Nicodemus only stood staring at Sheridan with his ice blue eyes, stroking the ends of his mustache. In the long, jade-hued greatcoat he wore, the Grandmaster was an imposing figure, and Leander admired not for the first time the mage's ability to remain calm under extraordinary circumstances.

Slowly, pensively, Nicodemus pulled his gaze away from Sheridan and turned his attention upward, staring at the circular staircase as though he could see through walls and floors to where Timothy would still be working, deep in the heart of the house.

"I want to see the boy," Nicodemus said.

Leander nodded. "Of course, my lord. Right away." He turned to the mechanical man. "Sheridan, find your young master and—"

The air itself was torn asunder with a shriek, a cry of battle that echoed off the walls, spilling down into the foyer from the stairs above. There was the crack of breaking wood and from somewhere distant, shattering glass. Leander looked up just in time to see the Asura warrior, Ivar, thrown against the wooden banister, splintering it. The savage fell end over end, the shadows slipping across his body, swallowing him and then revealing him again. Tribal markings moved fluidly across his skin. With stunning agility, Ivar twisted himself around in the air. As he plummeted toward the floor, he spun and lunged, and his right hand caught the edge of the stairwell below the level from which he had fallen.

Immediately the Asura began to scramble back upward.

"Alhazred's eyes, what is this?" Nicodemus barked. "That . . . that creature. It cannot be what it appears. The savages are all dead."

"Not all," Leander muttered, but he was paying little attention to Nicodemus now. Even as he started for the bottom of the staircase, he heard Edgar caw as the rook soared out over their heads, circling the crystal chandelier.

"Hurry, mage!" the rook cried. "Intruders! Caw! Caw! Assassins!"

The final word chilled Leander's blood. On the bottom step he looked up again. He heard Timothy call his name in the same moment in which he spotted the boy. Tim was running down the stairs, leaping them two at a time, sliding on the banister, anything to speed his descent.

Behind him came the intruders. *Assassins,* Edgar had said. Three, at first, then Leander saw a fourth and a fifth and at last a sixth. They were Cuzcotec, a guild comprised entirely of little sorcerers, men and women as small and slender as children, yet more barbaric than the myths had ever claimed of the Asura.

The Cuzcotec intruders ran low to the ground like animals, leaping down the stairs, one diving downward to catch hold of a banister below. Another vaulted upward to latch onto the chandelier, its crystals tinkling musically as it swayed.

Silently laughing, they set upon the boy. Timothy Cade, the un-magician, was helpless.

CHAPTER FOUR

The Cuzcotec attacker, its flesh the dark color and texture of a coarse-skinned milknut fruit, sprang at Timothy from its perch upon the banister.

Timothy halted his descent, watching as his ugly attacker lighted upon the step below. In a hand which seemed too large for his body, the assassin held what looked like a ball of liquid metal. It couldn't have been. He knew that. For liquefied metal would be too hot to handle. The rough-skinned creature chattered something in a language the boy could not understand, and he watched with a mixture of fear and wonderment as the object in the attacker's hand flowed into the shape of a cruelly curved dagger.

The creature thrust the blade at him with a savage grunt, but Ivar had taught Timothy well and he easily sidestepped this attack. There were beasts on the Island of Patience, some of them ferocious, and Timothy Cade had learned how to survive. Yet even as he dodged, the assassin's blade seemed to extend beyond its limit, as if suddenly elastic, stretching out to find its target. Timothy held his breath. No matter how often he saw it, magic always astonished him.

The creature's chatter had become a high, piercing screech, and his attacker slashed at him frantically with the elongating weapon. Again Timothy avoided the blade, jumping two steps farther up the stairs. Ivar's training again asserted itself as Timothy spotted an opportunity and shot a hard kick at the would-be killer's face.

It was as though the assassin had never even contemplated a physical attack, and had no idea how to counter it. Timothy's heel connected with the rough flesh of the creature's face, crushing its nose with a sharp snap. The killer cried out in shock and pain as it tumbled backward down the remainder of the stairs to lie in a broken heap at Leander's feet. The mage immediately dispatched the stunned creature with a blast of bluish flame from his outstretched hands.

Timothy had no idea how the tiny invaders had gotten into the house. He had been working on some new designs when they had erupted from the shadows, seemingly attacking from out of nowhere. He wanted to explain this to Leander, but he didn't get the chance. The tinkling of the crystal chandelier above alerted him, and he spun to see one of the assassins dangling there, ready to pounce.

"Back off, little man!" squawked Edgar. The rook was a black streak as he darted toward the invader clinging to the ornate light fixture. The ugly creature hissed, flecking its thin beard with bits of its last meal, and lashed out with another of those mystic blades, narrowly missing the fluttering, cawing bird.

Timothy heard Leander below him, barking a litany of guttural, unfamiliar sounds. A blast of blue light sizzled past the boy's face, struck one of the Cuzcotec, and turned it to stone. Timothy tore his gaze away from this breathtaking sight just in time to watch Leander lift one of his large hands and point at the chandelier. The big mage uttered several more snarling sounds and blasts of ruby fire erupted from his fingertips. The torrent of magical energy roared upward, struck the chandelier, and engulfed the distracted assassin.

The creature cried out pathetically as it toppled from the chandelier and landed with a crack and a thump upon the stairs, unmoving, petrified by Leander's spell.

There was further commotion from behind, and Timothy turned, half expecting to see more of the ugly little killers coming at him. And no doubt they would have been, if Ivar had not been there to stop them. The Asura warrior had positioned himself on the stairs to block their access to Timothy and was in the midst of fierce combat with a trio of the swift assassins. They shrieked and spat at Ivar in their ear-piercing dialect, and the Asura responded in kind. There seemed to be a connection between the two primitive tribes. *Perhaps an ancient rivalry,* Timothy thought, overwhelmed with awe as he watched Ivar fight. He knew that Ivar's people were great hunters and fierce warriors, for his father had spoken of the Asura people on numerous occasions, but nothing had prepared him for this.

There was a simplicity in the Asura's movements, every action seeming to come as a natural reaction. It reminded the boy of a dance, a dance with violent and bloody results, but a dance nonetheless. Ivar fought on the stairs with only the knife that Timothy had made for him in his workshop back on Patience. The Asura used the blade as an extension of his body, dipping and weaving from stair to stair, striking at his enemies with what seemed to be very little effort. The expression on Ivar's face remained void of emotion, as it often was. Only the dark, angular patterns that flowed across his pale body as he fought hinted at the fury raging within him.

The assassins did not stand a chance; even with their magical blades of liquid metal, they were easily outmatched. Ivar lashed out, his movements a blur, and two of the creatures fell, bleeding, to the ground, their lives slipping away.

The last of the small killers suddenly spun around and scrambled up the stairs, three at a time, with Ivar in pursuit. Timothy watched captivated as the assassin stopped at the top of the stairs, waving his hands in the air, fingers contorting.

"Caw! He's conjuring an escape route!" Edgar cried, diving and swooping in long circles high above the foyer.

But even as the rook raised this alarm, a tiny hole of solid black appeared in the air above the assassin. The black hole began to grow, and air began to rush into it with a loud, hideous sucking noise. The creature sprang into the opening, slipping into nothingness. Ivar reached out and snagged the assassin's ankle as a hissing bolt of white energy struck the circle of darkness. The escape route was violently closed and the fleeing sorcerer was severed midtorso.

Shocked and repulsed, Timothy turned to see where the deadly bolt of supernatural energy had originated and for the first time became aware of the stranger in the house. He was a tall, older man, thin and almost regal, with a long, silver mustache. The strange mage stood beside Leander; at his sides, his hands were still wreathed in a crackle of magical energy.

Timothy stared down from the circular staircase at this newcomer, who had about him an air of authority and power. "Who . . . who are you?" Timothy asked.

Leander seemed about to reply, but he was interrupted as the regal figure gave a curt bow of the head and began to speak.

"I am Nicodemus." His voice was rich and melodious. "Grandmaster of the Order of Alhazred."

The Grandmaster's piercing eyes focused upon the boy, and for the first time since arriving in his father's house, Timothy felt like an object of curiosity.

"I am most happy to make your acquaintance, Timothy Cade."

A terrible dread filled Leander Maddox. His chest felt tight, as though he could not get enough breath, and he felt cold, though he knew the house was quite warm enough. He watched Timothy's familiar glide across the room. A moment later Edgar touched down upon the boy's shoulder.

"Are you all right?" the bird asked. "They didn't hurt you, did they?" Edgar craned his neck, surveying Timothy's body for injuries.

"I'm fine, Edgar," the boy answered, a slight tremor in his voice. "Just a little shaken up."

Fine, yes. But had Nicodemus and I arrived any later . . . Leander did not want to entertain such thoughts. A terrible truth had begun to make itself clear to the young mage: His mentor, Argus Cade, had not been entirely wrong to think his son would be in danger should the world learn of his existence. By removing him from the Island of Patience, by bringing him through that secret dimensional door, Leander had put Timothy's life in peril. Though he'd had the boy's best interests in mind, his heart ached with the burden of guilt.

Now Leander moved toward the stairs and motioned for the boy to join them in the foyer. "Timothy, please come down here."

The boy descended the remainder of the circular staircase. Just as Edgar had done, Leander examined the child for injuries. Timothy had been lucky. The Cuzcotec were notorious for the savagery exhibited upon their chosen enemies. If the boy had been alone in the house . . . Leander couldn't even imagine the consequences.

"It's okay, Leander, really," Timothy said, managing to muster a small, nervous smile.

Leander brushed the boy's hair back affectionately. He had quickly grown quite fond of Timothy. He was brilliant, his father's son, and yet he was also open and warm and amiable in a way Argus had never been. *What a fool I was to doubt you, Argus,* Leander thought. *Yet now, what can I do to correct my mistake?*

Softly and with purpose, Nicodemus cleared his throat, capturing their attention. Leander placed a hand upon the boy's back and ushered him toward the Grandmaster.

"Nicodemus is the one I was telling you about, Tim," he explained to the youth. "Grandmaster of the Order of Alhazred. If there is anyone in all of Sunderlund who can help you with your . . . affliction, it is he."

Timothy glanced about nervously as he stood before the great mage, then he lowered his head to stare at his bare feet. Even though Leander had provided the boy with adequate footwear, he insisted on going about barefoot, as if still living upon a tropical island.

"I've heard great things about you, sir," the boy managed, still refusing to look up.

"And I, you," Nicodemus replied. The Grandmaster reached out and lifted the boy's chin, forcing Timothy to meet his gaze. A sad smile appeared upon Nicodemus's face. "You have your father's eyes. Argus was among the greatest of us, not merely in our own order, but in all the world. He is sorely missed."

Timothy nodded gratefully, visibly relaxing now that he grew more comfortable in Nicodemus's presence.

A whistling noise filled the foyer, startling Leander, who turned in alarm to find that it was no new attack, but merely a blast of steam from the angled pipe that jutted from the side of Sheridan's head.

The mechanical man clomped closer. "Where are my manners," he said in his echoing, metallic voice. "Can I get anybody some refreshments? An herbal decoction perhaps?"

"Not now, Sheridan, maybe—," Leander started.

"Yes," Nicodemus interrupted. "A warm libation would be just the thing." He clasped his hands behind his back. "And please have it brought to the study. This special young man and I have much to discuss."

Sheridan bowed his head and started off toward the kitchen

with the grinding of gears and a hiss of steam.

Nicodemus's feline familiar strolled into the lobby as if he had been living there for years, and leaped into the waiting arms of his master. Alastor began to purr as the Grandmaster stroked his hairless back. Leander's mind was in turmoil as he began to wonder how word of Timothy's existence had gotten out, why the Cuzcotec had attacked, and if there might be other enemies already on the hunt for the boy. Still, Nicodemus exuded a calm that was almost intimidating, and Leander felt that he must follow the Grandmaster's example.

"Well," he said, shaking his shaggy head to clear his mind. "Shall we proceed to the study then?" He motioned toward the hallway at their left and they all began to move in that direction. From the corner of his eye he saw that Ivar had cautiously descended to the foot of the stairs, his skin mimicking the colors of his surroundings, rendering him almost invisible. Despite having thwarted the attempt on Timothy's life, the warrior remained wary.

"It's quite all right, Ivar," Leander assured the Asura warrior. "We just need to speak with Timothy about some very important matters. He'll be safe with us."

Leander gestured for the warrior to accompany them, but Nicodemus frowned and glared at him.

"The primitive will stay outside the study," the Grandmaster of the Order of Alhazred proclaimed with obvious disdain. "Our discussion is not for his ears."

Timothy stopped, obviously startled. He glanced uncomfortably at Ivar. "But—"

"Come, boy," Nicodemus interrupted, and then he escorted the boy into his father's study at the end of the hall as though Timothy had never spoken.

Marks of jagged black flushed upon the warrior's passive face, the only real sign that he had been in any way affected by the Grandmaster's harsh words.

"I'm sorry for that," Leander said softly, embarrassed by Nicodemus's insensitivity. He was well aware of the order's lack of empathy for peoples of less civilized cultures. "He doesn't understand the relationship that you and Timothy share. Let me explain to him and—"

The Asura raised a pale hand, silencing him.

"This is fine, Leander Maddox," Ivar assured him. "Go and be with the boy. I sense that he is still very frightened." Abruptly the Asura turned and strode toward the scattered corpses of the Cuzcotec assassins. He lifted one of the dead off the ground and heaved the body onto his shoulder as if it weighed nothing. "I will dispose of our enemies' empty shells," he said. "It is my duty as victor." And he continued on his way up the stairs.

Leander hesitated only a moment before following Nicodemus and Timothy into the study. In moments, Sheridan had brewed a hot drink made from several herbs, and the rich, spicy smell of the refreshment filled the room with its soothing aroma. The metal man had then dismissed himself, saying that he was going to assist Ivar with cleaning up after the afternoon's incident.

Leander sat in a high-backed chair and gazed sadly about the study, its floor-to-ceiling bookcases filled with every conceivable kind of writing. This had been Argus's favorite room. He had loved to read and would often retire here to unwind after a long day. Now, with the discovery of Timothy, Leander understood all the more the pressures of being Argus Cade.

An individual pot of the herbed drink and a cup and saucer had been placed on a tray before each of them. Timothy had not yet touched his. He sat nervously next to Nicodemus on the long sofa; Edgar perched behind him. The Grandmaster sipped his brew and delicately placed his cup on the saucer. Alastor had curled into a tight ball on the great sorcerer's lap.

"I'll be blunt, Timothy," Nicodemus said, slowly turning his gaze to the boy. "Word of your existence has leaked to the outside world, and a panic has begun."

A shudder went through Leander. The Grandmaster had confirmed his fears.

Timothy twisted around to fix the Grandmaster in his gaze. "A panic? About me? Why would they be afraid of me?"

Edgar flapped his wings from his perch atop the back of Timothy's seat. "Yeah, well that pretty much describes the Parliament," the boy's familiar croaked, squawking voice laden with sarcasm.

"Hold your tongue, Edgar," Leander warned.

"Perhaps it was not only the primitive that should have been excluded from this gathering, eh, familiar?" Nicodemus noted idly, filling his cup with more drink from his brewpot.

For once, Edgar managed to be silent.

Leander leaned forward to set his empty cup and saucer down on the tray. "Grandmaster, I think Timothy is having a difficult time grasping how he might pose a threat to anyone."

Nicodemus continued to sip his libation, the hairless cat dozing in his lap. "In order to understand the guilds," he proclaimed, "one must have the ability to think like them. Certainly they will show great interest in your handicap, some decrying the cruelty of your fate and others thinking you a blight upon our race. There will be debate about you, boy, all of it regarding what ought to be done with you, whether you are an unfortunate child or an aberration of nature. But in secret, the debate will focus upon only one thing; whether or not Timothy Cade is a threat to the guilds and their power."

Timothy grunted in disbelief and confusion, shaking his head. "But I still don't—"

"It isn't that you cannot do magic, boy," Nicodemus noted, sitting slightly forward and stroking his long mustache thoughtfully. "What has them all skittish is what else they have heard . . . that you are unaffected by it. Undetectable. Invisible."

"And that's what scares them?" Timothy still wasn't sure of the meaning of it all. He had yet to see the entire tapestry of the problem, choosing instead to focus upon the single threads. "*That* makes me dangerous?" he asked softly.

"More than you can possibly imagine," Nicodemus said, gently stroking the animal on his lap. "Try to think as they do, Timothy," he said, tapping the side of his head with the tip of a well-groomed finger. "Imagine if somebody of your unique persuasion were used as a tool—a weapon against a rival guild."

The boy seemed taken aback. "Me? A weapon?" he asked incredulously. "But I could never—"

"And they would not believe you, even if you swore on the spirit of your dear, departed father," Nicodemus said, scratching Alastor behind one of his pointed ears. "The guilds wear a mask of solidarity when Parliament meets," he explained. "But there is always mistrust amongst them. Dozens of secret grudges and wars play out in the shadows."

Leander's heart ached for the boy. It was an ugly situation, but there was no use hiding it from him. "What Nicodemus says is true, Timothy," he said, speaking in his calmest voice. "Even now Parliament is investigating the disappearances of a number of sorcerers who were probably victims of the kinds of covert activity the Grandmaster is speaking of. Mages do not traditionally disappear with no reason. The guild masters are always suspicious of one another, but this is only making them worse. It's likely they're being killed. And thus for the investigation—"

Panic seemed to set in upon the boy, and he stood, fists

clenched at his sides. "Why are you telling me this?" he demanded. "Are you trying to scare me?"

Leander shook his head. "No, Timothy," he soothed. "We don't want to scare you, but you must be made aware of the dangers you face in this world." He paused, running his fingers through his thick, red beard. "On the way here the Grandmaster and I discussed ways to keep you safe. And after witnessing the Cuzcotec attempt on your life, I believe that Nicodemus's plan is most sound."

Timothy turned to Nicodemus. "And what is this plan exactly?" he asked warily.

Nicodemus narrowed his eyes, brows knitting thoughtfully. "It isn't safe for you here." The Grandmaster's tone was resolute, and as he spoke his feline familiar lifted its angular head and yawned languidly, displaying its needle-sharp fangs. "You will come and live at my estate where you can be properly protected. At least until we can be certain no one else will try to do you harm."

Timothy scowled and crossed his arms. "No, thank you. I want to stay here. This is my home now." The boy moved to stand beside Leander's chair. "Tell him," he said, and though the words formed a command, they were more of a plea. "Tell him that it will be fine for me here."

Nicodemus had first made the suggestion back at the ministry, and Leander had dismissed it, but that was before the attempt on the child's life. He reached out and took hold of the boy's arms, drawing him closer. He looked Timothy in the eyes. "I swore to your father that I would do everything in my power to protect you. If the Cuzcotec know of you, then others know of you as well."

Timothy's eyes had begun to well with tears, and he fought the show of emotion, lowering his gaze. "But Ivar and Sheridan can protect me," he said.

"Hukk! Don't forget the bird," said Edgar from his perch atop the sofa.

Leander ignored the rook and continued to speak to his charge. "Perhaps they could, but there is no way to be certain. We have no way to know who else might mean you harm, and how powerful they might be. I will not risk your safety. I could not bear it." He glanced past the boy to Nicodemus. The sage old sorcerer nodded his head in approval.

"What makes you think I'll be any safer with Lord Nicodemus?" Timothy asked, avoiding looking at the Grandmaster. "My father's house has safeguards. You told me so yourself. But those . . . those things managed to get in just the same."

Leander nodded. "All the more reason. Your father, may he rest, is gone. This manse is compromised. Nicodemus's estate is perhaps the most isolated, most secure home in all of Sunderlund. It would be almost impossible to enter uninvited, even if anyone would dare. Which is unlikely in any case. He is the Grandmaster of the Order of Alhazred. It would be tantamount to a declaration of war between guilds."

Nicodemus leaned forward, waking and dislodging Alastor from his lap. The cat leaped down and the Grandmaster steepled his hands beneath his chin, gazing at Timothy. "If you are not safe with me," he said, "then there will be no sanctuary for you anywhere."

The boy gave a short, bitter laugh. "Well, that's a comfort."

The following afternoon a carriage hovered weightlessly in the air at the foot of the stairs that led up to his father's home. Timothy stood on the last step and studied the floating vehicle that had been sent to take him away. It was the first time he would ride in one, and no matter how difficult things were, he could not stifle his excitement. It was sleek in its design, made of a golden metal that glistened in sunlight. Like Leander's carriage, it had the image of a dragon at each corner, and it bore Nicodemus's family crest on each door—a screaming eagle, its wings spread in flight. As a distraction from his anxieties, his brain attempted to devise a way in which a vehicle like this could be made to ride the air without the use of magic.

A familiar hiss of steam filled the air and Timothy turned to see Sheridan making his way down the steps with Ivar close behind. They were each carrying large satchels containing the boy's belongings. Behind them Leander was closing up the house with the aid of Nicodemus's personal assistant, a stout man named Carlyle. Timothy's eyes grew steely as he watched the men. In the short amount of time he had spent with the Grandmaster's assistant, he had decided that he did not care for the man even a little. Carlyle treated him like an oddity, meeting everything he said with a condescending smile and a nod.

I can't do magic, that's all! he wanted to scream at the man. *I'm not a simpleton.* But he was sure that even that would have garnered the same patronizing response.

Sheridan reached the bottom step.

"Let me help you with that," Timothy said, taking the bag from the mechanical man's hand.

Sheridan issued a cheery toot from his steam pipe. "Thank you, Timothy." The metal man studied the sky carriage floating in the air before them. "My, isn't it a wondrous craft," he said, the gears and such within his head whining and whirring as if there were insects trapped inside. "It's even larger than Master Maddox's."

The carriage's navigation mage, perched upon his seat at the front of the craft, turned to fix his stare on his passengers. He was draped in robes of yellow, similar to the hue of the vehicle itself.

His face, as with all transportation mages, was covered in a veil of a darker hue than his robes. Many wore their faces completely covered, using senses other than sight for navigation. But Nicodemus's navigator wore only a half veil, and his eyes glared intensely at them over the top of the veil. Timothy decided that this was not a person to be trifled with.

"The machine and the savage will ride in back," the navigation mage instructed in a gravelly voice, gesturing with an upraised thumb at a separate compartment that was attached to the back of the larger carriage. "Lord Nicodemus's orders."

Timothy's anger flared and his eyes narrowed as he stared at the navigator. "These are my friends you're talking about. Nicodemus may not think much of them, but he shouldn't be so narrow-minded. He's just going to have to—"

Ivar's firm hand fell upon his shoulder, and he felt the Asura's inner strength flow into him.

"It is inconsequential," the warrior whispered.

"Yes, Timothy," Sheridan said, taking the satchel from him. "A ride in the back will be more than sufficient. At least we don't have to walk."

A black shape dropped from the sky, landing on the roof of the carriage. Edgar cawed loudly and fluttered his wings. "He's got an interesting way of looking at things, doesn't he?"

The navigation mage glared at the rook, but Edgar paid him no mind, twitching his tail feathers and dancing from foot to foot.

"So, are we ready to go?" the black bird asked his master.

Timothy frowned, still not at all pleased at having to leave his new home. Then again, if Leander believed that it was necessary, who was he to argue. He had been born of this world, but he certainly did not understand it.

"I'm as ready as I'm ever going to be, I suppose." He took one final glance at the house, watching as Leander and Carlyle descended the stairs.

"If you have any questions at all, do not hesitate to contact me immediately at the university or at home—day or night," Leander told the Grandmaster's assistant.

"The boy will be fine," Carlyle assured Leander, aloof as always. He wore a smug smile that Timothy found unsettling. *It is inconsequential.* His Asura friend's wise words echoed in his mind, and Timothy made an effort to calm himself. Sheridan and Ivar were loading his things into the back of the rear carriage as Leander and Carlyle reached him.

"This is it, then," the burly, red-bearded mage said. In the brief time they had been together, Leander had become like family to Timothy, and now the big man seemed almost as nervous about their parting as he was.

"Yes," Timothy said, looking past the mage to the front of the house. He committed the sight to memory, every detail, no matter how small, would be there for him to remember anytime he wished. Timothy would keep the recollection close, until he was able to return. "I'd just gotten used to thinking of this as home. Patience seems so very far away."

"I know you don't want to hear it," Leander said, distracting him. "But no matter how dreadful this feels, it is all for the best."

Timothy focused on the face of his father's friend—*his* friend—and felt a pang of sympathy for the man. Leander only wanted to do what was right, and it was obvious that this decision pained him terribly.

"I understand." Timothy did his best to muster a smile. "And besides, it won't be forever, right?"

Carlyle coughed into his closed hand and then glanced at the timepiece on his wrist. "If you'll both excuse me," he said in an officious tone. "Master Maddox, we'll be in touch if the need arises." The Grandmaster's assistant offered the mage a slight bow. Then he turned his belittling gaze upon Timothy. "Young sir, I'll be waiting inside the carriage."

Carlyle climbed in and the door closed tightly behind him.

"Someone's in a bit of a hurry," Leander said, sniffing in annoyance.

"Seems like the type that always would be, don't you think?" Timothy watched the man through the window in the door and saw that he was scowling and again looking at his timepiece.

"You'd better be off then," the mage said with a halfhearted attempt at cheer. "Wouldn't want to keep the Lord Nicodemus waiting."

Timothy nodded. "No, of course not. The Grandmaster doesn't seem like he would have much more patience than his assistant."

They stood facing each other, hesitating. Neither, it seemed, wanted to say good-bye.

"Timothy," Leander began.

"Don't feel bad," the boy interrupted. "I know you just want to keep me safe."

The mage placed a large, comforting hand upon his shoulder and squeezed. "I wouldn't want you to think I was abandoning you—that I didn't care," he grumbled.

Timothy patted the man's hand fondly. "I would never think such a thing."

Silence came between them again. Then the carriage door swung open and Carlyle cleared his throat. "Timothy?" he called, and the boy knew that it was time for him to leave.

"I'll visit as often as I'm able," Leander promised as the boy climbed up into the floating vehicle.

Timothy raised his hand in farewell. "I would expect no less."

The spell that controlled the door of the floating vehicle did not recognize that anyone had entered the cab, so Leander passed a hand over it, purple sparks dancing from his fingers, and belatedly the door closed itself tightly. Then he stepped back as the craft began its departure. Timothy watched him and felt the loss of Leander's presence keenly, the departure aching his heart even more than he had expected. The house had provided him with a link to his father, now that Argus Cade was gone from this world, but in a sense Leander had provided an even more powerful link.

The navigation mage manipulated the crackling magics of levitation and they were off. Timothy turned away, not wanting to watch as the carriage descended the steep incline from August Hill toward the city of Arcanum waiting below. It was a panoramic vista that made his breath catch in his throat and his eyes widen in amazement. While he had not forgotten his sadness, it receded as they reached the base of August Hill and the sky carriage zipped along Arcanum's busy streets. The sights of the city were almost more than Timothy's senses could stand. He found himself closing his eyes periodically, protecting himself from the visual barrage parading past. Nothing could have prepared him for this.

"It's all so . . . incredible," he muttered, barely aware that he had spoken the words aloud.

Carlyle, who appeared to have been napping, gazed out the window as they passed a block of jagged, crystalline buildings that twinkled and glistened in the approaching dusk. Timothy wasn't sure if he had ever seen anything quite so breathtaking. They looked almost as though they had been grown upon that location, rather than built. It occurred to Timothy that no one here really *built* anything, not in the way he understood the word, and that it was more than possible that his instinct was correct. The idea that anyone could grow crystal towers made him shudder with giddy pleasure. This world was one discovery after another.

"Incredible," Timothy repeated.

"I suppose," the assistant said with disinterest, already slouching back into his seat.

They flew above a road that passed through the center of a bustling marketplace, and Timothy marveled at the brief glimpses of countless items he saw on display there. Amazing smells wafted up from many of the stalls. There were beautifully woven flying carpets, hoods and cloaks of myriad designs, racks of books and jars of herbs, and even stalls where the strangest of animals were tethered, awaiting purchase. Street magicians performed to the delight of children, dancing in the air, juggling multicolored flames, acting out scenes of high drama or low comedy, altering their clothes or their features with a flourish of a hand. Timothy would have given just about anything to spend some time wandering about the fabulous bazaar.

Carlyle had begun to snore, a high-pitched whining sound that reminded Timothy of one of Sheridan's straining servo-mechanisms, but he didn't mind. He had no interest in conversing with the man, especially when there were so many fabulous things to see outside.

The craft began to ascend, climbing so high that many of the taller structures and the spires atop them were suddenly at eye level. Timothy was anxious about the height at first, but his fascination with the architecture before him soon calmed him down. The spires in particular were marvels of magical creation—what Leander called conjure-architecture. They looked almost as though they had been sculpted from clouds, but were actually made of crystal or stone or wood, shaped and placed by sorcery alone. The speed of the carriage increased and soon they were gliding among those spires with unsettling speed. Timothy wondered how Ivar and Sheridan were doing; it was their first time in a sky carriage as well.

Abruptly they emerged from among the spires and only clear sky lay ahead. He craned his neck to look down and saw that below them the city had been replaced by a churning ocean of icy blue, so different from the waters that lapped the shores of Patience. No one had mentioned the ocean, and Timothy wondered where it was exactly that Nicodemus called home. Great watercrafts sailed across the sea below him, their prows jutting so high, flying the flags of the many magical guilds. Timothy had never been on a watercraft, and he felt a yearning in his heart as he gazed down upon them. One, a long, thin vessel colored the bright purple of vineyard fruit, sliced through the water so swiftly it seemed almost alive.

Beautiful, he thought, *but what are we doing out here?* He would have guessed that the Grandmaster of the Order of Alhazred lived in Arcanum—in one of the fabulous towers that reached into the sky above the clouds—above his followers.

"We're approaching SkyHaven," the navigation mage abruptly announced, startling him.

Carlyle came awake with a loud snort and rubbed at his eyes.

"SkyHaven?" Timothy asked with a puzzled frown, gazing out at the ocean below.

"The estate of Lord Nicodemus," the assistant responded, consulting his timepiece.

The vehicle banked to the right and Timothy grabbed hold of a leather strap on the door to prevent himself from sliding across the seat into Carlyle's lap. As the carriage tilted, the young boy, the un-magician, got his first glimpse of SkyHaven, the home of the Grandmaster. For a moment he held his breath.

Its towers and turrets twisted impossibly above the circular foundation of the mansion, as though the gray stone and black wood had been frozen in a timeless dance. Yet despite the formidable beauty of SkyHaven, what astonished Timothy most was that the entire estate—castle and fortress and the lush and verdant expanse of land beneath it—hovered, as if weightless, above the endless rolling waves of the azure ocean hundreds of feet below, earth and stone and roots dangling above the water as though they had just been ripped from the very planet itself.

"It's . . . it's incredible," Timothy said in an excited whisper as the air carriage flew nearer.

"Yes." Carlyle yawned. "Somehow I knew you would say that."

"The magics it must take to keep it aloft," Timothy said, more to himself than to his riding companion. This was business as usual for Carlyle. But for Timothy, well . . . it was more than he could comprehend.

The craft began its descent to SkyHaven. With amazing precision the carriage dropped out of the sky, passing beneath an ornate stone archway covered in thick flowering vines, to land in an open courtyard before the estate's most prominent structure.

Carlyle's door sprang open of its own accord, and he climbed down from the carriage. Timothy pushed his own door open, and as he stepped out he saw Nicodemus emerge from the castle, appearing as though from nothing in front of a pair of metal doors as tall as a Yaquis tree. They were ridiculously high, the boy thought, for who or what could the Grandmaster invite into his home that was as tall as that?

Nicodemus looked regal in long, flowing robes of vibrant green, and he carried his hairless feline familiar in his arms as he strode across the courtyard toward the carriage. Those two absurdly large doors swung open and an entourage of ten robed men and women emerged, bustling closely behind their lord and master.

"Welcome to SkyHaven!" the Grandmaster called out as he drew closer, a charming smile upon his distinguished features. "Welcome to my home! Do you like it?"

Timothy was certain that the grand mage could tell he was impressed just by reading the expression on his face, but he answered anyway, simply to be polite. "It's amazing!"

"More than three thousand, four hundred spells of weightlessness are perpetually maintained to keep my floating paradise aloft," Nicodemus said proudly as he stepped up beside Timothy, and then the two of them turned to admire the castle together.

Carlyle joined them, standing on the other side of the Grandmaster. "The boy was rendered nearly speechless by SkyHaven's majesty," the assistant said with an overly dramatic flourish of his hand.

Nicodemus chuckled. "Can you blame him, Carlyle? I conjure-built the estate myself, every tower, every room, and yet to me, it is still the most wondrous of sights to behold."

The door to the adjoining carriage swung open and there came a fluttering rush of wings. Edgar cawed loudly, angrily, and took flight from within, soaring above their heads, stretching his wings after being confined so long. Sheridan stepped out into the courtyard after the rook's abrupt departure, followed by a very cautious Ivar, who looked at the ground beneath his feet as though he did not trust it.

Timothy forgot all about the Grandmaster for a moment, and rushed to join his friends. "Can you believe this?" he asked excitedly. "It floats! Above the ocean!"

"Truly spectacular," Sheridan said, his head rotating three hundred and sixty degrees to take in all the sights.

"Caw! Caw!" Edgar cried. "I think the place has grown even bigger since I was last here," the rook said, surveying his surroundings from a branch in one of the many fruit trees that grew around the courtyard.

Ivar had not moved from the shadows cast by the sky carriage, and his entire body was a golden yellow, toned to blend with the color of the craft.

"It's all right, Ivar," Timothy said, approaching his friend and extending a hand. "We're going to stay here for a while."

The Asura looked about nervously, before gravely allowing himself to be drawn from cover. "This place," he said, his skin returning to its natural shade. "It is unnatural."

"Precisely the sort of reaction one would expect from a savage," Nicodemus sniffed. The Grandmaster strode toward Timothy and Ivar, the cat in his arms. He was not sneering, not cruel, but there was something cold in his eyes when he looked at the Asura. "It is we—the mages of the world—who determine what is natural and what is not."

Timothy felt the blood rushing to his face. He didn't like the way Nicodemus treated Ivar; not at all. "He's not a savage. He's the last of the Asura, a noble tribe of—"

Nicodemus made a dismissive gesture, then beckoned a pair of powerful men from his entourage toward them. "Yes, of course he is, Timothy. I'm well aware of your primitive friend's background, thank you." The Grandmaster seemed about to turn away, but then he paused and focused his gaze on Timothy, his eyes strangely sad, yet also, now kind. "You were born of this world, son, but you have never lived here. There is much you do not understand of our ways, our culture, and our history. Some things will delight you, others will disappoint you. This is the way of the world."

Two attendants stood on either side of Ivar, tensed as though expecting trouble. The Grandmaster gestured to them again and nodded.

"Allow my staff to show your . . . friend . . . where he will be staying," Nicodemus commanded.

"You mean, where *we'll* be staying?"

Nicodemus shook his head. "I'm afraid that cannot be. Rules of the house, you understand. The familiar may stay with you—and that toy of metal," he said pointing to Sheridan. "But the sav—Asura," he corrected himself, "will sleep elsewhere, and will be barred from the main chambers of my home. When you know more of this world, you will understand."

Timothy looked to Ivar, unsure of what he should do. "I . . . I don't think that's—"

The Asura signaled him to be silent. Ivar tilted his head slightly to one side and fixed Timothy with a steely gaze. "It is—"

The boy sighed knowingly. "Inconsequential," he said. And yet as he watched Ivar allowing himself to be led away to his quarters, he could not help feeling that it was not inconsequential at all. Ivar was sacrificing a great deal so that Timothy could be safe, and the boy felt the responsibility of that weighing heavily upon him.

"Come, my boy," Nicodemus said, his robes flowing around him as he turned and walked toward his residence. He lifted Alastor to his shoulder and the hairless cat curled itself around his neck and rested there. "Let me show you to your room so you may settle yourself before joining me for dinner."

Timothy hesitantly followed.

"A toy?" Sheridan whispered indignantly at Timothy's side. "I'd like to see a toy do half the things I can."

Edgar fluttered down from above to land on Timothy's shoulder. "If you thought the outside was impressive, wait till you see the inside."

They followed Nicodemus and several members of his staff up the stairs and through the doorway into a grand hall. Again

Timothy's breath was taken away by SkyHaven's opulence. The ceiling was at least fifty feet high and gilded with a strange design of spirals turning in upon themselves, radiating into a starburst at the apex of the concave ceiling. High arched windows of translucent energy allowed a view of the sky, which even now was darkening to the blue-black of evening. The moons and sister planets had never seemed so clear. Upon the walls of the grand hall were tapestries and portraits, sculptures and pictographs like those in his father's house.

"This way," the Grandmaster urged, and Timothy followed obediently up a winding staircase, constructed from smooth, white stone flecked with streaks of solid black.

They left the other aides behind, Carlyle included, and at once Timothy let out a breath. Despite Nicodemus's treatment of Ivar, he felt more comfortable with the great mage when no one else was around, when there were no servants bowing to him as a constant reminder of his power and stature.

With Sheridan clanking along the hall, emitting a peep of steam now and again, and Edgar riding upon his shoulder, Timothy followed the Grandmaster for what seemed miles along winding hallways, until they came to a wing of the castle whose door was made of wood and seemed imperfect to his eye, as though it had been carved by hand and not by magic. He found himself letting out a small breath, taking comfort in the presence of at least one thing that, like him, did not have the perfection of magic.

"Yes," the Grandmaster said, noticing Timothy's focus. "I thought you might like that." With a wave of his hand Nicodemus opened the door and led them into the small yet elegant foyer of a suite of smaller rooms. A door to another room stood warmly open and the Grandmaster went through it, gesturing for the boy and his mechanical man to follow. Edgar leaped from his shoulder and glided inside the bedchamber to perch upon a bureau of dark wood.

"Not bad," the bird croaked.

Timothy was shocked to see that his satchels were already there.

"Get acquainted with your new surroundings, my boy," Nicodemus said, stroking Alastor's head, the hairless feline still draped over his shoulders. "I'll send someone to fetch you as soon as dinner is served."

Then the Grandmaster departed and the door slammed closed behind him as though a great wind had blown it shut.

Timothy sat down upon the large, four-poster bed and glanced around the room, shivering, for it was strangely cold there. Though he had Sheridan and Edgar for company, he felt more alone at SkyHaven than he ever had on the Island of Patience.

CHAPTER FIVE

No matter how hard he tried, Timothy could not sleep. Carefully, so as not to disturb Edgar, who was perched atop the headboard of the bed, the boy threw back the bedclothes and padded toward one of the room's large windows. He chanced a quick glance over his shoulder to make sure the rook hadn't awakened. Edgar remained still, eyes closed, his perfectly streamlined head lowered to his feathered breast.

"Timothy?" asked a hollow voice from beside his bed.

The boy's finger shot to his lips. "Quietly, Sheridan," he whispered. "We don't want to wake up Edgar."

Sheridan shuffled away from the wall with a series of soft clicks and whirs. The mechanical man's eyes shone eerily in the darkness, and Timothy could hear the faint, sibilant sound of steam hissing from the release valve that protruded from the side of his head.

"You're right about that," the machine said, the volume of his voice lowered significantly. "An unrested Edgar is an irritable Edgar."

Timothy nodded knowingly and smiled at his companion. Sheridan was the boy's greatest achievement, the ultimate example of his mechanical aptitude. Certainly, he had built all manner of fabulous mechanisms, but in the creation of Sheridan, Timothy had built much more than that. He had built a friend.

"Are you all right?" Sheridan asked with concern in his metallic voice. "Why aren't you asleep? Nicodemus has a big day planned for you tomorrow, and you're just as grouchy as Edgar when you don't get your rest."

The Grandmaster of the Order of Alhazred planned to introduce Timothy to the masters of several other guilds in the morning, to prove that he was neither threat nor abomination. Just a less-than-ordinary boy who wanted to be left alone. Timothy was nervous. That was one of the things keeping him awake. "I'm okay," he told his friend softly. "Go ahead and shut yourself down for the night."

"Don't stay up too long," Sheridan cautioned before reversing his direction and returning to his place against the wall. "Good night, Timothy."

"Good night."

Timothy turned his attention to the sprawling estate outside the window. The celestial illumination cast by the night sky's myriad moons filtered through the magically conjured windowpanes, and cast the boy in a strange, rose-tinted light. He reached out to touch the window and the magical pane began to waver, and then was no more.

"What?" Timothy whispered, taken aback. He pulled his hand away, and the window reappeared. Timothy reached to touch the spell-glass again, and once more it wavered to nothing. Now he understood. His touch disrupted the spell that kept the windowpane in place.

Cool night air rushed into the room and Timothy sighed. "Of course. Magic."

The boy leaned his arms on the cold stone of the sill and peered out into the night. The castle fortress and all the lands of the estate hovered weightlessly hundreds of feet above the dark, churning ocean. There was a beauty to this bit of extraordinary levitation, and yet there was a terrible power in it as well.

Timothy gazed down into the cold waters, grateful that his

propensity to interfere with the validity of magic was very limited. Magic did not work on him, and his touch could disrupt it, canceling it out, but only if he actually had contact with the spell itself, with the substance of magic. He could not imagine how horrible it would be if that antimagic effect radiated beyond his touch, canceling out the work of a navigation mage driving a carriage, or even worse, undermining the spells that held SkyHaven aloft.

Timothy shuddered. He was learning to live with being an anomaly, a blank place on the matrix of magic that made up the world. But there was no one else like him anywhere, and this knowledge made him feel very, very alone.

He glanced at Hito, the farthest and smallest of the moons, hanging white and cold like a sphere of ice, and wondered at the mysteries beyond it. There had been a moon like Hito above the Island of Patience, but it had been alone in the sky. A simpler heaven above a simpler world. A pang of sadness washed over Timothy as he thought of the tiny island he called Patience. His father had made a home for him in that other world to keep him safe from this one. Gazing out that window, Timothy looked across the ocean to the radiant majesty of the lights and spires of the city of Arcanum on the far shore. *Fear me,* this new and awesome world seemed to say, and Timothy had no choice but to oblige.

The winds off the water picked up, bringing a raw dampness that hinted of storm. Timothy rubbed his hands across his arms to drive the chill from his flesh. He could hear the distant sounds of the horses in the stables below, carried on the wind, made nervous by the approaching storm. Timothy thought of Ivar, forced to stay in the stables with the animals. Nicodemus treated the Asura as though he were less than human, and though Ivar assured him it was not important, Timothy felt that it was. Ivar was his friend. It didn't seem right that he should be kept apart from other people because of who he was. Timothy wondered how it would be with the guild masters tomorrow, and he suspected that their treatment of him would help him understand how Ivar must be feeling, down there in the stables.

They would be afraid of you, his father had warned, *and from fear nothing good can come.*

"I'll be a freak," Timothy muttered, returning to bed. There was a spark and sputter from the window spell as the crimson panes of magic reappeared. And not a moment too soon, for the storm had arrived.

The boy listened to the threatening rumble of thunder out over the ocean—and the sound of something else, much closer. He stopped beside his bed and checked on Sheridan and Edgar. The mechanical man was motionless and the bird was still lost in sleep. But there was something, a queer feeling that he was no longer alone.

He gazed about the room, inspecting every darkened nook and cranny, and was about to chastise himself for such childishness—when two ominous figures suddenly materialized before the windows where he had just been standing. The boy stifled a gasp as he looked upon them. They were dressed in cloaks the color of dried blood, one slightly larger than the other. Their eyes glowed like tiny pinpricks of fire within the darkness of the hoods.

"Who—who are you?" he stammered. "What do you want?"

"Silence," the larger figure hissed as his pale, spidery hands emerged from inside the darkness of his cloak. "You do not ask questions of us."

Timothy could see that the tips of his fingers were blackened and charred. His father had told him of such men, reckless spell-casters who tapped too deeply into the natural magic of the world, who channeled more magical power than any ordinary mage could contain. An archmage could wield such power, but in others it corrupted the flesh. The charred fingertips were only one sign of such indulgence. And only one sort of mage risked such corruption.

More assassins, Timothy thought, an icy chill upon his flesh.

"Our masters have deemed you dangerous—too dangerous to live," said the smaller figure. He also removed his hands from within the folds of his cape, exposing fingers burnt black.

Timothy's mind raced as he heard the large figure begin to mutter a spell. It sounded like the angry drone of an insect trapped within a jar. A crackling blue energy began to flare about his blackened digits. Timothy dove onto the bed as a bolt of energy struck the spot where he had been standing. Fragments of the hardwood floor exploded into the air, awakening Edgar with a start.

"Caw! What's going on here?" the bird squawked as he flapped his large black wings. "Don't you know I need my beauty rest?"

"Not now, Edgar," Timothy snapped as he rolled across to the other side of the bed. He could hear the drones of the second assassin as he, too, prepared to cast a killing spell.

By then Edgar had noticed the hooded figures with the blackened fingertips. "Nimib assassins," the bird croaked. "Sound an alarm! Nimib assassins at SkyHaven!"

The massive rook took flight, the beat of his wings slapping the air. Cawing, he dove at the intruders, avoiding their attacks as he aimed his talons at their faces, distracting them for precious moments.

Using Sheridan for cover, Timothy flicked a tiny switch on the back of his friend's head to activate its audio sensors.

"Sheridan," Timothy hollered into one of the funnel shaped

receivers protruding from the side of the machine's head. "We need your help!"

Timothy looked away from the still inert machine as Edgar's shrill cries filled the bedroom. Again the rook was diving at the assassins, using his wings to beat at them, his talons to claw at their faces.

"A little help would be appreciated," the rook screamed as he evaded his attackers' flailing arms.

A blast of magic went wild, hitting the wall just above Timothy's head, and a rain of powdered stone fell down on him.

"C'mon, Sheridan!" He rapped on the metal man's head with his knuckles. "I know you're in there. Wake up."

Edgar cawed, a wordless shriek, as his tail feathers were singed by an explosion of greenish flame. The rook landed on the floor, fanning his smoldering backside with one of his wings, and the assassins returned their attention to their primary task. Their purpose was clear. They were here to kill Timothy, here to murder the un-magician.

As the sorcerers moved closer, the boy had no idea what to do. Frantically his mind raced, he looked around and his eyes fell on the rumpled bedclothes on his bed. Without even thinking, he reached down, snatched them up, and dove at the assassins, covering them in a makeshift net as he fell to the floor. The killers struggled beneath the multiple layers as Timothy climbed to his feet.

"Hurry, Timothy! We've gotta go!" Edgar squawked, flapping his wings above the bed.

"Sheridan, wake up!" Timothy exclaimed as he ran for the door.

The mechanical man suddenly sprang to life. His eyes blazed brightly as he looked about the room. "Yes? What's the ruckus?" he asked, confused, his electronic brain still dull from his time deactivated. His servomechanisms buzzed and hissed with steam as he strode away from the wall toward the pile of thrashing covers. "Is that you under there, Timothy?"

"No, Sheridan!" the boy cried from the door. "Over here!"

Before the mechanical man could respond, the writhing bed-clothes were engulfed in a supernatural fire that consumed the makeshift trap, revealing the enraged Nimib assassins beneath.

"Oh, my," Sheridan said, startled. He began to back away from the furious killers, whose hands crackled with arcane power.

"What manner of beast are you?" the larger assassin bellowed, one long finger pointing at the machine, dark magical energy sparking around his hand. His eyes blazed more brightly beneath his hood and in a glint of light from the killer's own glowing magic, Timothy thought he saw the gleam of several rows of sharp teeth.

"It is one of the boy's creations," said the other. "It is as our masters told us, Cade's offspring creates life with gears, cogs, steam, and springs."

"Another abomination," said the larger of the assassins as he extended his black-tipped fingers. "It, too, will die this night."

No! Timothy bolted toward Sheridan, Edgar squawking wildly above him. As if in slow motion, he saw the magical energies gather at the tips of the Nimib assassins' fingers, like fat droplets of water. Timothy screamed in defiance as he threw himself into the space between the deadly sorcery and the machine man.

The spell struck the boy square in the chest, dissipating on contact. Timothy stumbled backward, away from the assassins, and he crashed into Sheridan, the two of them tumbling to the floor.

"It is done," Timothy heard one of the killers say with finality, and wondered what he meant.

The boy climbed to his feet, gazing at his chest where the sorcerous energy had struck. He touched the area, which tingled slightly from the warmth that the blast had generated before it had been disrupted. He did not want to think about what it would have done to him if he was vulnerable to such an attack.

"What wizardry is this?" the smaller one whispered, staring at his own hands for some defect that might have interfered with the potency of their spellcasting.

"Impossible," growled the larger one. His hood had fallen away to reveal a pale, older man, his face adorned with the black tattoo of a dragon. "Warriors and kings have fallen before our skills."

"It is as our masters feared," said the other, voice hushed with fear as he pulled his cloak tighter around him, as if to warm himself from a sudden chill. "The boy cannot be cursed or hexed. Magic cannot touch him."

The assassins were so bewildered they seemed almost to have forgotten Timothy was there. He reached down and hauled Sheridan's metal form up from the floor. "Come on," he said, "while they're trying to figure out why I'm not dead."

They ran for the door. Edgar was frantically beating his wings against it, but the rook did not have the magic to open it. Timothy gave it a shove and it swung wide. He raced into the murky, candlelit hallway. From behind him, Timothy heard a loud whistle of steam. He spun to see Sheridan paralyzed in midstep, glowing with mystical energy, dark, ugly light as purple as a bruise. Sheridan's face was capable of little expression, but over the years Timothy had learned to read it well. At that moment, there was only regret on the mechanical man's features.

"I hate to be a bother yet again, young Tim, but—"

The older assassin smiled a yellow grin. "The boy is immune

to our dark magics, but perhaps his own creation could be used against him."

In unison the Nimib began to chant. Their eyes flashed, and the aura around the mechanical man turned from a bruised purple to an icy blue.

"Oh, my," Sheridan said pitifully as his metal frame began to tremble and clank. "Something is most definitely wrong here."

Edgar perched on Timothy's shoulder in a panic. "We have to get out of here or we're done for," the bird warned.

The boy kept his eyes on Sheridan. Constructed to be a helper as well as a companion, the mechanical man was equipped with all manner of tools—tools that had the capacity to be used for harm. And the Nimib had control of him, so now it appeared that Sheridan was going to be used to harm *him*.

"I'm so sorry, Timothy," the mechanical man said helplessly as he lunged forward, swinging fists like sledgehammers. A buzz saw blade on a spindly arm sprang from the machine man's chest, whirring as it sliced toward him.

Edgar squawked with surprise, taking flight as Timothy dodged quickly to one side. The saw cut a gash across the doorframe, narrowly missing him. The boy scrabbled along the ground, avoiding the swinging hammer arms that whisked past his head, and a blowtorch whose spitting flames nearly set his hair afire. Timothy reached out to lay a hand on Sheridan's leg. It was a risk, but he had the idea that perhaps his—*curse*—could be used as something other than an impediment.

His fingers touched the cool metal of Sheridan's leg as he rolled to one side to avoid a fist that could very well have crushed the life from him. The effect of Timothy's contact was immediate. The mechanical man stopped his destructive actions, the spinning blades, hammer fists, and blowtorch returned to the proper compartments in his body. The spell was broken.

"Oh my, that feels much better," Sheridan said with an exhausted metallic sigh.

Timothy scrambled to his feet and dragged Sheridan into the hall. Seconds later, the assassins emerged from the bedroom in an explosion of supernatural fury. Bolts of crackling magical energy erupted from their bodies, reaching out like tentacles.

"Cade!" the dragon-faced assassin bellowed. "You cannot elude us forever!"

Timothy could feel the electric tendrils of magical power snaking above their heads as they fled down the long, darkened hallway toward the stairs. "Go, go, go!" he shouted, pushing Sheridan along as Edgar glided above them.

He chanced a look back to see how closely the Nimib were following and was chilled when he found that they were almost upon him. Timothy was startled to see that the smaller assassin's hood had fallen away to reveal a boy only a few years older than himself. A tattoo of a crescent moon adorned the left side of the snarling boy's face.

"If we cannot slay you with magic," proclaimed the older Nimib, "there are other ways."

The assassins reached inside their robes, and from within the folds, each produced a curved, gleaming dagger. Timothy increased his speed, pounding toward the stairs, certain that his immunity to magic would do nothing to stop a sharp blade from cutting him open.

At a landing below, the stairwell turned sharply to the right. Timothy was in the midst of a frenzied descent behind Sheridan, whose eye-lights illuminated the path ahead, when a stocky shape appeared from the darkness below to block their path.

"Caw! Another one!" Edgar croaked.

The unknown figure grunted in response and Timothy knew

immediately who it was. Ivar climbed the final step onto the landing, into the light thrown by Sheridan's eyes. The warrior held an intricately carved wooden staff in his hand, a weapon he had brought over from the Island of Patience.

"I heard your cries," he said, his voice like the growl of a great, jungle cat. His skin, now a deep forest green, seemed to glisten wetly in the dim light thrown from the ghostfire candles on the walls.

"They're Nimib assassins," Timothy explained breathlessly, glancing back up the way they had come. "I think they want to kill me."

"You *think* they want to kill you?" Edgar asked incredulously as he flew above their heads. "What could possibly have given you *that* idea?"

"Quiet, bird," Ivar commanded, studying the two cloaked men who were descending the stairs toward them, weapons in hand.

The Nimib stopped when they saw Ivar and held their knives before them. "We have no fight with you, great warrior of the Asura," the older Nimib said with a courteous bow of his head. "Step away from the boy so that we may complete our sacred mission."

Timothy gasped as Ivar stepped back, exposing him to his attackers.

"What are you doing?" he exclaimed.

"It is a holy mission," the warrior answered. "It is not my place to stand in their way."

Timothy stared at Ivar in horror. "So you're not going to stop them from killing me?"

They were on the stairwell landing, the Nimib coming down toward them. A corridor led away from the landing, deeper into SkyHaven, and from the corridor came the glow of ghostfire lamps, their light gleaming off the bald pate of the Asura as he shook his head and cast a hard look at Timothy. The wisdom that was always in his eyes was joined now by mystery.

"No. *You* are going to stop them from killing you." He offered the boy his staff.

"You're kidding, right?" Timothy asked as the Asura placed the intricately carved wooden staff into his hands. He could see the calm in Ivar's eyes, the confidence there, and he knew that his friend had no doubt that he could defend himself. But Timothy was not so sure.

"I'm glad you believe in me. Really, I am," the boy said. "But what if you're wrong about me? What if I can't beat them? What if they kill me?"

Ivar shook his head. "I am not wrong. I am your teacher. I have taught you many things. Now it is time to see how much you have learned."

Timothy turned to face his grinning attackers.

"Ivar, do you really think this is wise?" Sheridan asked politely. The Asura only frowned at him.

"Of course he thinks it's wise!" Edgar cried. "Caw! He thinks everything he does is—caw!—wise! That doesn't mean he's always right!" The rook touched down on the mechanical man's shoulder. "Those leeches are going to kill our boy."

"Quiet, bird," Timothy heard Ivar say. "The Nimib are used to killing with magic, their physical combat skills should be on par with Timothy's. It will be a fair fight."

Staff in hand, Timothy stiffly approached the Nimib assassins. Dragon-face snickered, his eyes turning to slits as he lowered his body into a fighting stance. "What you are sickens me," he spat, and lunged.

Timothy dodged, but the curved blade passed dangerously close to his throat.

"Remember what you were taught," Ivar coached. "Choose your first attack wisely."

He began to replay the Asura's endless lessons on self-defense through fevered thoughts, and for once wished he had paid closer attention. The younger assassin was next to move. The crescent scar on his face gleamed as he darted forward, feigning an attack to the left, then switching to the right. Although Timothy made a valiant attempt to block the knife slash with the staff, he was hesitant, his reaction time too slow, and the blade cut a nasty gash through his nightshirt and the tender flesh beneath.

Timothy hissed in pain and stepped back. Sheridan and Ivar had stepped out into the corridor, leaving him to face the two assassins on the broad stairwell landing by himself. If he let himself be forced down the stairs, he knew that they would have an advantage over him.

The shallow cut stung and he could smell his own blood.

Ivar sighed. "Choose your first attack wisely," he repeated, stressing each word.

Timothy took a few deep breaths, holding the staff up warily, the two assassins eyeing him, looking for an opening. In those precious seconds, the meaning of Ivar's words began to gradually sink in. Timothy's anger tempted him to strike out at the younger assassin, at the one who hurt him, but he guessed that the Nimib with the crescent moon tattoo on his face was the lesser of the two fighters.

Timothy lunged toward the grinning boy, who seemed eager to continue their conflict. Then, abruptly, the un-magician changed his direction and swept the staff out, catching the older assassin by surprise. The dragon-tattooed man grunted as the staff connected with his face, spinning him around, baring his back. Timothy brought the staff above his head with swiftness born of years of practice, and cracked it down upon the assassin's spine.

The younger Nimib, seeing his comrade in danger, attacked again, but carelessly this time. Timothy blocked the young assassin's wild attack with ease, following through with a satisfying roundhouse kick to the boy's tattooed face.

"Oww! That's going to leave a mark!" Edgar cawed.

Timothy wanted to laugh, but the older sorcerer had recovered.

"The Asura has passed some of his skills on to you, boy," the killer said as he switched his razor-sharp dagger from one hand to the other. "It saddens me to think that valuable knowledge will be gone when you are no longer breathing. Such a waste."

The Nimib lunged again, this time the knife poised to pierce Timothy's heart. The boy stepped to the side and drove the staff into the assassin's gut, then rapped his skull with it, driving the Nimib to the ground, unconscious.

He spun away from his fallen foe, well aware that the battle was not yet done, preparing to meet the attack of the second assassin. The younger Nimib crouched, circling the landing warily, knife in hand. Their eyes locked, and Timothy could feel the cold hatred radiating from his opponent. Never had he experienced such intense, savage emotion.

The young assassin came at him again, the shriek of a wild animal upon his lips. The crescent-scarred Nimib slashed out with his dagger. But this time Timothy was quicker, and he struck the young assassin's wrist with a swift blow from the staff. The boy screamed, clutching the injured wrist to his chest. He scrambled to his partner's side. The one with the dragon-tattoo moaned as he began to regain consciousness.

Timothy watched them, his gaze unwavering. "Why?" he asked, abruptly losing his taste for combat. "What have I done to you?"

The older Nimib shook himself awake and rose to his knees, his hand slowly reaching inside his cloak. The assassin removed a glowing orb from within his cape. "Our magic could not kill you, but perhaps if we bring this whole structure crashing down into the ocean . . . then we would succeed."

The Nimib held out the sphere of crackling energy. "Our kind do not fail. It is inconceivable." The sphere began to emit a high-pitched whine, growing louder, as if the dreadful magic within it was building to a critical state. He held the sphere above his head. The crescent-scarred youth clasped his hands before him and gazed up at the shrieking object in awe.

Timothy's thoughts were in turmoil. If he tried to grab the sphere, would he be able to cancel out its explosive properties in time? He started forward, about to lunge for it, but he froze as a whipcrack of rolling thunder boomed through the hall, as if the storm outside had somehow touched down within the building. Above it all, a voice bellowed in rage.

"How dare you!"

Timothy spun to see Lord Nicodemus descending the stairs toward them with Alastor in his arms, a roiling cloud of supernatural energies drifting behind and above him. Clothed in an intricate dressing gown of gold and emerald green, the aged magician scowled.

The Nimib reacted immediately, hurling the screaming ball of magic at the Grandmaster.

"You are too late, mage," the dragon-faced one cried madly, over the deafening churning of supernatural forces that filled the stairwell and seeped off into the side corridor. "Your secret weapon shall never be unleashed against your brothers in magic."

Timothy backed toward his friends, amazed at the speed with which Nicodemus reacted. The ancient mage dropped his cat to the floor and extended his arms. Arcane words spilled from his mouth and the orb of energy paused in midair, its momentum interrupted, hanging frozen before the sorcerer, a miniature sun, blazing brightly.

"You endanger my houseguests, and now you have the audacity to threaten my home?" Nicodemus bellowed, his anger terrifying to see. "That will be all from you, I think."

A sound like ripping fabric filled the air.

"Well, what do you know?" Edgar muttered in wonder from his perch on Sheridan's shoulder.

The air before the mage shimmered and ripped apart, a fissure opening in reality, a window to a red-skied, storm-churned dimension. Timothy was familiar with the concept of alternate dimensions—had lived most of his life in one—but he had never witnessed anything like this. The Nimib's energy sphere was sucked into that red-skied world, and as quickly as he had torn it open, Nicodemus sealed that fissure in time and space with a dainty flourish of his age-spotted hand. The stairwell was disturbingly quiet, only the sound Alastor's affectionate purring as he rubbed against his master's leg and the whir of Sheridan's gears interrupting the silence.

The Nimib assassins sprang to their feet and pulled their cloaks tight about their bodies. Timothy could hear the spell they uttered and watched with wonder as they began to gradually fade away.

"Oh, I think not," Nicodemus whispered ominously. He extended his arms and silver, fluid magic flowed from his hands like liquid metal, engulfed the assassins. Tendrils of silver magic wound about the assassins' heads, gagging their mouths, preventing them from uttering any further spells.

"Are you all right, Timothy?" Nicodemus asked, his tone heavy with worry.

"I—I'm fine," he answered, staring at the captive assassins, his gaze locking on the younger Nimib's terrified eyes. "Maybe just a little scared."

Alastor sprang up into Nicodemus's waiting arms. "And so you should be, my boy," the sorcerer said, stroking the hairless head of his pet. "If they would dare send assassins into my home . . . well, action must be taken. This is simply unacceptable."

"What are they so afraid of?" Timothy asked, gazing at the two helpless assassins held in the grip of Nicodemus's magic.

The old man wandered closer to the struggling Nimib, studying the men who dared to invade his home. "They are afraid of what you may become," he said, looking away from the assassins, his pale blue eyes connecting with Timothy's. "You're the world's first un-magician, boy. You could hurt them, if you wanted to. That's why they fear you."

A little laugh of amazement and disbelief bubbled up out of Timothy's lips before he could stop it. He shook his head. "Me, hurt them? I don't understand."

"Think, Timothy. The guilds that comprise the Parliament of Mages work together in public, but in private there are suspicions, there are grudges, and quiet power struggles always in play. They spy on one another. And they fear you because they realize that your uniqueness makes you the perfect spy, capable of evading their glamours and exposing their nasty little secrets."

The words amazed Timothy. He had never even considered that he might have a role to play in the politics that his father and Leander had always been involved with. A spy? It seemed ridiculous. And yet a part of him was thrilled by the suggestion.

"Who sent them? Which of the guilds?" Timothy asked, studying the struggling captives. Even though there wasn't the slightest possibility that they could escape Nicodemus's magic, still they tried to fight it.

"Their sort never reveal such things," Nicodemus said with a snarl. "That is one of the reasons that the Nimib are still thriving after so many centuries. Their secrets die with them."

"There is honor in that silence," Ivar spoke up, his golden eyes intense as he stared at the ancient magician, his flesh gleaming damply in the corridor's torchlight. "It is a shame that there are not more that hold honor in such high esteem."

Nicodemus glared at the warrior, his nostrils flaring as if the very act of his speaking was an insult. "Such wisdom from the mouth of a primitive." He scratched a wrinkled area of pinkish flesh beneath Alastor's ear. "Perhaps the anthropologists studying your people were correct all along. Perhaps the Asura were smarter than other animals. If only slightly."

Timothy felt Ivar tense beside him, and he placed a calming hand on the warrior's muscular arm. The two of them stood with Sheridan just inside the corridor, off the stairwell landing. Edgar was perched atop the mechanical man's head now, and they all stared at the tableau before them, the horrible sight of the sorcerer assassins writhing in the grasp of Nicodemus's magic.

"What will you do with them?" Timothy asked, trying now to avoid the gaze of the young Nimib assassin. "Give them over to the Parliament?"

"No," Nicodemus answered abruptly, turning his attention back to the assassins. "Those who sent these two into my home must be taught a lesson."

"I don't like the sound of that," Edgar whispered to Sheridan.

"Nor I," the mechanical man concurred.

Nicodemus again dropped his cat to the floor. He cracked his knuckles and wiggled his fingers, an amused grin spreading across his features. But his eyes were cold.

"What are you going to do?" Timothy asked uneasily.

The sorcerer did not answer, instead beginning to weave a spell that consisted of exaggerated flourishes and the uttering of an incantation that sounded more like the breaking of glass than a language. From behind their gags of magic, the Nimib assassins began to scream.

"What are you doing to them?" Timothy shouted anxiously. He started to advance toward the mystic master, wondering if his ability to negate a spell on contact would stop Nicodemus, but Ivar's rock hard grip fell upon his shoulder.

"That would not be wise," the Asura warned.

The Nimib assassins' muffled shrieks continued, and Timothy watched in horror as they writhed in agony.

"This is awful," Sheridan said. "I think I'll turn my eyes off." And he did; the additional light they provided winked out and left only the gloom of the corridor's ghostfire lamps to cast their illumination into the stairwell landing.

"I wish I could do the same," Edgar whispered, and his wings fluttered softly.

The assassins' bodies began to shrink, their clothes swallowing them up as their plaintive cries became nothing more than grating, high-pitched squeaks.

"Is it over?" Sheridan asked, his head swiveling around, searching for somebody to give him an answer so that he could again activate his visual receptors.

"It's over," Timothy rasped, his own eyes wide with shock. "They're . . . gone."

Nicodemus turned to look at them. "Gone?" he asked. "They're not gone at all."

It was then that Timothy noticed that the piles of clothing

were moving. He stepped closer. "What have you done?"

"I've changed them into something more befitting their true nature," Nicodemus answered haughtily. Alastor sat at his master's feet, tail twitching eagerly.

A pair of white-furred rodents emerged from within the garments. Timothy gasped in shock as he saw the tiny tattoos upon the faces of the rats. The small creatures sniffed cautiously at the air, and Timothy wondered if they were even aware of what had happened to them.

"Word of the Nimib's failure will soon get back to those who acquired their services," Nicodemus said slowly, squatting down beside his pet, who watched the rodents with unblinking attention.

"Then . . . then they'll leave me alone," Timothy said hesitantly, pulling his attention away from the rodents to the sorcerer. "Right?"

"On the contrary, boy," said the master of the Order of Alhazred. "It may very well compel them to pursue you with even greater vigor."

Timothy felt his heart sink. To have to endure another night like this might be more than he could handle. "What are we going to do?" he asked, dreading the response.

"The only way to keep them at bay is to make them even more afraid of you than they already are. They fear you. Show them that they have reason to fear you, even greater reason than they know. Show them what you can do to them if they continue to pester you."

Nicodemus smiled. "Become exactly what they feared you would become."

"A spy?" Timothy asked.

Nicodemus snapped his fingers and Alastor leaped from his master's side with a flick of its naked tail and an eager hiss.

Timothy could only stand and stare, stunned, as the cat pounced upon the squealing rodents—ending their lives with needle-sharp fangs and tearing claws.

The sorcerer nodded his head, a smile upon his thin, bloodless lips as he watched his pet dispose of the rats in his house.

"A spy, yes. And so much more."

CHAPTER SIX

Timothy did not sleep well the rest of that evening. What dreams he had were fraught with horrid images of cloaked men with charred fingertips and tiny creatures with needle-sharp talons bent on taking his life, slicing him open. Disturbed by these nightmares he rose with the first light of dawn but did not wake Sheridan or Edgar.

The rook was perched atop the headboard, his beak buried under one wing. Timothy thought he could hear the sound of light snoring coming from beneath the bird's feathers. Sheridan was simply off, powered down, no lights in his eyes and no steam coming from the release valve at the side of his head. It always disturbed Timothy to see his friend this way. Sheridan was so much a person, so much an individual, that at times Timothy forgot that the mechanical man was not actually alive, and he hated to be reminded of it.

He stood at the window and gazed down at the ocean, at the sun glinting off the tips of the blue waves, and across the gulf that separated SkyHaven from the mainland. Arcanum at night was beautiful, extraordinary. Its lights made it ethereal after dark. Yet Timothy had been here only days and already the city by day-light seemed ordinary to him.

Ordinary. There was something about the ordinary that was powerfully attractive to him. He wanted to go to Arcanum and explore it during the day, to eat its food, walk in its shops and markets, be among its people and hear them speaking and laughing and crying. This was a yearning that he had felt often in his life, and yet he had always buried it deep in his heart, knowing that it could never be. The few friends he had on the island were to be his only real companions.

Now all of that had begun to change. It was both thrilling and terrifying, because that change had already twice endangered his life.

Across the ocean in Arcanum, dark powers were at work—struggle and conflict and competition that most of the citizens of that city, of the nation, would never understand or bear witness to. Leander and Lord Nicodemus had tried to explain it to Timothy that night at his father's mansion when he had first been attacked. It had been so foreign to him, difficult for him to understand that beneath the veneer of peace and openness presented to the public by the Parliament, there was a deeper relationship comprised of ancient grudges and feuds. The guilds were constantly at odds, making and breaking alliances, each striving for dominance in Parliament.

Thus the need for assassins, for lies, and for spies.

Though he had been taken in by the Order of Alhazred and the Grandmaster had vowed to protect him, Timothy did not feel as though he was actually a part of the order. How could he be? He was the un-magician, after all. But Leander was a part of the order as well, and Lord Nicodemus had befriended him, offered him sanctuary, such as it was. They were, he believed, his one chance at survival in this world.

But the others, they're going to keep coming after me, he thought. *I can't stop them.* Nicodemus had made it clear that the other guilds had reason to fear him, that Timothy was capable of discovering their secrets, of hurting them politically. He would never have considered doing such a thing, but his attackers did not know that. He wanted to fight back, to defend himself. *And there's only one way to do that. If they're attacking me, I have to attack them. I have to be exactly what they're so worried I'll become.*

Still, despite all Nicodemus had done for him, Timothy could not feel entirely comfortable in the Grandmaster's home. Not when Ivar was still confined to the stables deep within the fortress. If Timothy was going to stay at SkyHaven and train to be an agent of the order, he would have to speak with Nicodemus about Ivar's treatment. He did not like resting in a comfortable bed while one of his only friends slept with the animals.

A loud rap at the door interrupted his musings. With difficulty Timothy tore his gaze away from the churning ocean.

"Enter!" he called.

With a soft crackling noise the door swung inward, and a pair of the Grandmaster's aides appeared. They wore cloaks of green with gold stitching, but beneath these, Timothy could see they wore dark-colored breeches similar to his own pants. He wondered what this signified. Most of the mages wore robes whose various colors seemed to represent their families or guilds or a certain magical discipline. With their cloaks, these two looked almost like guards or soldiers, and he wondered if that was the intended effect, and if that had anything to do with the fact that some of the other guild masters were visiting today to assess Timothy.

Then Nicodemus entered the room and all other thoughts were brushed aside. It was impossible of course, but the Grandmaster seemed taller, larger than Timothy had ever noticed before. He wore golden robes similar to those Timothy had seen him in before, but these were shot through with green stitching, the arrangement the precise opposite of the gold-on-green of his aides' cloaks.

The Grandmaster stroked his mustache, brow furrowed with worries that Timothy could only begin to guess at.

"Good morning, Lord Nicodemus," he said, standing up straight and raising his chin, trying to be as respectful as he could. In the few days he had been here, he had tried his best to learn manners and protocol from those around him.

"That remains to be seen," said the Grandmaster. He narrowed his gaze and studied Timothy. "You have not yet dressed for the day."

Uncomfortably the boy glanced down at his nightclothes, then over at Edgar and Sheridan. They were still asleep. He himself was still in his pajamas. Dawn had come and gone perhaps three quarters of an hour earlier. He had not imagined that the guild masters would arrive this early.

"I'm sorry, sir," Timothy said. "I can change quickly. I need only a few minutes."

Nicodemus shot a quick glance at the snoring Edgar, beak under his wing, and at the still and silent form of Sheridan. "A few minutes are all you have. The other guild masters are waiting. Yurick and Faulkner will bring you to the aerie when you're ready."

With a flutter of his cloak hem, the Grandmaster turned to take his leave, but he paused just outside the door.

"Timothy?"

The boy stood up even straighter. "Yes, sir?"

His face was thin and severe and often Nicodemus could appear cruel. But he softened now, and there was an almost fatherly air about him. His eyes were gentle as he gazed at the boy.

"You were impressive last night. I'd no idea the Asura had trained you for hand-to-hand combat. With that and your capacity for invention, I think you are going to make a remarkable spy."

Lord Nicodemus said this last in a hushed voice, obviously

unused to giving compliments. Then his features hardened again. "Unfortunately only seven guild masters have answered my summons. Some have stayed away because they abhor you, others because they do not like the idea that you are a part of the Order of Alhazred, but not all of them wish to do you harm. What we must discover, then, is who our enemies are. Do not assume that those who have stayed away are against you, nor that those who have answered my summons and gathered here today are your friends."

Timothy nodded, anxious and confused. How did he become the nexus for so much bitterness and suspicion? The answer, when it came to him, unnerved him: *Simply by being born.*

The Grandmaster disappeared into the corridor and his aides, Faulkner and Yurick—though Timothy could not tell one from the other—retreated beyond the door to give him privacy while he dressed.

Of the seven guild masters who had answered the summons of Lord Nicodemus, only three piqued Timothy's interest. He knew he ought to be curious about all of them, particularly in light of Nicodemus's warnings that any of them might be an enemy or a friend, but four of them seemed almost interchangeable. Two of these were men and two were women, and all of them had varying flesh tones. Yet despite their robes, and their high offices, and the responsibilities they held, there was something, dare he say it, ordinary about them. Certainly they dressed in sorcerous finery appropriate to their status, but each was middle aged and not physically remarkable. He had expected all of them to have a certain presence and austerity, the way Nicodemus did. And, truth be told, he had expected a certain exotic quality to these powerful men and women.

Had only those four been in attendance he would have been

sorely disappointed. Fortunately for Timothy—though he was aware it might not be to his good fortune—the other three guild masters who had answered the summons were more in line with his expectations.

Lord Foxheart, Grandmaster of the Malleus Guild, was no larger than Timothy himself and completely bald, right down to a lack of eyebrows. He had the blackest eyes Timothy had ever seen, and too-sharp teeth that made the boy shiver every time the man opened his mouth to speak.

Mistress Belladonna, Grandmaster of the Order of Strychnos, was a tall, elegant woman whose skin was the earthy red hue of the sand on the Island of Patience. Timothy found himself mesmerized by her—he had seen precious few women up close since being brought to this world—but she did not favor him with the slightest of smiles, only watched him with one brow arched warily.

Finally, there was the mage Timothy wished most to avoid looking at. Lord Romulus was a massive man—if he even was a man. The mage was gigantic, no less than nine feet tall and perhaps more. Grandmaster of the mysterious Legion Nocturne, he wore a gleaming silver helmet that covered his entire head, save for an opening in the shape of a cross that revealed his eyes, nose, and mouth. The helmet had been fashioned from magic of course, not in some crude forge the way Timothy had taught himself to work metal. And yet it did not have the smoothness that so many magical creations had. The metal was rough and a pair of spikes jutted from it, making it appear as though Lord Romulus had sprouted horns.

For just a moment Timothy wondered if the gigantic mage truly did have horns, and the helmet had been fashioned to cover them along with the rest of his head. The giant mage wore a chest plate of the same metal, though it shimmered with color, imbued with an enchantment. Over his shoulders was thrown a cloak that had been made from the pelt of an enormous, furred animal. The way the fur had been cut, it was obvious that whatever the dead creature had been, it had not been killed by magic. The cloak was a trophy of some sort, and the idea chilled Timothy while at the same time intriguing him, as it indicated that there were, at least, some mages who were not completely disinclined to work with their hands rather than with spells and charms and curses.

Foxheart, Belladonna, and Romulus. Those were the three who drew his attention. The others were both less interesting and less vocal. In fact they said almost nothing at all, leaving the debate and the inquiries to their more colorful counterparts. Timothy picked up what information he could about the various guilds and their masters merely by observation, but he intended to find out more about these three after the conference was over.

"What I would like to know is how such a thing could happen," said Mistress Belladonna, her voice quiet and lilting. Everything she said seemed to arrive at his ear as a whisper meant only for him. "The world is an ocean of magic. You cannot immerse yourself within it without getting wet. You cannot be a part of this world and not be touched by magic."

In his high seat, set above the others, Lord Nicodemus tugged at one end of his long mustache, his hawklike features more severe than ever, the blue veins beneath his pale skin giving him the appearance of having been crafted from marbled stone.

"And yet," Nicodemus said, inclining his head toward Timothy. "There he sits."

A ripple of mutterings went around the room. Several of the guild masters commented, but Timothy found that despite his being the topic of discussion, most of what was said was repetitive and boring. Even with all that was going on in that room, he found himself more fascinated by the chamber itself than with the proceedings.

Lord Nicodemus called the room the aerie, and Timothy had already decided it was the greatest room he had ever been in. The word "room" was hardly sufficient to describe it. SkyHaven was already a kind of miracle, floating above the ocean. The aerie was the one place in SkyHaven that really took advantage of the beauty inherent in this powerful magic.

It was a meeting hall, and clearly had been constructed for no other reason than for Lord Nicodemus to impress his guests with an example of how powerful he was. Thus the conference table at the center of the aerie was not so much a table as a ring, with chairs for visitors and dignitaries around its circumference, and nothing within that circle.

Nothing at all. No table. No floor. No ground at all. Within the circular space was a hole in the base of SkyHaven that was more than thirty feet wide. Daylight seeped into the room from below, reflected off the rolling blue ocean. All around the room were beams and nooks that had been created to provide perfect roosting places, and dozens of seabirds had shown their appreciation by building nests there. Even as the conversation droned on, Timothy watched the birds fluttering and cooing in their nests, flying across the high ceiling of the chamber, then dipping to glide out through the hole in the base of SkyHaven.

It was beautiful, really, and though Nicodemus could be harsh, the knowledge that the man had built such a chamber in his home gave Timothy hope that the Grandmaster was gentler at heart than he seemed upon the surface. Edgar had accompanied him, but the rook had taken flight only moments after they entered the aerie, disappearing to investigate both the massive chamber and to fly down through the foundation of SkyHaven and soar above the ocean waves. Timothy could not blame him. He wished he could have been anywhere but there. If he could fly, he would have done precisely the same thing as Edgar.

An image appeared in his mind, an image of wings and rotors and gears. Timothy smiled to himself.

His reverie was interrupted as Lord Romulus smashed an enormous gloved fist down upon the ring table. Timothy jumped and stared, wide eyed, at the giant mage who was pointing at him.

"The boy is a blight upon the face of this world!" Romulus snarled, his voice flat and tinny inside his helmet. Yet he was no less terrifying for it. "Why do you think Argus Cade hid him away? He was ashamed, as well he should have been. If an animal is born into your stables lame or filled with the madness, do you not destroy it? Of course you do. And so must this boy be destroyed. You risk the scorn of all the guilds by harboring him, Lord Nicodemus."

Murmurs of assent whispered around the ring-shaped table. Lord Foxheart was seated beside Mistress Belladonna, almost directly across from Romulus in the circular space. She whispered something to him, and the sharp-toothed little man— whom Timothy now realized reminded him of the hairless cat, Alastor—rapped his knuckles lightly on the table to draw attention.

"Beg your pardon, Lord Romulus," Foxheart said, his voice deep and insinuating, "but the Legion Nocturne is well known for its love and respect of ancient ways. You are to be commended for remaining dedicated to the righteousness of a simpler time. But there must be some progress in the world and in a case such as this, when a boy's life is in question, there is no place for antique ideas.

"Have you no pity, sir? Is the Legion really so primitive, so barbaric, that you would sentence a child to death for the crime of being different?"

Foxheart kept his gaze firmly on Romulus, with Lord Nicodemus shifting his attention back and forth between them. Belladonna, however, glanced over at Timothy, a sweet smile blossoming upon her ash-red lips. Timothy could not help but smile back, but he regretted it instantly. Lord Romulus had noticed it, and now the gigantic sorcerer leaped to his feet with a speed that belied his massive size and pounded upon the ring table once again.

"I would destroy him myself! With my own hands, had I not vowed there would be no violence in Lord Nicodemus's home."

Timothy froze. All of his fascination with the guild masters, and with the aerie and the seabirds who lived within it, was driven from his mind. His mouth was dry and he blinked, staring incredulously at Lord Romulus. The man wanted to kill him. Not to order his execution, but actually to kill Timothy himself, with his own hands.

"Caw! Caw, caw!" came the shrill call of the rook as Edgar soared up through the round hole in the floor and began to circle the ring table. He fluttered to a landing on the back of Timothy's chair.

"Over my dead body," the bird declared.

Lord Romulus's eyes narrowed inside that horned silver helmet and he lowered his head. A snarl came from deep within his chest as he spun on Nicodemus. "What is this, sir, that you would allow a familiar to speak thus to a grandmaster in your home?"

Now it was Nicodemus who stood, cocking his head slightly to one side and regarding Romulus with a warning glare. "You've threatened his master. How would you have him react?"

All of the guild masters muttered in amazement, some actually letting out epithets of surprise.

"You cannot be serious," said Lord Foxheart, staring at the rook.

Lord Romulus sneered across the gulf, the reflected sunlight gleaming up to glisten upon his helmet. "The boy is not a mage, yet he has a familiar?"

Edgar cawed loudly. "Hukk! Yep! And I'll tear your eyeballs out if you get anywhere near my boy."

"I'm not sure I believe any of this," Foxheart said. He shot Romulus a look. "My esteemed friend of the Legion Nocturne, the Grandmaster of the Malleus Guild asks you to put aside your ire for a moment so that we may ask what ought, perhaps, to have been our first question." The little man bared his rows of needle teeth. "How do we know this boy truly is an un-magician?"

Timothy was tired and afraid and saddened. None of this was accomplishing anything. It was all bluster and posturing. If it was true he could not even gauge his allies and enemies by the behavior of these people—the few guild masters who had even answered Nicodemus's summons—then what purpose did any of it serve? He wanted it to be over.

"Try me," he said.

All of the mages around the ring table turned to stare at him. Behind his head he heard Edgar chuckle softly as the bird settled more comfortably onto the back of the chair.

"Timothy—," Nicodemus warned.

But the boy would not be deterred. He stood and looked defiantly at Foxheart and then at Nicodemus. "Try me," he said again. "I invite you to use your magic on me. Attack me. Transform me. Levitate me. Silence me. Whatever you like. Try."

Mistress Belladonna stared at him. "Young Master Cade, do you really think this is wise?"

Foxheart grunted. "I don't think this is appropriate at all," he said, and he glanced up at Nicodemus. They were all staring at the Grandmaster of the Order of Alhazred, waiting to see what his response would be.

"All right. Do your worst, my friends."

Timothy's heart fluttered like rook's wings in his chest, but it was too late to take the words back. Still, only one of the guild masters seemed inclined to take him up on his challenge, even with the consent of Lord Nicodemus.

"Very well," Romulus agreed. "Thus my concerns are dealt with far more swiftly than I anticipated." He glared at Timothy. "You are an accident, boy. An unnatural thing. It is no fault of your own, but you cannot be allowed to pollute the magical fabric of this world."

Timothy sighed and rolled his eyes. He was afraid, but he was also tired of the gigantic mage's raving.

"Go on," he urged.

Lord Romulus opened his mouth wide and spewed an arcing stream of fire across the chamber. It scorched the ring table and burned the air above the opening in the floor. Edgar squawked loudly and took flight, darting into the air and up into the eaves of the aerie. The magical flames washed over Timothy, engulfing his upper body and his face.

They did not even feel warm.

When Lord Romulus clacked his jaws closed and the fiery blast subsided, the Aerie was silent save for the cooing of seabirds and the gentle lull of the ocean waves far below.

Nicodemus stood, arms crossed upon his chest. He inclined his head in a ritual gesture of respect. "And now that your questions are answered, my friends, let it be known that Timothy

Cade is a member of the Order of Alhazred and remains under the protection of the order, and my personal protection as well. This is to honor the memory of his father, but also in sympathy with a bright, unique child who wants nothing more than to learn about a world that he has been deprived of his entire life.

"Timothy Cade has come home," Lord Nicodemus said, and the Grandmaster's eyes seemed to burn with grim warning. "And he will be left in peace. Or I shall be very displeased."

The Grandmaster took a last look around, then glanced at Timothy. The boy could not hold back the smile that bloomed upon his features then. Much as he might be humorless and set in his ways, Lord Nicodemus was a true friend.

"And now," Nicodemus said, glancing at the others, "I thank you all for coming. Safe journey home."

The bright sun shone warmly down upon SkyHaven and her banners flapped and waved in the ocean breeze. The water was a deep, rolling green and the sky a pale blue that seemed to hint of clouds yet to come. If there was a storm to come, however, there was no sign of it on the horizon.

Leander Maddox stood upon the battlements of the fortress, the wind whipping at his hair and ruffling his bushy beard. The view to either side—the spires of Arcanum or the vast ocean—was breathtaking, yet his focus was entirely upon the activity in the courtyard below. A flock of seven or eight fanquail paraded about, digging grubs from the lawn, their rainbow plumage spread behind them. Songbirds fluttered in among the leaves of the trees on the far side of the courtyard, where a horticulture mage wrung rain from the air above his gardens with a flourish of his fingers, using the sorcery that was unique to his specialty.

Leander paid little attention to the wildlife or the horti-mage. His attention was occupied by the graceful violence unfolding below him. As several lower-caste Alhazred mages looked on, arms folded within their robes, Timothy sparred with Ivar. From the way the boy moved, fluidly and yet with a firmness and confidence that seemed out of place for someone so small and lithe, it would have been obvious to any observer that the Asura had trained him. There was a synchronicity between them, a familiarity that made the sight of their combat one of elegance.

Ivar's flesh was the color of the grass. It was difficult at times to keep track of his movements from above. Timothy seemed not to have a problem doing so, but by now he must have been used to the chameleon qualities of the Asura. Against an opponent unfamiliar with his tribe, Ivar would have an immediate advantage. Leander was glad they were allies.

With a feint that even the Asura warrior believed, Timothy tricked Ivar into lunging for him, then dodged out of the way. He tapped his mentor in the back of the skull with a closed fist, then danced swiftly aside before Ivar could respond.

The Asura smiled and bowed, then stepped aside and gestured toward the four Alhazred mages who had gathered. Leander could not hear what was being said from this height but when the mages removed their cloaks, one by one, he realized what was happening. Timothy was going to spar with Nicodemus's followers. The boy seemed vulnerable in the blue breeches and loose white shirt Nicodemus had provided for him. In the uniforms of their rank within the order, the mages were imposing. Four full-grown men against one teenaged boy.

Leander blinked with surprise and felt a tremor of alarm go through him. It was uncommon for Alhazred mages to be trained in hand-to-hand combat, but not unheard of. If they had been trained, however, he was certain there was reason for it, that Nicodemus would have ordered it to enhance their capacity as security operatives at SkyHaven. Their training would have been completely different, however, from Timothy's. As the boy's self-appointed guardian, Leander feared for him. He was, after all, still a child in so many ways.

As the four mages began to encircle the young un-magician, Leander decided he must put a stop to this exercise. He spun on his heel, searching his memory for the fastest route of descent from battlement to courtyard, and an animal yowl filled the air as he nearly stepped on Alastor, the Grandmaster's hairless familiar.

Nicodemus stood perhaps twenty feet away, his hair and long mustache blowing in the breeze, hands hidden inside the sleeves of his robes. In the bright sunlight he was pale as a corpse and his pink eyes now seemed nearly as white as a blind man's. Leander was taken aback by his appearance and startled by his mere presence. He had not heard the Grandmaster arrive and had thought himself alone upon the fortress wall. They gazed at one another in silence for a long moment, there atop the battlement, high above SkyHaven.

"You worry for Timothy." The Grandmaster strode to the edge of the battlement and looked down on the courtyard. "You should not."

Leander stepped up beside him, hesitant and anxious, worried for Timothy, ever aware that with Argus Cade dead, Leander was responsible for the boy's well-being. But when he glanced into the courtyard again he gave a sharp intake of breath and blinked several times as if doubting what he saw. Two of the Alhazred mages were on the grass, one of them cradling an injured arm, while a third wisely retreated. Even as Leander watched, Timothy darted toward the fourth and final opponent. The mage struck out at him, but Timothy sidestepped the blow as though the man were moving at half speed, hooked a foot around the man's ankle, and gave a firm shove, knocking him onto the grass.

Those mages already on the ground laughed good-naturedly at how easily their last hope had been bested. Off to one side, blending almost completely into the landscape, Ivar watched with an air of approval, but not a trace of surprise.

"You see," Nicodemus said. "Nothing to be concerned about. There is danger, certainly, but the order will do whatever is necessary to protect him, even as we discover how prepared he is to protect himself."

Leander glanced at the Grandmaster, whose eyes squinted against the light.

"This is Timothy's life now."

In one of the lower levels of SkyHaven, not far from the quarters that Lord Nicodemus had reluctantly set up for Ivar, the Grandmaster had also allowed Timothy to construct a workshop not unlike the one he had had on the Island of Patience. There was a forge and bellows, and there were windows that looked out over the ocean. With all that had been going on since his arrival, Timothy had had time to do little more than assure himself that all of the crates he had packed up at his father's home had been placed in the workshop.

Until today.

Inspired by the new purpose he had been given, Timothy had enlisted Sheridan's help in moving crates to locate the project he had been in the midst of building before the first assassins had come after him at his father's home. The model he had constructed back on the Island of Patience had turned out to be a perfect template, at least so far as he could tell.

The air was thick with the scent of oil and far too warm. A mage could have commanded the spell-glass to disappear, but the windows would only open for Timothy if he touched them, disrupting their magic. Each time he wanted to cool off he had to take a short break and go to the window, negating the spell-glass to get a breeze into the workshop. Eventually he would have to ask Nicodemus to alter the spell on the windows, but for now he kept at his work. Beads of sweat rolled down his back and forehead as he stoked the fire and let the rotor blades for his new creation heat in the flames. Then he laid the metal flat on the anvil and hammered it down, the clang and spark of his hard work making his heart leap. How he had missed this!

Timothy took in the shape of his gyrocraft, its small, gliding wings already firmly fastened into place. Edgar fluttered his own black-feathered wings and walked along the craft, investigating the contraption with the abrupt, inquisitive jerks of the head that were a reminder that no matter how intelligent the familiar was, he was still a bird.

Timothy took a rest and wiped the sweat from his brow with the back of his hand. He set the rotor aside to let it cool and walked over to the workbench where Sheridan was carefully joining together the links of the small chain that would be part of the moving heart of the gyrocraft.

"How is it coming?" the boy asked.

The mechanical man's eyes brightened and his head swiveled around to look at Timothy. Steam sighed from the release valve on his metal skull. "I will be done with this task shortly, Timothy. But I must ask you again to reconsider. You are putting yourself in a great deal of danger, in a craft that is untested."

Timothy smiled and wiped his hands on his apron. "Come on, Sheridan. The only way to solve the problem of it being untested is to actually test it."

With a loud flutter of wings, Edgar flew the short distance across the workshop and alighted atop Sheridan's head. "Caw, caw!" the rook cried. "I'm with him. If people were supposed to fly, they'd have wings."

The boy put his hands on his hips. "My father brought me many books on the island, Edgar. I know there are plenty of birds who have wings but can't fly."

Both of his friends were agitated and Timothy appreciated their concern, but his mind was made up. He was about to tell them this when Sheridan's head swiveled quickly toward the door of the workshop and a blast of steam tooted from his release valve.

"Hukk!" Edgar cried, feathers ruffling. "Company."

The massive silhouette that filled the doorway was cloaked in shadow, but Timothy recognized Leander instantly. A moment later the mage stepped into the workshop, smiled at Timothy, and glanced around, shaking his shaggy mane.

"Never seen anything like it," Leander said. "Your workshop on the island was extraordinary, Tim, but the speed with which you have adapted this space is even more impressive." He spotted the frame of the gyrocraft. "And that . . . you're actually building it, eh? Amazing."

With a grin, Timothy bounded toward him and threw his arms around the mage. "I saw you earlier, while I was sparring outside, but I thought maybe you had left already." He pulled back and shot Leander a menacing glare. "Of course, I would have had to pummel you. It isn't the same around here without you."

Leander's smile flickered, faded, and then disappeared completely.

A trickle of sweat slid down the back of Timothy's neck and he shivered with dread, a frown knitting his brows. "What?" he demanded. "What is it?"

The mage forced his smile to return. "It's nothing. Nothing for you to worry about. And I'm glad to see you as well. I had some business at SkyHaven today, and I thought perhaps we might dine together this evening. By all accounts, you're doing well. I heard how you handled yourself this morning in the aerie, and I'm proud of you, Timothy. I'm certain your father would be as well. It is a difficult situation you find yourself in, and you have given an admirable accounting of yourself thus far."

Timothy stared at him grimly. "Stop that."

Leander arched an eyebrow. "Stop what?"

"Tell me what's on your mind right now. Is there some new danger Nicodemus hasn't told me about? Have some of the other guild masters come? What's going on, Leander? Don't leave me in the dark. That's far more dangerous than anything else I'm up against."

At first the mage began to shake his head again. Sheridan clanked and whirred and hissed steam as he walked over and crossed his arms, eyes glowing brightly as he, too, glared at Leander.

"Caw! Caw, caw! What's on your mind, Master Maddox?" Edgar crowed.

Leander ignored the rook and the mechanical man, his eyes focused on Timothy. "I'm afraid for you, boy. That's all. With so many guild masters shying away from the conference this morning—and even among those who showed themselves—it's impossible to know who can be trusted. Especially with . . ."

Once again he shook his shaggy mane of hair and reached up to stroke his beard. "Never mind. I didn't come here for—"

"Leander," Timothy said firmly, gazing up at the massive mage. "Please. Speak your mind."

The mage sighed and glanced away. He hesitated a moment before turning back to them, his eyes alight with intensity. "What I tell you in this room must remain in this room. There are things even the Grandmaster does not know."

"Of course," Timothy replied.

Leander glared first at Sheridan, who nodded once with only a whisper of steam, and then at Edgar, who cawed his assent. With this, the mage seemed to shrink slightly, settling down into his own skin. He glanced at the others again before at last refocusing on Timothy.

"Lord Nicodemus and I have both told you of the recent disappearances in Arcanum. Mages from many guilds have gone missing. The fact is that more than two months ago I was engaged by the Parliament to investigate this mystery. They came to me in secrecy so complete that not even my own Grandmaster—not even your father, my friend and mentor—were told of my work for the Parliament."

Edgar hopped to the ground and walked toward Leander, talons scritching the floor. "And what have you discovered?"

Dejected, Leander threw up his hands. "Precious little thus far, I'm afraid. They might well be running off to form a new guild. It has happened before, but not for more than three hundred years."

Timothy heard the doubt in his voice. "But you don't think so. You think something awful's happened to them."

Slowly the mage nodded. "I do."

"I don't understand," the boy said. "If it's supposed to be so secret, why are you telling us? I'm glad you did. I just don't understand why."

Even in the mix of firelight from the forge and the twilight that gleamed in through the windows, Timothy saw that Leander's face reddened. The mage glanced away, as though in shame, and it was several long moments before he looked up again.

"I fear for you, Timothy," Leander said. "I don't approve of you becoming involved in the espionage that you and the Grandmaster have planned. Yet I know that you can do it, that you will likely be very successful at it. And as much as it pains me to confess it, I fear that one day soon, I may need to endanger you further by asking for your assistance in my own clandestine affairs."

CHAPTER SEVEN

The gyrocraft is ready, Timothy thought as he finished tightening the last of the bolts on the lightweight frame. *But am I?*

Nicodemus had told him during supper that this would be the night his special skills would be put to use, and Timothy had felt as though he might be sick. He had expected it to be soon, but not *this* soon. He'd hardly touched his meal, then excused himself from the dining chamber and headed to his workshop. If tonight was indeed the night, he had to be certain that his flying craft was in perfect working order.

Timothy stepped back and admired his work. He had conceived and designed it ages ago, but now at last he had been able to complete it. The workshop Nicodemus had set up for him was everything he could have hoped for, tucked away on the southern side of SkyHaven, away from prying eyes. All he had to do was spy for the Order of Alhazred and everyone would be happy—well, almost everyone.

Throughout making the final tweaks to the gyrocraft, Edgar had fluttered nervously about the workshop, black eyes gleaming with disapproval. Now, as Timothy gave a spin to the large rotor on top of the craft, the rook croaked loudly from atop a workstation covered with leftover parts. "I know you haven't asked for my opinion. I'm just the familiar, after all. But I have to tell you, Timothy, I don't care for this one bit."

The tiny propellers attached to the short wings and to the tail of the gyrocraft were fastened well enough, but Timothy checked and double-checked the main roof rotor one final time.

Though in an emergency he could jettison the rotor and simply glide to a landing, he did not like to entertain that possibility. Better safe than sorry.

Edgar cawed loudly.

"I'm sorry," Timothy said sheepishly. "I'm not ignoring you. I just want to make certain I don't miss anything. That . . ." He smiled. "That would be bad."

The rook's feathers ruffled. "Caw! If you're trying to make me less worried, you're really bad at it."

Throughout his work on the gyrocraft, Sheridan had been his loyal assistant. Now the mechanical man hissed a sigh of steam, and with a whir he raised his chin. It was obvious he shared the rook's fears. Timothy handed his wrench to Sheridan.

"I know how you feel, Edgar, but I don't have much of a choice," Timothy explained. "They've tried to kill me twice now, and if I don't find out who's responsible, the third time might be the end of me."

The bird cocked his head, light reflecting off his black beak. "I still don't like it." With a rustle of feathers he turned his back on Timothy. "You're just a boy, not a spy—and look at how he's dressed you."

With a frown Timothy glanced down at himself, at the midnight black, tight-fitting clothing Nicodemus had provided him. He reached up to touch the hood that was bunched around his neck.

"It's so I don't get caught," Timothy said to his disgruntled familiar as he studied himself. "It'll help me blend with the shadows—that's what Nicodemus said, anyway."

With a jerk of his head, the rook twisted to fix him with a dark, riveting stare. "It scares me."

A whistling geyser of steam was released from the side of Sheridan's head as the mechanical man began to tidy up the workroom. "Edgar speaks for all of us," he said as he picked up Timothy's tools. "We are all anxious about this sneaking around business."

Timothy was annoyed. This wasn't what he needed to hear. He already had his own doubts about this assignment, and his friends' fear wasn't increasing his confidence any.

"I have to do this."

"Do you?" came a wizened voice from across the room.

Timothy glanced over to find that at some point Ivar had slipped into the workshop. Now he stood silently at a window looking out at the night, his skin as white as the moons that hung weightless in the sky.

"Oh, Ivar, not you, too," Timothy said. "I thought that you would understand."

As always, the Asura thought carefully of his answer before responding. Then he spoke directly from his heart, for he was incapable of lying. "I know of the hunt, of confrontation and battle—of victory and defeat," he said as he looked away from the quiet beauty outside SkyHaven. "I know what it is to skulk in shadows in the camp of my enemy, or to elude capture. But to spy upon your allies because you suspect duplicity . . . There is no honor in this."

Timothy flushed, momentarily ashamed, but then he frowned deeply and shook his head. "This is more complicated than that. I haven't been among other people very long, but with mages it seems pretty obvious that it's difficult to tell who's an ally and who's an enemy. I know you're all concerned for my safety, but without magic, I have to take any advantage I can get. In this world, that means knowing what the guild masters are up to. I'm sorry, but I have to do this. I'll be careful."

Timothy approached his craft for yet another inspection. "I'm going to fly in, take a look around and hopefully find out something that will help Lord Nicodemus weed out those who want me dead. With my special abilities—" He smiled at his own choice of words. "Or, without any, I should be practically invisible to their security systems. And since there's no magic built into the gyro, they won't be able to sense that either.

"I hope."

Edgar flew up from the table to land on Timothy's shoulder. He squawked as he examined the invention. Its framework was made from lightweight metal tubes, one of which rose up from the craft's center. The lower part of this shaft was connected to a series of gears that would enable it to turn, and its top was adorned with three long horizontal blades—the rotor. There was a single seat in front of the shaft, and behind it a specially designed engine that drove both the rotor and the small propellers on the tail and each wing.

"You're really going to try to fly? With this?" the rook asked.

Timothy crossed his arms, growing frustrated with Edgar's continued doubts. "That's the plan."

The familiar ruffled his feathers with uncertainty. "Not only are you un-magical," he said. "But I think you might also be a little crazy."

The boy chuckled, not unfamiliar with the bird's lack of confidence in his abilities. He leaned toward the gyrocraft and used a rag to wipe a smudge of grease from its gleaming frame.

From somewhere close by, a clock tolled the hour, a mournful sound that reminded Timothy of the task he had yet to accomplish this night.

There came a sudden rapping at the door, and before any could respond, it swung slowly open to allow Lord Nicodemus to enter.

"I was wondering when he was going to show up," Edgar grumbled, just loud enough for Timothy to hear.

Ivar crouched on the floor beneath the window and his skin turned the color of the gray stone wall at his back. Timothy had stressed the importance of Ivar's presence to his work and Lord Nicodemus had grudgingly allowed the Asura to travel this wing of SkyHaven freely. But Ivar knew that it did not please Nicodemus in the least and thought it best to blend into his surroundings whenever the master mage was near.

The Grandmaster was eerily silent as he entered the room, the door closing behind him.

"Good evening, Lord Nicodemus," Timothy said with a slight bow of his head.

The Grandmaster was clothed in elegant, high-collared robes the color of a fiery sunset. Timothy had never seen him in the same outfit twice, and absently wondered how much clothing a single person could have. Then he felt foolish, realizing that a mage of Nicodemus's skill could easily alter his garments to appear however he wished. A small smile rippled across the boy's face as he realized how vain the Grandmaster must be.

"Timothy," Nicodemus responded. His gaze ticked toward the boy's invention and he studied it with a curious eye. "Is this the device in which you will . . ." He moved his hand through the air in front of him.

"Yes, my lord," Timothy responded proudly. "I haven't tested it yet, but I'm sure that—"

"You shall have the opportunity tonight," Nicodemus interrupted, strolling around the craft, taking in every detail. "Fascinating," he said as much to himself as to anyone else in the room. "Do you have a name for it?"

"How about, *It'll Never Get Off the Ground*," Edgar commented, softly enough so that only Timothy could hear.

The boy swatted him from his shoulder.

"Caw! Hukk! Hukk!" Startled, the bird fluttered across the

room and perched upon a workstation. "Kid's kind of touchy when it comes to his gadgets," grumbled the rook.

"I call it a gyrocraft," Timothy said.

"Gyrocraft," Nicodemus repeated, letting the word roll around on his tongue. "Are you sure that this . . . gyrocraft will perform as you designed it to?" he asked as he clasped his hands behind his back.

Timothy looked at his invention, his mind taking it apart piece by piece, screw by screw, and then putting it back together again. "I trust it with my life," he responded with certainty.

"Excellent," Nicodemus answered. "That level of assuredness will be necessary for your success."

A germ of doubt began to grow in Timothy's mind, but he quashed it. Ivar had trained him well—the order's combat mages had learned that very quickly—and as he was invulnerable to magic, he had nothing to worry about. *And if I just keep telling myself that, I'll be fine.*

As Timothy and his friends looked on, the Grandmaster wiped his hand across the air. Where his fingers passed, an image shimmered and began to take form, a grand tower rising up from a lush forest on the far outskirts of Arcanum. Yet this was no ordinary tower, not even one of the glittering spires of the city. It was not built from stone, nor of metal or wood, but rather, appeared to be organic, alive, as if it had sprung up from the earth rather than been constructed.

"It is the Order of Strychnos I wish you to investigate tonight," Nicodemus said, and with a wave of his hand changed the image from the organic tower to the lovely, exotic features of the Strychnine's Grandmaster. "Mistress Belladonna," Nicodemus uttered softly. "As beautiful as she is deadly."

"She didn't seem all that dangerous," Timothy said, referring to the guild masters' meeting where he'd first seen Belladonna.

He had found her strangely alluring then, as he did now.

"That is but one of her many weapons, dear boy," Nicodemus explained. The Grandmaster moved his hands again, and a closer image of the living tower appeared. Timothy silently marveled at the magics of the Strychnos guild to have created something so impressive.

"The Strychnine exhibit a mastery over plant life. This fortress tower was grown from a single seed of the long-extinct Maximus tree. All things rooted within the earth respond to the Strychnine's commands and the members of the guild share a fondness for poisons."

The image changed again to show Mistress Belladonna in a vast garden, surrounded by all manner of greenery, the wild and unusual, as well as the mundane. The guild master was collecting clippings from the various plants and placing them inside a basket she carried on her arm.

"Belladonna is a true master of crafting poisons derived from plants."

Timothy continued to watch the elegant, red-skinned woman as she moved among the lush vegetation.

"At one time or another, all the assassin guilds of the world have used the poisons of the Strychnos," Nicodemus said, as he, too, eyed the image of the woman before him. "Including the Nimib."

Timothy slowly nodded, now understanding why the Strychnos order had been singled out.

The Grandmaster waved away the images he had summoned. "You will use this craft of yours to infiltrate the living tower," he said, looking from Timothy to the gyrocraft and back again. "Once inside, you will seek out any evidence that might prove the Order of Strychnos was involved in the attempts on your life."

Lord Nicodemus narrowed his gaze. "And there is one more small chore," he said, raising one long finger.

"A chore?" Timothy asked, the muscles in his stomach tightening with unease.

Nicodemus stepped away from the gyrocraft, hands again clasped behind his back. "Many years ago the Order of Strychnos stole something from me—from the Alhazreds." He stopped before the boy, his expression grave.

"I would like you to get it back."

The cold night air whipped his face, but Timothy's cheeks burned with the warm current of fear that flowed through him. His every nerve seemed to buzz with anticipation of what he had set out to accomplish. In a way, his trepidation annoyed him, for if he hadn't been so anxious, he would have been ecstatic. The gyrocraft was functioning exactly as anticipated, but the thrill of the contraption's success was severely limited by his destination. Perhaps on the return trip he could exalt in the wonder of flight, at the uniqueness of his own invention.

But not yet.

The engine purred and the propellers were nearly silent. The rotor was louder than he would have liked, but there was nothing to be done for it now. Timothy passed above the agitated ocean waters and navigated between a pair of oceanside structures nearly as tall as the spires of Arcanum. In his mind Timothy reviewed the three-dimensional map that Nicodemus had conjured before his departure, the route from SkyHaven to the living tower illuminated in scarlet. Carefully he piloted the craft northward toward the wild forest on the outskirts of the city, where the tower grew.

With the gyrocraft's hand controls he gained elevation, rising hundreds of feet as he left the harbor behind. The city of

Arcanum passed beneath him, and Timothy was dazzled by the sight. From his bedroom window in SkyHaven, he had marveled at the countless ghostfire lights twinkling in the distance, but it was nothing compared to this. Everything was close enough for him to touch, to feel, to experience. He wished he could land the craft and explore the thriving city, soaking up the sights, smells, and sounds of the wondrous place. But that was for another time, when there were less pressing matters to attend to than sneaking into the headquarters of a sorcerous guild and stealing some kind of valuable supernatural artifact.

Well, all right, it wasn't *exactly* stealing. The Box of Vijaya had been stolen from the Order of Alhazred. Timothy was just going to take it back. According to Nicodemus, the box could be used for divining the future and had been in the possession of the Alhazred guild for well over a millenium. It had gone missing during the extravagant ceremony held to mark the raising of SkyHaven, an event attended by all the guilds. The Grandmaster had long suspected the Strychnine were responsible for the theft. They had always been jealous of the advantages the box had provided for the Alhazreds.

The lights of a sky carriage blinded him momentarily, and Timothy expertly manipulated the controls of the gyro to climb higher. It wouldn't do to be seen in such an unusual, nonmagical craft, so he maneuvered his invention upward into a thick cloud of mist and hovered as the sky carriage passed harmlessly beneath him.

Timothy dropped the craft out of the mist, the gyro as well as his black clothing now dappled with glistening moisture. His mind flashed back to the moments before his departure, as he climbed aboard the gyrocraft and Sheridan wheeled it to the open window in his SkyHaven workroom.

"To blend with the darkness one must be as the darkness," Ivar had said, demonstrating by shifting the color of his skin to a solid black.

"Some of us have to make do with what we have," Timothy had replied, tugging the black hood up over his head.

But the Asura warrior had frowned, displeased with the boy's response. Ivar had reached over to Sheridan, sticking his fingers between the joints of the mechanical man and pulling them away covered in a dark lubricant. "Be as darkness," he had stressed as he painted Timothy's face with the oil.

Timothy had left without looking back at his friends, not wanting to see the fear or disappointment in their eyes. He had chanced a look at Nicodemus though, and saw that the old man was smiling.

Now he shivered with the recollection of that smile, and attempted to distract himself by peering down at the ghostfire lights of the city below. The structures were more spread out now, and far less modern in their design. He guessed that he was nearing Arcanum's northern provinces and searched the horizon through squinted eyes for any sign of the Strychnos tower. Ahead, he could just make out a thick bank of fog that seemed to rise up from the ground below, the blanket of gray, shifting moisture covering a large portion of forested area, a place called the Khabanda Weald. Rising up through the mist, like the finger of some great, elemental deity, was the tower of Strychnos.

Timothy's heart raced and for a moment he hesitated, a new reluctance stalling him. The concerns of his friends and Ivar's disapproval weighed heavily upon him. The rotor cut the humid air and, as if for effect, the night sky growled and lit up with a flash of lightning. Timothy flinched, but it was enough to shake him from his cautionary paralysis. He set his jaw, teeth clamped tightly together, and increased the output of power on the craft's engine. If there was a storm coming in, he wanted to reach the tower before it arrived.

He flew the gyrocraft into the fog bank that hung over the dense forest as the sky rumbled and flashed, oddly grateful for the thunder, as it would mask the sound of the rotor. The nearer he got to the tower, the more impressive became the sight of the Strychnos guild's base of operations. Nicodemus's conjurings of the tower had not allowed him to appreciate its massive size. The tower's dark green exterior was covered in a thick bark that reminded the boy of scales on a fish, and in its multiple windows were dots of ghostfire light that glowed within its body. It was truly an awesome sight. Timothy slowed his progress as the winds increased. He didn't want to come in too fast and crash into the building's side.

At first he thought the sound was coming from the gyrocraft, a low buzzing noise that hinted of malfunction. Quickly checking and rechecking his instruments, he realized that the droning sound was not coming from the craft at all. He turned his attention to the mist surrounding the organic tower, just in time to see something fly toward him out of the concealing mist.

Timothy's reflexes were sharp, and he dipped the gyrocraft to one side as the object buzzed past. It was an insect of some kind, the shell of its body a smooth, emerald green that glistened brightly in the flashes of lightning. Its veined, transparent wings beat the air so quickly that it produced a vibrating sound.

Before he knew it, they were everywhere, flying around and past him at incredible speeds. He hadn't a chance to maneuver the craft out of their path, but it didn't seem to matter. The bugs avoided him with ease.

Timothy watched in wonder as the insects whizzed past him; some stopping abruptly in midair, hovering very much like his gyrocraft was doing at the moment. They paid him no mind as they hung there, wings beating the air unmercifully. The bugs were eyeless, with long, segmented antennae that seemed to stroke the mist as if searching for something. He guessed they were some sort of aerial sentry, sensitive to traces of magical energies that did not belong in the vicinity of the tower. But there was nothing magical about Timothy's presence, and they took no notice.

After several long moments, during which he clutched the controls of the gyrocraft so hard that his knuckles went white, the sentries turned their antennae in other directions and flew on. Timothy let out a long, shuddering breath and ascended up the outer wall of the tower until he could look down through the fog at its rooftop, where he recognized the elaborate garden from the Grandmaster's conjured image. Bringing the craft down toward the lush vegetation, he realized Nicodemus had not mentioned insect sentries, and with a sinking feeling in his gut, Timothy wondered what else his mentor had failed to mention, what other surprises he might encounter this night.

Timothy landed his craft with the utmost precision in a small clearing. Swarms of large beetles flew up from the thick vegetation, dipping and weaving about him as if he were one of their own. He unhooked himself from his seat and climbed from the flying machine. Gathering some dried leaves, tall grass, and Yaquis fronds from the ground, Timothy concealed the gyrocraft. Then, satisfied that it was invisible to the casual observer, he turned and searched for an entrance to the tower.

He found it in the shape of a large, grass-covered mound. Within the mound was a door adorned with a magical insignia, and if he had been an ordinary citizen of Arcanum attempting to enter the Strychnos headquarters uninvited, he would have gotten no farther. But Timothy wasn't an ordinary citizen, and the magical wards on this door did not apply to him. Others would have required a key to enter. Instead he placed both hands against the surface of the door and simply pushed.

A warm, moist air, tinted with the sweet aroma of cut flowers, wafted out from inside as the door opened onto a winding ramp spiraling down to the next level. The walls were damp and the ramp beneath his feet soft and springy, as if comprised of moss. Slowly he descended, feeling as if he were not in a building at all, but inside some gigantic living thing. At the end of the ramp, he encountered a door. In his mind he reviewed the diagram he had seen in the privacy of Nicodemus's study. The blueprints had been quite extensive, and when he'd asked the Grandmaster how he had come to have this information, Nicodemus just chuckled. "The concept of spying is not new to the Order."

On the other side of this particular door would be a series of corridors that would lead him to what the Strychnine called the sanctum, a chamber that housed precious artifacts and ancient materials for research. Nicodemus was almost certain that the box would be there. According to the Grandmaster, it had been specifically designed to be used only by the mages of the Order of Alhazred, so the Strychnine were unlikely to have managed to use it for their own ends.

Timothy clung to the shadows as he moved stealthily through the quiet halls. He rounded the last corner and faced a set of large, double doors, the symbol of the Order of Strychnos etched upon them both, a flowering vine wrapped around a simple representation of the world. Timothy slowly approached. *So far, so good,* he thought. He took a quick look over his shoulder, then carefully pulled on one of the doors, opening it just a crack. The sound of conversation floated out from within.

"Well, I'm done here," came a weary voice. "It's time for me to retire for the night. Can I get you anything before I turn in?"

Pulse racing, Timothy tensed to run, to retreat, but something held him back. He had not given himself away. They weren't aware of his presence. He remained where he was and listened.

"Set me over by the window, would you?" asked another voice, this one reedy and slow, as though the speaker was quite old. Something about that voice made him shiver. "You know how much I enjoy the sunrise."

Cautiously Timothy pulled the door open a bit wider. A large man dressed in the dark red robes of the Strychnine was placing an ornate box of lacquered gold upon the windowsill. The boy's breath caught in his throat. The fancy box was exactly as Nicodemus had described.

"There," the man said, turning to leave, his body set in a slight, bestial hunch. "Until morning, then." He started across the room toward the doors.

"Good night," said the other voice—and it seemed to be coming from the direction of the box.

Quickly Timothy turned and pressed himself against the wall. The double doors opened wide, hiding him from view as the Strychnos disciple left the sanctum. The boy remained utterly motionless, silently hoping that the mage would not look back. Otherwise he would have to rely upon his black garments and the door to hide him.

The mage had nearly reached a bend in the corridor and Timothy needed only to wait a few more seconds, but the doors to the sanctum were swinging shut and he was out of time—he would be discovered. As quietly as he could manage, staring at the retreating back of the mage, he moved out into the corridor and slipped into the sanctum, just as the doors shut behind him.

The room was dark except for a few ghostfire lamps upon the wall, but they burned low and cast deep shadows. Even so, Timothy could see that the place was a cluttered mess. Ancient books, stacks of paper, scrolls, both rolled and not, were sprawled across desks and tabletops as far as the eye could see. There was a mustiness in the air that reminded him of his father's study back at his house, and suddenly he longed to be there. *Soon,* he thought. *I'll be back there soon.*

"Is somebody there?" a rasping voice whispered.

Timothy whipped around, startled, his throat going dry. He felt himself shudder and he ran his tongue across his lips to moisten them. The voice had come from the windowsill, from the ornate, gold box.

"Hello?" came that eerie voice again.

Timothy carefully picked his way across the room. His gaze darted about, but it was clear that there was no one else in the room.

"I know you're there," said the voice again, and this time Timothy was certain of its location. "Why don't you step closer so that I can see you."

Timothy stood before the golden box on the window sill. It was set at a slight angle, its top opened toward the window. He reached up and touched its ornate surface, and slowly craned his head around to take a peek inside. The boy gasped. Within the box was a human head, its eyes wide and staring right at him. It appeared to be trying to speak to him, but all that came from its mouth were guttural squawks and gasps, even as its eyes began to roll back in its skull.

"Daargg, putthu duuuuuuarrrrrrrrr," the head said, its sunken face contorted, a rivulet of drool slipping from one corner of its mouth.

Timothy moved closer, confused and more than a little alarmed. He was reluctant to touch the head, but felt he ought to do something. Then he had a thought. He turned the box so that he could still see inside it, then moved back a few paces.

Immediately its eyes cleared and an alertness returned to its expression.

"That's better," it said. "For a moment there, I couldn't seem to think straight. That has never happened to me before. I must be getting old."

The bizarreness of the situation suddenly struck Timothy. Here he was secretly inside the tower citadel of one of the most powerful guilds, in the early morning hours, about to have a conversation with a decapitated head. It was enough to make him long for the tranquil sameness of Patience. At least on the island, things seemed to make a certain amount of sense.

"What . . . what are you?" he asked the head, keeping his distance so as not to cause any problems with its answer.

"I?" the head questioned. "I am the Oracle of Vijaya. And who, may I ask, are you? You are not of the Order of Strychnos, of that much I am certain."

"Timothy," the boy said as he studied the head.

It appeared to be very old: a paper-thin covering of spotted, yellow skin stretched over an angular skull, white wisps of hair springing up in sparse patches atop its head. It should have been quite frightening, but there was something warm and friendly about its large, deep brown eyes. They seemed to put him at ease.

"Timothy?" the oracle asked. "Merely Timothy? You have no surname?"

"Cade. Timothy Cade."

The head smiled, revealing a jagged row of brown teeth. "Argus's boy? I'd heard his wife was with child—but then again, that was some time ago, not long before I was stolen away."

He considered telling the oracle about his mother's sad fate and his father's recent death, but the oracle already seemed to know.

"It's all so very sad," the head said dreamily. "Both of them gone, and you all alone." The oracle was suddenly silent, its mouth slack, its eyes glazed.

For a moment he wondered if he was still too close. "Oracle?" he called, moving back a few more steps.

The head came awake. "I'm sorry, Tim," it said. "It's just so nice to be seeing for an Alhazred again. I shut myself down after I was brought here, damned if I was going to divine the future for the poisonous Strychnine."

The Oracle of Vijaya again seemed to drift off—*gazing into the future perhaps,* Timothy thought.

"You have the potential for a very interesting destiny," the head said to him. "And your gift—it could very well change the world."

Timothy wanted to know more, but caution told him that time was of the essence, and he should gather his prize and leave. He had yet to find proof of the Strychnos order's involvement with the attempts on his life, but the fact that they were indeed thieves certainly had to count for something.

"I'm going to take you back to SkyHaven—to Nicodemus," he told the oracle, "but in order for me to do that, I'm going to have to carry you—your box, and it will probably affect you. You see, I have this problem and . . ."

The Oracle slowly blinked its wonderfully kind eyes. "I understand, Timothy," he said. "It will be good to leave this place, to be back where I belong." Then the head closed its eyes. "I look forward to speaking with you again soon."

Timothy reached for the box, gently closing it, and snapping shut the latch. On his belt he had brought another of his inventions. It was similar to something he had crafted on Patience using the webbing of a Sundin spider. It was a net of sorts, and on his island home he had used it to help him carry the fruit from various trees as he climbed them. It kept his hands free.

Timothy slid the ornate box inside the netting and attached it to his belt, where it hung at his side. Satisfied that it was secure, he made his way toward the doors.

He was about to push them open when he heard a sound from the hallway. Curious, Timothy pushed open the door a crack, pressing his face against the cool wood to look outside. He was expecting to see more Strychnos mages, so the sight of the two massive beings standing in the corridor outside stunned him. They were dressed in body armor and fur, their heads covered in fearsome helmets, adorned with spikes and horns.

Legion Nocturne, he thought. They had to be. As he peered at them, one of the soldiers reached into his cloak and produced a rectangular block of a rough, yellow substance, perhaps some kind of cheese. He broke off a small piece and handed it to his comrade.

"I don't feel right leaving him with that witch," muttered the Nocturne soldier who had accepted the cheese. He brought out strips of dried meat from a leather pouch and offered them to the other man in turn. "What if she uses her poisons on him? The Strychnine cannot be trusted, and Belladonna least of all."

The other grunted, taking a piece of meat for himself. "We have been promised safety while we are here," the warrior said. "Why else would we be allowed to wander these halls?"

"I don't like this place and I don't trust them. I'm uncomfortable with their sudden hospitality," the first growled, taking a bite from his dried meat.

"It is not our job to trust. We are to follow the orders of our superiors. That is how the legion has always endured."

What are they doing here? Timothy wondered as he watched the warriors through the door, remembering what Leander and Nicodemus had said about the various guilds' intolerance for one another. Could this alliance be the kind of evidence that

Nicodemus was searching for? He backed away from the door carefully, allowing it to close completely.

His curiosity was piqued, but he decided that it was best to return to the gyro and escape with the oracle. But how to do that with the Nocturne soldiers right outside the door? His mind raced with possible options.

Why not ask the oracle? he thought.

Timothy removed the box from the netting at his side and placed it upon a scroll-littered desk. He unlatched the lid and pried it open to gaze upon the head stored inside. Timothy still found the sight of it disturbing, but realized that he was getting used to it. Stepping back, he called out to awaken it from its rest.

"Oracle?" he said in a whisper, not wanting to arouse the attention of the warriors outside.

"Hm? Are we at SkyHaven already?" the oracle asked, eyes springing open. "Did they actually manage to get it up into the air? I can't wait to see—"

"We haven't left yet," Timothy explained. "There are Legion Nocturne soldiers outside the door." He pointed to the double doors behind him.

"Hmm, yes. I did see that. Didn't pay it much mind though. What are we going to do? "

"I was hoping you might have a suggestion. Could you look into the future a bit and see how we get out—if we get out that is?"

"A few minutes ahead you say?" the oracle asked. "Don't see why not." And then he went abruptly quiet, his rich brown eyes glazing over. They cleared a moment later and the ancient, withered face of the oracle smiled. "You are a clever one, Tim. Perhaps it's because I haven't any body, but it never would have occurred to me to use the air ducts."

Timothy looked about the room and found a circular opening high up in the wall. It was covered in a sheer membrane that pulsed in and out, as if the tower was breathing—yet another reminder that the citadel was not some structure crafted of wood or stone, but a living thing.

With a grin, the boy thanked the oracle and closed up the case to return it to the carrier at his side. He approached one of the desks and quietly pushed it over to a spot beneath the wall opening. Timothy hopped up on the desktop to be at eye level with the duct. He felt the warm, moist air upon his face and reached out to tear at the sheer netting that covered the opening. It must have acted as a kind of filter, he thought, examining the silklike material in his hands; the inventor part of his brain was fascinated. Tearing the delicate sheath away, he hoisted himself up into the circular hole in the wall and scrambled inside.

It was dark and cramped in the circular passage. A steady breeze passed over him like the breath of some great, mythical beast, carrying the sounds of the tower. The shaft was soft and moist beneath his knees, and he began to crawl through the winding passage. Occasionally coming upon another opening, he would peer through the membranous filter covering it, trying to assess his whereabouts. For what seemed like an eternity, he made his way through the ducts, and was just considering consulting the oracle again when the conduit suddenly opened up into a junction of sorts, with a gaping hole above him. Figuring that was the way to the roof, Timothy prepared to climb, but then he heard a familiar sound—a voice carried upon the breath of the Strychnos citadel.

The voice was drifting out from one of the passages before him. Timothy struggled with the idea of ignoring it, of hopping up into the tunnel above him and climbing to freedom, but his curiosity got the better of him. *If I'm going to be a spy, I might as well act like one,* he thought, leaving the junction to crawl down the shaft to verify a suspicion he'd had since first seeing the Legion Nocturne soldiers.

The voice was loud, bearish, and filled with intimidation. There was no mistaking its source. Another speaker joined the first as Timothy cautiously made his way to a membrane-covered opening. The second voice was softer, calmer, and he was surprised that it didn't have a more soothing effect upon the other.

"It is as I've said for decades," proclaimed the first. Timothy squatted in the tunnel, peering into the chamber below. "The Grandmaster of the Alhazred cannot be trusted."

Lord Romulus and Mistress Belladonna faced each other in what appeared to be her private chambers. The Grandmaster of the Strychnos guild casually sipped something from an ornate, green goblet that appeared to have been grown rather than cast in metal or blown from glass. She watched as the menacing Nocturne leader paced, his black, fur-collared cloak billowing out behind him.

"Even if the boy is an innocent, Nicodemus's motives are to be questioned," he said, stopping before her. "It would not at all surprise me to see the youth used for ill gain."

Belladonna set her goblet down on a serving cart, turning to walk toward a high-backed throne upon a raised dais. "I am glad you have brought these suspicions to my attention, Romulus," she said, taking her seat of authority. "The recent disappearances of guild mages have begun to pique our curiosities as well." She stroked her lips with long, delicate fingers the color of Patience soil. "Isn't it interesting that none of those missing has affiliations with the Order of Alhazred? Passing strange, wouldn't you say?"

Romulus nodded his helmeted head in agreement. "The Alhazred bear watching, Belladonna," he said to his supposed rival, his voice a bestial growl. "If my suspicions are correct, we may all soon find ourselves in grave danger."

Timothy was stunned. Doubts that he had harbored from the moment he had met Lord Nicodemus rushed to the forefront of his thoughts, and he found it hard to breathe. *Maybe the Strychnine aren't the ones I should be spying on,* he thought as he backed away. He needed time to think.

Quickly he crawled back to the opening he believed would take him to the roof. Sinking his fingers into the soft flesh of the tunnel, he hauled himself up into the shaft and began the long climb.

CHAPTER EIGHT

The storm had come, a fierce rain driving down from the tumultuous sky in gray sheets. The wind howled around Timothy like some great, crazed beast, beating against the gyrocraft as if trying to swat it from the air. He struggled to keep his invention aloft, at the same time fighting the inner squall that had been whipped up by the foreboding discussion he had overheard in the Strychnos tower ducts.

. . . none of those missing has affiliations with the Order of Alhazred . . . Passing strange, wouldn't you say?

The words echoed in his mind and a chill crept through him, deep to the bone. *Is it possible,* he wondered, *that what the guild masters said is true?*

Lightning knifed across the sky in front of him, jagged spears of white-hot fire descending from swollen gray clouds to illuminate the sleeping city of Arcanum below. The rain continued to pelt his face, and he took one of his hands away from the craft's controls to wipe away the water that spattered the circular glass of his flight goggles. Timothy was glad that he had decided to bring them; it had been hard enough to pilot his invention earlier in normal weather conditions, never mind in a driving rainstorm.

He was supposed to return directly to SkyHaven, but he was not at all certain he wanted to do that. *And what if I do? Should I just tell Nicodemus what Belladonna and Romulus were saying, ask him if it's true?* Timothy thought it would be wiser to just keep it to himself, at least until he could discuss it with Leander.

Lightning tore across the sky again, followed by a bellowing rumble of thunder. He wiped rain from his goggles and was surprised to see the large, looming shape of the SkyHaven estate floating not too far off over the churning sea. Timothy had been so preoccupied that he had barely noticed the journey.

Then, impossibly enough, over the din of the storm, he heard his name being called.

As he squinted through the rain, he saw a black shape in the distance, growing larger as it flapped toward him. "It's about time, kid!" Edgar was cawing loudly to be heard above the storm. "We were getting pretty worried."

Timothy smiled; it was good to see his friend again. It had been only hours, but it felt as though he had been away for a very long time.

"Keep an eye on me and I'll guide you in," the rook promised. He glided in front of the gyrocraft as they drew closer to SkyHaven.

Two lanterns of ghostfire had been lit and hung on either side of the window opening, lighting his way, and Timothy began to gradually decrease his speed as he prepared to land.

"Almost there, kid," he heard Edgar say, the words sucked away by the wind.

The window grew larger and more defined as he approached. This was the tricky part, not to allow the spinning rotor blades to come in contact with the sides of the opening. *Total concentration,* he thought, slowing his forward progress all the more, now practically hovering before the open window. He felt the weight of the box that contained the Oracle of Vijaya at his side, but could not muster any sense of accomplishment this early morn. It had been tainted by the foreboding conversation of Lord Romulus and Mistress Belladonna.

"Timothy, be careful!" Sheridan cried out in his metallic

voice, snapping the boy's wandering mind back to the here and now.

He was drifting to the right, his spinning blades dangerously close to the window frame. Timothy's heart raced as he tugged the controls, focusing again just in time to bring the gyrocraft to a graceful landing inside the workshop.

That was too close, he thought, angry that he had let his mind wander at such a crucial moment. He was tired and anxious, but he knew that his lapse could have gotten him hurt, not to mention his friends. It troubled him deeply and helped him make up his mind as to what he ought to do next.

"Caw! Caw!" Edgar cried as he flew around the gyro. "Had us worried there for a bit," the bird said as he looked for a place to land.

Silently Timothy unhooked himself from his seat restraints and climbed from the vehicle.

"Glad to have you back, Timothy," Sheridan said, his metal feet clumping closer. The mechanical man released a whistling cloud from the valve on the side of his head. "I've been holding my steam until your safe return, I must say."

Timothy didn't respond, checking inside the netting at his side to make sure that the oracle's case was in one piece. It appeared fine, and he removed the ornate box carefully.

Ivar emerged from the shadows, ghostlike, his skin a luminous white. "Timothy," he said, his dark gaze seemingly reading the boy's troubled demeanor. "Is all well?"

It was a unique trait the Asura warrior had, to be able to read his mood—to know when something was wrong.

Timothy shook his head, moving past them all to make his way from the room. "I'm not sure," he said, pushing open the door and stepping out into the hall. "But once I am, you'll be the first to know."

Timothy rapped on the door to Lord Nicodemus's study before entering. Normally the enchanted door would have announced the arrival of a guest, but Tim was, as always, invisible to the magic.

"Come in, Timothy," Nicodemus called out.

It is not an easy job I have been elected to perform, my boy, Nicodemus had said to him when they studied the designs of the Strychnos tower. *The fate of so much weighs heavily upon my shoulders, but now you have come, and I see that there is much that we will accomplish together to provide for the safety of the world.*

Timothy had felt important that night, as if he suddenly had a purpose and was no longer an aberration to be pitied. The Grandmaster of the Order of Alhazred had recognized him—Timothy Cade—as being important. But now, stepping into the room, he wondered about the validity of those feelings.

Nicodemus rose from his chair before the hearth of dancing ghostfire. There was no warmth from the supernatural flames, but they danced and shifted color within a magical field of containment. In addition to being a source of light, he'd heard that many used the mesmerizing movements of the supernatural flame as a means to relax. Nicodemus's familiar, Alastor, had been curled up on his master's lap and now jumped to the floor without a sound.

"Thank the stars that you've returned safely," the Grandmaster said, a concern in his voice that Timothy had not noticed before.

The hairless cat padded across the ornately woven rug to rub against the side of the boy's leg.

"It appears Alastor is pleased that you've come home safely as well."

Home. Timothy had never thought of SkyHaven as his home before, had never really considered it a possibility. He'd always imagined it as a brief stopping point, before being allowed to return to his father's house. He wasn't sure if he really cared for the idea of living here permanently.

Yet there was a warmth in the Grandmaster that Timothy had never seen before, and suddenly the suspicions he had carried back with him from the Strychnos citadel seemed foolish. Leander trusted Lord Nicodemus, and Timothy's father had as well. The man was the Grandmaster of their order. There had to be a logical explanation for the insinuations and concerns of the other guild masters. There had to be. Both Nicodemus and Leander had told him about the pettiness and the infighting between the guilds. He could not allow himself to be taken in by idle gossip.

Timothy was about to begin his report, his step-by-step review of what he had done this evening, when the Grandmaster cut directly to the chase.

"By the looks of the box you have beneath your arm, I gather that your mission was at least partially successful?" Nicodemus asked, a wry smile upon his aged features.

"Very successful, Lord Nicodemus," Timothy responded, feeling a brief moment of pride.

"You entered their domicile unimpaired, walked the halls unnoticed, and relieved them of a priceless supernatural artifact?"

Timothy nodded.

The Grandmaster played with the ends of his mustache. "And as you skulked about their tower did your ears happen upon anything of interest?" he asked. "Dire plots that would perhaps incriminate the Order of Strychnos in the attempts to take your life?"

"Nothing about me," he said, glancing away as he chose not to reveal the conversation he had heard. Nicodemus was so pleased that Timothy did not want to give the old mage the impression that he had doubts. He looked up quickly. "Lord Romulus was there, though. With some of his Legion Nocturne. He was having a meeting with Mistress Belladonna."

The pale, slender old man knitted his white brows. "Was he indeed? That is interesting. But not terribly unexpected. I imagine they're all trying to figure out what to do about you." Lord Nicodemus's gaze ticked toward the ornate box in Timothy's hands. "And you returned with a prize. The oracle?"

"Yes, sir," Timothy said quickly, presenting the box to the Grandmaster. "Proving that you were right about the theft."

"So it does," Nicodemus replied, as he accepted the ornate, golden case that held the clairvoyant, disembodied head. "You've done remarkably well on your maiden mission, my boy," he said, turning toward a circular table across the room that looked as though it had been hand carved from a single piece of veined, milky white stone. The mage crossed the room and carefully set his prize down upon it.

Alastor hopped up onto the stone table, rubbing the skin of its hairless neck affectionately upon the box as Nicodemus prepared to open it.

Timothy let out a long breath, as though he had been holding it for a very, very long time. "I have to say, I was a little shocked when I saw what the oracle was," he said, caught up in the Grandmaster's excitement. "A talking head, I couldn't believe it."

Nicodemus pulled his hands away from the box's latch and turned to stare at the boy, ice in his eyes. "Did you speak with the oracle?"

Alastor continued to rub his furless body against the outside of the oracle's case.

A tremor of nervousness went through Timothy. "Well, yes. Or, actually, it spoke to me. When I found it, the box was open— and it spoke."

The Grandmaster narrowed his eyes as he digested this information. "How could it be? When you touched the box, the aura of negation that surrounds you should have disrupted—"

"It spoke to me before I touched it. And when I realized I was . . . affecting it, I stepped away," he replied. "Have I done something wrong?"

The Grandmaster was about to answer when the box containing the Oracle of Vijaya sprang open, the locking mechanism triggered by the attentions of the Grandmaster's familiar.

"Alastor!" Nicodemus snapped, startling the cat, which leaped down from the table to hide in a shadowy corner of the room.

The oracle's eyes fluttered open, and a smile blossomed across its withered face as it saw Timothy from across the room.

"Hello there, Timothy Cade," the oracle said cheerily as it began to look about its new surroundings. "I see you've succeeded in bringing me back to—"

The head stopped abruptly when its gaze fixed upon Nicodemus, who loomed above the box. The oracle's eyelids became hooded and started to flutter, its mouth twitching, just as it had done before, in the Strychnos citadel. It was seeing the future.

The Grandmaster reached down to close the case just as the oracle's eyes grew wide.

"What have you done, Nicodemus?" it cried, sheer horror in its voice. "What have you done?"

The old mage slammed the box shut, double-checking its latch. His movements were jittery, anxious, and Timothy felt his stomach churn and a chill go through him as he wondered what exactly it was that the oracle had seen.

"The Oracle of Vijaya has been in the possession of an opposing guild for far too long," Lord Nicodemus said dismissively, but it was several moments before he looked Timothy in the eye. "It must be examined thoroughly before it can be allowed to divine for the Order of Alhazred again."

Timothy slowly nodded, his misgivings over what he had heard at the tower again heightened. "Who knows what the Strychnine might have done to it?"

"Exactly, Timothy," Nicodemus said, pushing the golden case of the oracle to the far side of the table. Alastor had emerged from the shadows and now mewled at his master's feet.

"Well, you must be tired," Nicodemus stated softly, stroking the head of his animal. "I suggest you return to your quarters for a well-deserved rest."

"I am very tired," Timothy lied, yawning. Fear and doubt were like a fire racing through his veins. He couldn't remember the last time he'd felt *less* tired. It would have been impossible to sleep even if he had wanted to.

"Very good then," Nicodemus said, escorting the boy to the door. "We'll talk further in the morn, and discuss your next endeavor." The Grandmaster smiled, pushing open the study door. "Good night, Timothy. You've served the Order of Alhazred greatly this night, and I'm sure your father would have been quite proud."

As Timothy walked the dimly lit corridors of SkyHaven he became convinced that his father would not have been proud of him at all. In fact he was sure the man would have been quite disappointed.

His friends were waiting for him back in his workshop, so Timothy did not go straight back to his quarters as Nicodemus had suggested. Instead he began to descend through the floating island fortress to the only room in SkyHaven where he felt even remotely comfortable.

As he made his way through the lonely hallways, he began to feel as though he was being watched. The boy was certain that it was all just nerves brought on by his newly aroused suspicions about his benefactor, but he could not help but search every shadowy nook and cranny that he passed for a pair of spying eyes.

He descended the winding staircase that would take him to the room that Nicodemus had made his workshop, passing long, open windows that looked out onto the ocean that surrounded the floating estate. The storm had passed. If only the same could be said about the tumult in his life at the moment.

Timothy pushed open the wooden door to his workshop and stalked inside.

"So?" Edgar greeted. "Was the old bird impressed or what? Bet he's going to name a street after you."

Timothy didn't reply. He was lost inside his head.

"Is something wrong, Tim?" Sheridan asked with concern. "Your rather cryptic words to Ivar before you left have certainly left all of us speculating."

Timothy did not feel safe in SkyHaven anymore. No matter how hard he tried to convince himself that he was letting his imagination get the better of him, that he should get a good night's sleep before doing anything rash, the ominous words of the guild masters kept intruding. He had been ready to dismiss them, but when he saw the oracle's expression as it looked upon Nicodemus, he knew with absolute certainty that something was amiss.

He felt Sheridan's metal hand fall gently upon his shoulder. "Timothy?"

The boy sighed. "Tonight I heard some things about Grandmaster Nicodemus—bad things—and I think they may be true." A kind of relief washed over him now that he had voiced his fears, and yet speaking them aloud also gave them a new weight.

Ivar emerged from the shadows, arms crossed and eyes narrowed sagely. There was a strength and firmness in his manner, and Timothy took a deep breath and tried to draw on that, to learn from the Asura's example.

Edgar fluttered down to perch atop Sheridan's head, careful not to scald himself on the escaping steam. "Do you know what you're saying, kid? This is Nicodemus you're talking about."

"I know what I heard—and saw, Edgar," Timothy told his familiar. "I need to speak with Leander right away—he'll know what to do."

The rook was strangely silent, studying him with quick cocks of his pointy head. "You're serious, aren't you?"

"Very," he answered.

"Then so am I," Edgar responded. "Fill me in and I'll fly to Leander's house and—"

"No," Timothy interrupted. He glanced over at Ivar, who nodded slowly in understanding. "I don't think it's safe for us here anymore," the boy explained. "I . . . I'm afraid for you, my friends, even more than I am for myself. We should all go. Right now. Before Nicodemus decides he didn't believe the answers I gave him about tonight."

Timothy went to his flying machine, flipping the hatch open to check the engine and the fuel level. "We'll use the gyro," he said. "Dawn is just arriving. Maybe it will be a while before anyone notices that we're gone."

"You expect that contraption to carry all of us?" Sheridan asked as he shuffled across the stone floor toward his creator.

Timothy nodded, inspecting the inside of the gyrocraft. "Edgar can fly on his own, and if we're careful, there should be just about enough room behind my seat for you and Ivar to squeeze—"

Sheridan shook his head from side to side, gears clicking, servos whining. "No, Timothy," he said, a soft hiss of steam leaking from one of his valves.

"What do you mean, no?" the boy asked. "We have to leave."

"I'm too heavy, and you know it. Pile me into your sky craft and it will crash into the surf within yards of your departure. You must go without me."

The mechanical man's words triggered a flurry of ideas. Sheridan was right; the gyrocraft would not support the weight of all of them, but with some adjustments, he thought he might be able to increase the craft's power.

"I have an idea," Timothy said, going to his workstation.

"You always do, my friend. But there is no time, Master Timothy," Sheridan said. "If your suspicions are true, you need to reach Leander as soon as possible."

"But I can't—," the boy began, horrified.

"You must," Sheridan said with a curt nod of his head. "Come back for me later."

"And so we have a plan," Ivar noted quietly.

Edgar fluttered his wings, still perched on Sheridan's metal head. "Not a plan that I like, mind you, but I don't think we have much of a choice."

The flesh of Ivar's body undulated with symbols of stark black, indicating his deep concern. "I will stay, and Sheridan will go," he said with finality.

Sheridan walked over to the warrior, reaching out to touch his arm. "Thank you, my friend, but I would still be too heavy for the flight. No, it is decided."

Timothy knew that Sheridan was right, but it pained him greatly. "I will come back for you," he promised. "I'll find a way."

"I know you will," Sheridan responded. "Now go on your way, so that you can return for me all the faster."

Without another word Timothy leaned into the gyrocraft and flicked a switch to activate its engine. The machinery whirred to life, the blades atop the craft and the small wing propellers slowly beginning to spin. Ivar went to the vast window, unlatched the wooden shutters and threw them wide.

From the corner of his eye Timothy detected movement on the ledge outside the window. Something had been out there, watching them, listening to their conversation. He didn't think himself quite so foolish about his paranoid feelings anymore. Ivar leaned out the window. He had seen it as well.

"It is the Grandmaster's familiar," he said over his shoulder as he pulled his knife from the scabbard at his side. "Depart quickly. I will deal with the creature before it can inform its master of our plans."

The Asura sprang up onto the window ledge, but Edgar launched himself into the air. "Caw! Caw!" the bird cried out, black wings flapping. "Get into the flying machine with the boy. I'm better designed for heights. I'll take care of the snooping cat and catch up with you as soon as I'm done."

Timothy watched as the rook darted out the window into the waning darkness. "Ivar, come on!"

The Asura nimbly leaped down from his perch on the sill and cautiously approached the gyro.

"Get in the back," Timothy told him.

Ivar stared at the machine with wary eyes.

The boy reached out and grabbed the warrior roughly by the shoulder, giving him a shake. The Asura glared at him, but there was no time for subtlety. "Please, Ivar, you need to get in right now—we can't afford to waste any more time."

The Asura grumbled something beneath his breath in the guttural tongue of his people and slid his bulky frame into the space behind the pilot seat of the flying machine. Timothy climbed in and gripped the gyro's controls.

Checking the instruments to be certain that everything was functioning properly, he spared one final glance at Sheridan. He could not help but think that the mechanical man seemed sad, even afraid, though his features were incapable of revealing much emotion. "I'll see you soon!" Timothy yelled over the whine of the gyro's engine.

Sheridan responded with a thumbs-up and a burst of steam from his head.

Manipulating the controls, Timothy lifted off from the floor of the workshop and steered the craft toward the open window. With the extra weight of Ivar added to the mass of the machine, the gyro did not respond as quickly, or as easily, as it had before, but he took all of this information into consideration, clearing the window and navigating the machine out into the open air.

The storm had subsided, but the night air was still cool and ripe with moisture.

"We have to find Edgar," Timothy yelled over the sound of the gyro's motor as he worked the craft's control stick. The flying machine banked to the left, arcing back toward the hovering estate.

"There!" Ivar cried out, and it took a moment for him to spy what the expert hunter's eyes had seen almost immediately.

Edgar, blacker than the diminishing darkness, flapped his wings furiously, hovering at a ledge not far from the window they had just left. As Timothy moved the craft in for a closer look, he saw the hairless Alastor balanced on his two back legs on the outcropping of stone, his front paws swatting at the bird. The rook beat his wings crazily at the feline familiar. The cat hissed fiercely, lashing out with its hooked claws as Edgar dipped, wove, and fluttered in the air, narrowly avoiding the cat's strikes. But Alastor proved cunning. He feigned a strike to the left, then spun around to lash out to the right with his other paw. The claws ripped across Edgar's wing, sending feathers fluttering in the early morning breeze.

The rook screeched, then retreated, flying back from the ledge to collect himself. The cat saw its opportunity, slinking along the stone sill, on its way to the next open window and back into SkyHaven.

"Edgar!" Timothy cried out.

The familiar flapped in the air, glancing over his shoulder briefly. Their gazes connected, and Timothy was certain that the rook was well aware of the importance of stopping Alastor from getting back inside. Edgar spread his wings, and angling his body toward the estate, dove at the hairless cat, his earsplitting battle cry filling the air.

Timothy held his breath as the two familiars raked at each other with claw and talon, unable to tell where the cat ended and the rook began. The furiously fighting animals seemed to be suspended in the air, their cries and hisses a cacophony of battle—and then they began to fall.

Purely on instinct, Timothy dipped the gyrocraft toward the plummeting figures still locked in combat. "Hold on, Ivar," he warned.

Suddenly Edgar unfurled his impressive wingspan to slow his descent and reached out with his talons to grip the loose, pale flesh around the neck of Nicodemus's familiar. Edgar flapped furiously to keep aloft with the struggling feline. He flew out over the cold ocean, opened his claws, and dropped the flailing cat into the water below.

Timothy watched as Alastor was swallowed up by the churning sea, but felt a spark of relief when the cat's head broke the surface, and it began to paddle toward the distant shore. *That should give us plenty of time,* he thought.

Edgar landed on the smooth surface of the gyro's nose and

began examining the missing patch of feathers on his wing. Just as the sun broke over the horizon, spraying spears of gold across the surface of the ocean, the rook looked up at Timothy with his dark eyes.

"I suggest you hurry."

CHAPTER NINE

Leander Maddox shifted in his favorite chair, and with a sigh, prepared to view the next student presentation. The crystal eye of Xanthari hovered in the midst of his study and now it blinked once, clearing away the images it had just shown and preparing to display the next.

"All right, Desmond," the professor said wearily. "Show me what you've learned this semester."

The image of a rotund youth, his golden robes pulled tight against a pronounced middle, shimmered to life before him. The young man was about to perform a spell of transmutation—transforming a block of stone into wood. Leander doubted he would succeed, having taught at least three others of the boy's family. He would have wagered that this difficult enchantment was far beyond the young man's magical abilities.

Leander reached for his goblet, eyes carefully studying the way Desmond's hands moved when calling forth the mystical energies. Distracted by a sudden noise from outside, Leander pulled his hand away from the wine goblet and sat up straighter. He listened, but heard nothing over Desmond's droning voice. The mage moved a forefinger about in the air and the crystal eye immediately shut down, plunging the room into silence.

Leander had been jumpy of late. With mages mysteriously disappearing in Arcanum and in other cities as well, one couldn't afford *not* to be overly cautious. Extensive investigations yielded no explanation as to why these mages were being taken, and the level of concern in the Parliament continued to rise.

He heard the sound again. A spell of defense on the tip of his tongue, he left the study and moved down the darkened corridor toward the back of his modest home. His housekeeper, Miss Fogg, had left hours ago after serving dinner, so he knew he should be alone. But there were faint noises coming from the back of the house—from his solarium. The magician's blood began to boil with anger. Somehow, someone had managed to bypass the wards of security that he himself had conjured. Clearly, whoever the intruder was had no idea who lived within. This evening prowler was in for a rude awakening.

Leander softly began the first syllables of a defensive spell that made the tips of his fingers tingle and carefully approached the door to his sunroom. He could hear voices within: two, maybe three intruders. This spell was one that he hadn't used in years. Leander was not a violent man, but when push came to shove he could conjure spells that would make the most battle-hardened combat magician stare in awe. He uttered the last of the incantation, the explosive power of magical force collected at the ends of his fingers, just waiting to be released.

The intruders were moving closer to the open doorway where he waited. *How dare they break into my house and skulk about,* he thought, enraged. Leander snapped his arms forward, his fingers extended, and let the supernatural energies flow.

"Did you think you would catch me unaware?" he bellowed, the magic cascading from his hands to engulf the first of the intruders. The room was bathed in an eerie supernatural light, and Leander finally saw the invaders clearly.

Timothy Cade's eyes widened in shock as the raging magical energies struck him square in the chest, with no effect at all.

Leander drew back in surprise. "Timothy," he said, dropping his smoldering hands to his sides. "Whatever are you doing here?"

With nary a whisper, Ivar emerged from the shadows with Edgar perched on his bare shoulder. Leander scanned the remainder of the sunroom for Sheridan, but the mechanical man was not to be found.

Then Timothy began to speak. It was as though Leander's question had opened a floodgate and words began to flow from the boy's mouth in jumbled torrents. What he could discern from the young man's fevered ramblings filled the mage with dread.

"Calm yourself, Timothy. Obviously there's trouble afoot, but panic will not cure it. Let's go to my study and settle down, and you can explain yourself at a more understandable pace."

Leander showed them to the study, urging them all to be seated as he himself sat down in his favorite, high-backed, leather chair. The Asura squatted on the floor, tensed as if waiting for something to happen. Edgar was strangely silent as he fluttered his wings and perched atop a marble bust of Lexius II, one of the most famous of Arcanum's mayors. Timothy was the only one who took a chair, but he set himself on its edge as though he was about to jump out of his skin.

"Now, Tim," the professor said in his most calm voice. "Slowly. You went on your first mission for the order, spying for Nicodemus. What went wrong?"

"I . . . I think that Nicodemus . . . he might be doing something bad."

The mage chuckled, attempting to put the boy's fears at ease. "Now why would you think that?" he asked. "What did you hear that would make you believe that Lord Nicodemus could ever—"

"Mistress Belladonna and Lord Romulus believe that he can't be trusted—that he's going to use me as some kind of weapon against the guilds."

Leander frowned. Suspicions played at the edges of his mind and he was short of breath, as though a gigantic hand was squeezing his chest as the words spilled from the boy's mouth.

"Well, of course they would think that. Neither of them are beyond suspicion either. And, after all, in a way the Grandmaster is using you as a weapon, isn't he?"

The boy shook his head. "That's not the way they meant it, I'm sure of it. And there's more. They suspect he has something to do with the mages who are disappearing, the ones you're investigating."

Timothy's accusations were unbelievable, treasonous, the thought of them carrying any truth a nightmare. "You do realize, Tim, that the guilds are often at odds with one another and—"

"You didn't see the look on the oracle's face," Timothy said, his voice a whisper filled with genuine fear.

"The oracle?" Leander asked.

"The Oracle of Vijaya," he explained. "I think it was having a vision, and it had something to do with Nicodemus."

Leander's mind was racing again. "You saw the Oracle of Vijaya?" he asked the boy, moving to the edge of his chair.

Again Timothy nodded. "Nicodemus said that the Strychnine had stolen it, and that I was to take it back for the Alhazred."

Amazing, Leander thought. The Oracle of Vijaya had been lost to the Alhazred order for twelve years. Before it had gone missing, it had been one of the most important magical items in their arsenal. Its visions were often deadly accurate. "What did the oracle say, Tim?" he asked, hoping there was a logical explanation for the boy's fears.

"It asked him, *'What have you done?'* and you should have seen the look on its face, Leander," Timothy said, his face twisted with the recollection. "Whatever the oracle was seeing, whatever it thinks Nicodemus did or will do—it must be really horrible."

The oracle's question reverberated through the mage's troubled thoughts, becoming his own.

"What *have* you done, Nicodemus?" he muttered.

Sunlight washed over Leander's face as he sat in the back of his sky carriage being carried across the city of Arcanum. It was a beautiful day, the sky crystal clear. He should have been light of heart. Instead Leander's mind was in turmoil.

For years the accusations had been whispered among the Order of Alhazred and even among the Parliament of Mages. There had been many petty complaints about the Grandmaster, suggestions that Nicodemus had used unsavory practices to manipulate some of the lesser guilds into voting with the Alhazred on Parliamentary matters. Leander had heard them and dismissed them as exaggerations of the truth, but now he was being forced to rethink his view.

The beauty of the new day, the morning sky above Arcanum, was lost upon him. Leander was far too preoccupied with the concerns Timothy Cade had expressed to him that early morning.

Timothy had been genuinely distraught, and Leander had done everything in his power to calm the boy, to get him to remember everything exactly as he had experienced it. He wanted all the facts to be accurate, for the implication of those facts was unthinkable.

Leander gazed out the window, for the first time this morning actually taking note of his surroundings. They were over the ocean now; it wouldn't be long before he reached SkyHaven, and hopefully some answers to his questions.

The boy and his companions had wanted to accompany him back to the floating fortress estate, to return for their mechanical friend, but Leander didn't think it wise. If Nicodemus *was* secretly acting out against certain guilds in Parliament and he learned that Timothy had been responsible for exposing him, there was no telling how the Grandmaster would react. No, Timothy and the others would be better off elsewhere. Leander had insisted that they be brought to the Cade mansion as a precaution. He hoped that the magical wards of protection at Argus's estate would be enough to protect the boy and his friends from harm.

"We're approaching SkyHaven, Master Maddox," his driver communicated from his perch atop the carriage.

"Fly around back, please, Caiaphas," he told the navigation mage. "I'll use the staff entrance. I'd rather not have it known that I've come to pay a visit."

"Very good, sir," the driver replied, and Leander felt the craft tilt to the right as it traveled around the always impressive expanse of SkyHaven.

The carriage gracefully dropped toward the garden at the rear of the estate. A fine, early morning haze rose up from the rich, green land around the fortress, dispersing as the skills of the navigation mage brought the craft in for a gentle landing before the back entrance. It was still quite early in the morning, and the grounds were abandoned. Leander opened the carriage door on his own and climbed out.

"Should I wait, sir?" Caiaphas asked, the hands usually sparking with the energies of supernatural transport now resting in his lap.

Leander gazed at the back of the estate, at a large wooden servants' entrance that would take him inside.

"No, that will be all for now, my friend," he said, a creeping unease growing in the pit of his stomach. For a moment, he thought he might be sick. Leander had not the slightest idea of what he would find inside the fortress, or what he might learn upon confronting the Grandmaster, but there was no other way. For the continued safety of all the guilds, he could not allow this to go unexamined.

"Master Maddox?" the driver ventured from his seat. "Are you well?"

With a deep breath, Leander nodded. "I'm fine, old friend. Too much on the mind." He tapped the side of his head with a finger. "Off with you then. I'll send a summons if I should need you to return for me."

Caiaphas bowed his head, extended his arms, and lifted the craft up into the air and away. Leander watched his carriage depart. He adjusted his robes as he prepared himself, standing before the door. He waved his hand before the door's eye-shaped locking mechanism. The magic within the lock recognized the man for who he was, a frequent visitor to SkyHaven and a dignitary, a high-ranking member of the order. The door opened to admit him.

Silently he padded down the hall, cautious as he passed the doorway leading into the kitchen, not wishing to be seen. He could hear the sounds of the kitchen staff as they bustled about, preparing breakfast for their master.

Nicodemus had often spoken about his morning ritual of rising before the sun to review the matters of the day before he would settle down for breakfast. The Grandmaster held the belief that only after he had contemplated what was expected of him that day could he truly enjoy his morning repast. Leander intended to give him plenty to fill his mind with this morning. Stealthily he proceeded to the Grandmaster's office study.

As he moved into the main body of the house, he wove a glamour of concealment about himself. It would be best to confront Nicodemus without giving him an opportunity to prepare for the questions Leander wished to ask him.

The staff was already hustling about SkyHaven, beginning their daily duties for the order. Leander sidestepped secretaries, secretaries' assistants, assistants to the assistants, maids, and maintenance workers on his way to Nicodemus's study. SkyHaven was coming alive, and he needed to quicken his pace if he was to catch the Grandmaster in his office before breakfast was served. Winding staircases and seemingly endless hallways were the course to his destination, but eventually the mage reached the place he sought.

Standing before the door to the Grandmaster's chamber, he composed himself, dismissed the glamour of concealment, and brought his hand up to knock. The door to the study clicked open before his knuckles could land upon the wooden frame, and Nicodemus's voice drifted out for him to hear. The Grandmaster was in the midst of conversation.

Leander stepped into the office. Nicodemus had his back to Leander. The Grandmaster was dressed in splendid robes of emerald green, facing a magical window that hung shimmering and pulsating in the air.

"In fact he's just arrived," he heard Nicodemus say to the one he conversed with on the other side of the mystical portal. The Grandmaster turned his head slightly and gestured to Leander that he would only be a moment longer.

A chill ran through Leander. Somehow Nicodemus had learned that he was coming. He squinted, attempting to discern the identity of the person on the opposite side of the communication, but to no avail. Magical windows could be used for spying, or for mages to converse over vast distances. They were meant to allow the speakers to see one another, but the image of whomever Nicodemus was conversing with was blurred and dark.

"Have no fear," the Grandmaster assured the mysterious figure beyond the portal. "The minor annoyances will be dealt with, I assure you." Nicodemus bowed.

"Be sure that they are," said the cold, cruel voice from the other side.

Leander felt the hair at the back of his neck stand on end as he watched the window collapse in upon itself with a sound very similar to that of breaking glass, leaving behind only a pin-prick of light. And then that, too, was gone.

The Grandmaster turned, a warm, welcoming smile upon his face. "Enter, Professor Maddox. Please."

"I find it hard to believe that you've been expecting me," Leander said, voice firm, posture straight; he would not be intimidated. If the Grandmaster of the Order of Alhazred was involved in dark deeds, he would be held accountable.

"When I learned that the boy and his friends were missing, I assumed that they had gone to you," Nicodemus said with a hint of a smile. "It seemed only logical that I would find you upon my doorstep this morning."

A pale shape leaped up onto the Grandmaster's desk, startling Leander. It was Alastor. The animal did not look at all well. Its skin was a sickly gray and tracks of a dark fluid leaked from the corners of its eyes.

"Is there something wrong, Leander?" Nicodemus asked. "Did I do or say something to cause the boy to flee my hospitality and nearly drown poor Alastor?" He took the cat from the desk and held the hairless animal lovingly in his arms.

There was a tension in the room that he'd never felt in the presence of the Grandmaster before, as if a storm was about to break.

"Timothy told me of his mission last night. And he told me of a conversation he overheard between the leaders of the Strychnos and Nocturne guilds."

The Grandmaster slowly stroked the body of the cat as it nestled in his arms. "The Strychnos and the Nocturne—do tell?"

Leander shook his head. "They suspect you of deeds most foul. Their words suggest that you have a connection to the string of disappearances in Arcanum, and beyond."

"Oh, my," the Grandmaster said, startled. He set Alastor down on the seat of a nearby chair. "No wonder Timothy ran off."

Nicodemus returned to his desk, his eyes scanning the cluttered surface, searching for something. "And what are your feelings on these indictments, Leander?" he asked idly. "Do you believe there is any truth to them?"

Leander kept his focus on the Grandmaster. He did not know what to believe. Everything that mattered to him was challenged by these suspicions, but he dared not ignore them.

"He also told me about the oracle—and what it said to you."

The old man froze, his hand hovering momentarily over something on the desktop before snatching it up.

"I see," Nicodemus replied darkly. He sighed and turned to face his guest. "I can't blame you for coming like this, Leander." The archmage sat tiredly in his chair, the item he had picked up still clutched in his hand. "These charges are most dire. Does anyone else know of them?"

A tremor of guilt and regret went through Leander. He thought of all the things Nicodemus had done for the order, all the years he had been grandmaster. "I know how wild this all sounds, my lord, but it cannot be ignored. Still, I wanted to hear your explanation before I made a report to the judiciary council."

With his free hand, Nicodemus pulled at his long, gray mustache. "As you must, I suppose. I appreciate your candor."

The Grandmaster opened his other hand to reveal the object he had lifted from his desktop. It appeared to be a small bell.

"I'm going to share a secret with you, Leander," Nicodemus said, and he proceeded to ring the bell.

It wasn't as pleasant a sound as one would expect from a bell so small and delicate. It was far louder than it should have been, its tone lingering in the air like an offensive smell, and the sound filled Leander with an overwhelming sense of dread.

"I know the truth about each of the disappearances you refer to," Nicodemus said as he set the bell back down upon the desktop.

Leander was stunned.

"And I'm forced to admit, I am indeed responsible," Nicodemus confessed, as thick wisps of what appeared to be smoke snaked up from the floor surrounding the Grandmaster's desk.

Alastor rose from where he rested upon the chair and arched his back, hissing at what had begun to coalesce before them.

"I am old, you see," the Grandmaster continued. "Older even than you know. Mages live long lives, but still, not long enough. Worse yet, as we age, our power wanes. And I simply could not allow that. I have ambitions that could not be fulfilled by some weak old fool. I needed more power. More magic. And so I found those who would stand against me, and with a bit of ancient sorcery known to very few, I stole their power and added it to my own."

The smoke furled itself into the shapes of men and women, ghostly apparitions that swayed in a nonexistent breeze before the Grandmaster's desk, glaring at him with eyes bulging and vacant.

"The only failure to the process of extracting a mage's magical essences is that it doesn't quite kill them. Not completely. It leaves a bit of tainted soul behind, wraiths that can be controlled, commanded. Bad for them, but good for me."

Leander knew these pitiful shades before him. In his investigation into their disappearances, he had gazed upon their pictographs numerous times. He felt as though he knew each and every one of them personally.

"At first I thought this might be a problem, but I learned that in this form they were quite malleable, and also very aggressive. They are hungry, you see. Hungry for what has been taken from them."

The wraiths began to wail, their mouths opening to emit a high-pitched scream that made Leander's bones vibrate.

"How could you do this?" Leander said, his hands going to his ears to block out the ululating cries of misery.

"A new power is on the rise in Arcanum, my friend," the Grandmaster said, standing up from his chair, little more than a wraith himself. "And I have every intention of sitting at its side."

"We . . . we'll stop you," Leander said. It was becoming difficult for him to speak, even to think. The wraiths' screams were inside his head, and he was finding it hard not to fall to the floor and curl himself into a ball.

"*Who* will stop me?" the Grandmaster asked, emerging from behind his desk. "You, Leander? I seriously doubt that. The boy? Timothy Cade, the freak of nature? All I see in that one is a useful tool to achieve my goals. And if he will not assist me in achieving them, he will be put to death."

Leander struggled to unleash a spell of defense. The words fluttered from his lips and his hands began to glow like twin suns.

"Your timing is excellent, Professor," Nicodemus said. "I am weak, you see. I have not leeched a mage in many days. I thank you for saving me the effort of hunting for one."

Suddenly the wraiths stopped their cries and in an eyeblink— before Leander had the opportunity to unleash his conjuring—

the ghostly creatures pounced upon him, tearing at him with ghostly talons. It felt as though all the warmth, all the life was being drawn from his body. Leander fell to the floor, the wraiths swarming hungrily about him.

"They are starved, Leander. Starved for what has been taken from them," Nicodemus said. "They feed upon magic. But you've probably already guessed that by now." The Grandmaster frowned and focused on the wraiths. "Slowly, my pets. Only a taste for you. The rest is mine."

Leander held on for as long as he could, but soon he was pulled into the embrace of unconsciousness, the wails of the damned dragging him down into a realm of eternal darkness.

And it was cold there. So very, very cold.

"Are you sure?" Timothy demanded, springing up from the kitchen chair in which he had just barely managed to get comfortable. It nearly toppled to the floor.

"Caw! Caw!" Edgar cried, wings fluttering as he hopped across the table. "Very sure. Someone just opened a dimensional portal in the house."

Leander had brought them here, to Timothy's father's home—to Timothy's home—and had instructed them to wait for his return. Timothy was not certain if Leander going to SkyHaven alone was the right thing to do, but the burly mage had seemed to think he owed it to Nicodemus to confront him, to hear him out before speaking of it to anyone else. Timothy had not argued with him, but now he regretted it.

"How can you know that?" he asked his familiar.

Edgar cocked his head to one side and eyed Timothy coolly. "It's a little something I picked up while serving your father. I can smell when a dimensional rip has occurred."

Timothy was standing beside the long, wooden table where

they had just shared a small meal of bread, cheese, and tea. Despite the tension, he'd almost allowed himself to relax. *How foolish.*

"Did you smell the last one?" Timothy asked, referring to the attempt on his life that took place in this same house.

"That one caught me off guard," Edgar admitted. "Must not have been paying attention. But this one I can smell for sure. It's coming from this floor." The bird craned his head toward the doorway. "Down the hall—in the study maybe."

Ivar had already risen from his seat on the floor, knife in hand, the black, fluid patterns flowing across his pale skin signifying possible violence to come. He moved stealthily toward the doorway.

"No," Timothy said to him. The warrior turned and gazed at him with dark eyes. "We'll all go. It's safer if we stay together."

He didn't give Ivar a chance to argue, moving around the table and out into the hallway. Timothy didn't have to turn around to know that the Asura was following close behind. Edgar flapped above and past them, perching where he could, checking the air for the lingering aroma of a dimensional rip.

"Definitely from the study," the bird said, landing atop the head of one of the two carved wooden gryphons that decorated the posts at the base of the grand staircase in the entryway.

Timothy felt his pulse quicken as he realized that there was a chance he was again stepping into danger. *Is this how it's going to be from now on?* he wondered. He thought of the life he had left behind on the Island of Patience and wondered if it might not be best for everyone if he went back there.

He looked about the lobby for a weapon, and his eyes fell upon a metal container in the corner by the front door. The container was filled with ornate canes, rare things that had been made by hand instead of by magic. In his father's waning years, as his health declined, he had needed to use a cane to help him get around. Timothy darted to the container and selected one made from rich, dark wood, its head decorated with the body of a silver dragon. Timothy hefted the cane and then swung it like a club. Then he gestured for the others to follow him to the study just down the hall.

As he prepared to push the door open, he checked to see if Ivar and Edgar were ready. The bird was perched upon the Asura's shoulder, and Ivar wore the fearsome markings of battle. *And so danger arrives again,* Timothy thought as he looked away from his friends, placed the flat of his hand against one of the double doors, and pushed. It never seemed to end, the danger in this new world he had chosen over the old.

Timothy entered the study, memories of the first discussion he'd had there with Nicodemus fresh in his mind. He held the cane like a club, ready to strike out at anything that came at him.

Across the room, its back to him, there stood a large, hooded figure. The intruder had pulled a leather-bound volume from among the thousands of books arrayed upon the floor-to-ceiling bookshelves and appeared to be reading it.

"You don't belong here," Timothy said in his most menacing voice. He could sense Ivar at his back and, even though the intruder appeared quite large, was confident that he and the Asura could handle themselves.

"Put the book down and explain your presence."

The figure closed the book, returned it to its place on the shelf, and slowly began to turn toward them. Timothy tensed, ready for just about anything, but nothing could have prepared him for what followed. The intruder was impressive in size, its body covered from head to toe in a dark, coarse material. From beneath its hood, eyes like twin balls of Hungry Fire burned.

It brought its hands up and pulled back the hood to reveal its monstrous countenance. Timothy gasped.

"It just doesn't get any easier," Edgar muttered.

Timothy could not pull his gaze from the creature before him. He had never actually seen one in the flesh, but his father had told him stories of the race of beings called the Wurm. Its skin was the color of stone and multiple yellow horns of various sizes jutted from the top of its angular head. Trails of oily black smoke drifted from two nostril slits above its fanged mouth.

"Cade," the creature grumbled as it began to crouch. With a speed that should have been impossible for a creature of that size, it lunged across the room toward them, massive wings unfurling, his name again upon its lips.

"Cade!" it bellowed, mouth opened wide enough to show what appeared to be a churning inferno burning within its throat. Timothy raised the cane to defend himself, knowing it would do him little good.

CHAPTER TEN

With a cry that seemed to claw at the very air itself, Edgar flew straight at the monster, darting down to rake his talons across the intruder's face. The rook's wings beat the air in an urgent, angry flurry. Timothy's eyes went wide when he saw that the bird's talons barely nicked the creature's thickly plated hide. Its flesh was like armor. Edgar was doing more to annoy it than to harm it.

And the towering monstrosity *was* annoyed.

It snarled, plumes of fire curling from its nostrils, and turned its attention on the bird.

"I seek Argus Cade!" it roared. The heat issuing from its bellows of a mouth was enough to sear Timothy's face, even as the boy backed away. "Where is Argus Cade?"

"Caw!" the rook cried. "He's where the likes of you can't do him any harm, Wurm! And I won't let you harm his boy, either."

In the momentary distraction, Ivar blended in with the room, nearly invisible in the shadows and the dark, rich earth hues of the study. Frantic, pulse racing as he tried to figure out how to help, how to fight the monster, Timothy glanced around and caught the silhouette of the Asura warrior slipping behind the Wurm.

"Damn you, bird!" the intruder roared. "I want Argus Cade!"

"Caw! Caw!" Edgar continued to beat his wings in front of the beast, talons scratching that stony hide. "Timothy, run!"

"Edgar, fly!" Timothy shouted, fearful for his friend.

The Wurm opened its mouth and inhaled deeply, snorting.

Tendrils of black smoke issued from within its jaws, where the glow of fire had diminished. But only for a moment. It shuddered, eyes lighting up as though the flames blazed behind them, and it braced itself as though to scream.

What came from its mouth was not a scream but an inferno.

Timothy shouted for Edgar to escape as fire jetted from the Wurm's mouth. The rook soared low across the study, wings beating the air, feathers singed with flames as it tried to stay ahead of the stream of fire. Timothy could hear the rook screaming in pain and terror, and he felt numb and cold. He began to shake his head back and forth, even as the Wurm paused to take another deep breath, its eyes tracking the flight of the black-feathered bird through the room.

"No!" Timothy snapped. Heedless of the monster's fire breath, he lunged across the study and swung his father's cane at the side of its head with both hands and all the strength he could muster. It connected with an impact that resonated through his entire body, the wood splintering across the bony ridge behind its horns.

The Wurm grunted and staggered a step forward, colliding with an ornate chair that shattered under its weight. With twin jets of fire streaming from its nostrils, the monster shook off the blow and turned toward Timothy, the rook now forgotten.

Timothy froze. Brandishing what was left of the broken cane before him, he backed away, eyes wide. His gaze shifted toward the study door, but he knew he had no hope of reaching it if he ran. A chill went through him, a sadness he had never felt before.

He was going to die.

Teeth clenched, brow furrowed, he stopped retreating and raised the splintered cane higher. Fire burned behind the Wurm's eyes, and Timothy was mesmerized by it. The monster let out a short burst of charnel breath, then it began to inhale again, the inferno churning at the back of its throat. Timothy clutched the cane, preparing to dive toward the monster, to try to penetrate its scaly, plated hide with the jagged shaft of wood.

Ivar spoke then, his voice seeming to come somehow from nowhere and everywhere all at once. "There has been a mistake," the Asura warrior said, the words heavy with regret and warning.

The Wurm narrowed its eyes, clamped its jaws shut, and spun in search of the source of those words. Black smoke plumed from its nostrils, forming a cloud much larger than before, a cloud that enveloped Ivar, revealing his silhouette. The Asura bowed to the confused Wurm, but it snarled and its jaws snapped open. A burst of flame erupted from its throat, charring its own black teeth, arcing across the room.

As though dancing with the fire, Ivar twisted himself out of the way of the attack. Then, with one swift motion, he stepped forward, grabbed the creature by its horns, and drove it to the ground. The floor shook beneath its weight. The Wurm thrashed at Ivar, who tumbled onto his back and turned the momentum into a somersault that brought him back to his feet in a crouch a moment later.

"Damn your eyes, Asurahi!" the Wurm roared, rising to its full height, quivering with rage.

Ivar tilted his head to one side, still in a crouch, and deftly brought his hands up in front of him. With his thumbs together, palms outward and fingers fanned like a bird's wings, he put his hands in front of his face so that he seemed to be peering through a mask.

"Let calm prevail," Ivar whispered.

Shaking, fire leaking out from the corners of its eyes and dripping in ropy tendrils of liquid flame from his mouth, the Wurm took several long breaths, chest rising and falling like a bellows.

At last its rage seemed to recede, and it nodded slowly at Ivar.

"All right, Asurahi. Let calm prevail, as it did between our tribes in days of old." The monstrosity curled its upper lip back from its ebony fangs and glanced at Timothy for a moment before its gaze ticked back toward Ivar. "But now I must have an answer. Where is Argus Cade?"

With a flutter of wings Edgar appeared from behind a chair in the far corner of the room. He hopped, flying just a few feet before landing awkwardly, feathers singed.

The Wurm turned to glare at the bird.

"Caw! Caw!" Edgar chided it. "You've got a lot of nerve, lizard. You're the intruder here, let's not forget. And you just charred my tailfeathers. I have half a mind to—"

"Edgar," Timothy snapped.

The rook glanced up at him, black eyes widening in surprise.

"That's enough." Timothy dropped the broken cane and strode over to Ivar, who rose at his friend's approach. The boy turned toward the Wurm, a strange calm settling over him despite the fire-breather's ferocious appearance. "I am Timothy Cade. Argus Cade was my father. I deeply regret having to inform you that he is no longer with us. He has passed through that gate from which none of us returns."

Timothy had heard the words spoken before—by his father, by Ivar, and by Edgar—but this was the first time he had spoken them himself. He found within himself a strange, melancholy peace. One day he would pass beyond that same gate and join his father on the other side. Until then he hoped to live with courage and conviction, and without fear. He met the Wurm's gaze with his own and did not waver.

A change came over the creature then. Its expression contorted, altered by a sadness that mirrored his own. The beast seemed crestfallen and its head sagged, eyes narrowing, so that for the first time it seemed not at all horrid to him. With a flourish it brought both hands up to its face in the same gesture of respect and peace that Ivar had used, fiery eyes gazing out between its talons.

"I am Verlis of the Wurm, Timothy Cade, and I am sorry for your loss," it said, its voice bubbling with the liquid fire that still boiled in its throat. "My tribe and I share your grief, for without Argus Cade, there is little hope for us."

Verlis narrowed its eyes, black teeth flashing as it spoke. "I am sorry to have intruded, young Master Cade. With your father gone, you and the rest of the Alhazred have troubles of your own."

Timothy frowned, shot a glance at Ivar and Edgar, who was now perched on the Asura's shoulder, then looked back at the Wurm. "What do you mean? What troubles?"

The Wurm gazed at him curiously. It dipped its head in an odd sort of nod, as if displaying its horns to him for inspection. Then Verlis gave a short jerk of its head, a motion that Timothy interpreted as the Wurm's idea of a shrug.

"Of course you must know. You are the son of Argus Cade. How could you not know? Without your father, there is nothing to keep the terrible, withered sorcerer Nicodemus from pursuing his dark intentions."

Timothy felt as though he could not breathe. The shadows in the study seemed to deepen and he shivered, a new chill seeping into the room. His suspicions had churned in his mind and gut ever since he had fled the citadel of the Strychnos, and his encounter with Nicodemus had only strengthened them. But now, to hear the accusation stated so flatly, so boldly, he shook his head.

"I don't understand. What do you mean, 'dark intentions'?"

Verlis swayed, serpentlike, gaze drifting a moment as though deciding how much he wished to say. At length he glanced up at Timothy again. "Nicodemus has greater ambition than he has revealed. Your father knew this, and opposed him, but only in secret of course. Nicodemus wants the Order of Alhazred to usurp the government so that he can destroy the other guilds and force their members to join his own order, to follow him."

In that moment it felt to Timothy as though a great weight had been laid across his shoulders. He sagged, deflated. Moments before, he had determined to live courageously, and he would . . . he would. Yet it was difficult for him to let go of the hopes that he had held in his heart. His life on the Island of Patience had been one of loneliness and solitude. When Leander had brought him back into this world, he had cautiously allowed himself to believe that there might be a way for him to become a part of the society of mages, despite his uniqueness. That there might come a day when he could be happy here.

The truth was difficult to take: that he had been happier alone.

A low, trilling murmur came from Edgar, but the rook said nothing. Ivar reached out and laid a comforting hand upon the boy's shoulder. Slowly Timothy looked up at the burning, fire eyes of the Wurm.

"How, Verlis? Tell me exactly what Nicodemus has in mind."

The chamber of the Grandmaster was filled with a high, eerie whistling noise, as though whatever remained of the souls of the mages he had murdered were crying out in pain and despair. Leander had awoken and now stood at the center of the chamber. He raised his hands as though he might defend himself against these poor shades, these wraith creatures.

The old mage dropped the pretense of pleasantry, the smile disappearing from his face. His already pale skin grew ashen, and his eyes lit up with an uncanny glow that seemed to dim the other light in the room. Alastor hissed and began to creep slowly across the stone floor toward Leander, the hairless feline baring fangs that dripped with a pearly venom.

That whistling cry of sadness wrenched Leander's heart, filling him with grief. Though they were but shades, he saw in the wraiths around him the features of mages he had known, members of other guilds whose acquaintance he had made. Some of them he recognized only from the records he had examined in his investigation into their disappearance for the Parliament.

Nicodemus stroked his long mustache, his slender body now wreathed in a golden energy that buffeted him like a strong wind and raised him up off the ground. Even weakened, his magic was astonishingly powerful.

"Restrain him," the Grandmaster said, his voice thick with revulsion and disdain, his upper lip curling. "Do not concern yourselves with being gentle. I won't mind at all if you break bits of him in the process. But do not leech too much from him. He is mine."

The coldness of that voice shook Leander deeply. With the wraiths that had gathered in the chamber all around him, there had been something unreal about the threat he faced. And in his heart, there had been a kind of surrender, a bitterness that made him feel as though he had no hope. Now he narrowed his eyes and wondered how much of that feeling was his own heart, and how much was some kind of magical control Nicodemus was attempting to exert over him.

The wraiths floated toward him, encircling him with no expression at all on their haunting features.

Leander drew a long breath, his massive chest filling, and his nostrils flared with hatred and the pain of betrayal. He reached up and slid the hood of his cloak over his head, the spells woven into the fabric casting his own body into shadow, so that he was barely more than a wraith himself.

"What is . . . no!" Nicodemus snapped. "Stop him!"

The wraiths wavered, but their senses were not limited to those of a human. They continued to gather around him, several darting forward with their shadow mouths open as though they intended to rip his soul out with fangs of sharpened darkness. Yet it seemed to him that they were uncertain of his precise location, so perhaps the enchantment of his cloak was more effective than he'd hoped.

"You underestimated me," Leander growled. "An error you often make. It will be your undoing."

He dropped both hands in a slashing gesture, as if he could have carved the air with his fingers. But it was not the air that he was attacking. Nicodemus would have hexed the doors and windows of this chamber so that there was no hope of escaping that way. Leander did not waste the time to even attempt it.

"Eternal entropy," he whispered, and a silver dust sprinkled from his outstretched hands onto the stone floor.

Instantly the floor aged thousands of years, the stone weakening, eroding, and the wood beneath it rotting. With a great, thunderous crack, a segment of the floor just under him gave way. The wraiths screamed in that soul chilling whistle and whipped after him, but Leander was falling, tumbling through the hole in the floor even as it sifted into nothing more than sand beneath him.

The wraiths clawed and bit him, darting in with shadow fangs, and where they drew his blood, he felt a cold unlike any he had ever known, and his bones went numb. But Leander would not stop.

As he crashed down into the chamber beneath the Grandmaster's—the dwelling of several of his acolytes—he let the magic flow through him, buoying him, levitating him just enough to keep him from shattering his legs. It slowed his fall, and in the eyeblink of a moment, before his feet would have touched the floor, he performed the entropy spell again. It was powerful magic, something Argus Cade had taught him, and which very few mages in modern times had ever mastered.

The floor crumbled to nothing.

Leander continued to fall.

The wraiths screamed and pursued him. The massive mage looked up into their faces and he wept for them, knowing that even if he survived, they were beyond help. Their souls were tainted, corrupted, their bodies destroyed, their magic gone, their spirits in chains, leashed to the cruel hand of Nicodemus. Leander tried not to feel the betrayal that ate at him, the knowledge that this man whom he had trusted, the master of the guild to which he had given his life, had a black, venomous heart.

In the air, Leander tucked himself into a somersault, becoming calmer, more in control of the magic now. He plummeted headfirst toward the wooden floor of the chamber below, part of the servants' quarters, and with a gesture he rotted the floor to nothing.

His heart ached, the pain thrusting deep within him.

Drained, he thought. *I'm being drained.* And though he told himself it was the magic, that any mage would be shaken and weakened by what he was doing, he knew that it was the wraiths who were draining him, feeding off of him, taking back in sips and scrapes what Nicodemus had taken from them. And the worst of it was, he could not blame them.

He crashed through the next floor and into a storeroom whose shelves were piled high with scrolls and dusty artifacts. Some of the wraiths clung to him now, their hungry mouths fastened to his flesh like leeches. He trembled, his magic beginning to fail.

"Eternal entropy," he rasped, spraying silver dust upon the floor. It gave way and once more he tumbled through it.

This time he had no more strength to keep himself aloft.

Leander crashed into the ring table in the aerie, the meeting chamber at the base of the floating fortress. His left arm shattered on impact and streaks of darkness slashed across his vision. He nearly slipped into unconsciousness but would not allow it, forcing himself to remain alert. He had to escape.

The outer walls and the floors and ceilings of SkyHaven would have nearly unbreakable charms by which Nicodemus could keep him from escaping. But the round aperture in the base of the aerie gave way to the open air beneath SkyHaven and the churning ocean waves below. If only he could reach it.

Leander forced himself up. He might not have enough strength left to survive the fall, or to get himself to shore . . . but it was his only chance.

His fingers grabbed the inner edge of the ring table. He pulled himself toward it, breathing in the fresh ocean air.

Then the wraiths tugged back his hood. Shredded his cloak of shadow. One after another they began to feed on him.

And the darkness claimed him.

In the front parlor in his ancestral home, Timothy Cade leaned upon the window sill and gazed out at the blue sky, and at the sun-splashed city of Arcanum that stretched out far below at the bottom of August Hill. A chill breeze whispered through the window—its spell-glass eliminated by his presence—and he gratefully inhaled the fresh air. With a soft sigh he traced his fingers along the wooden window frame and his gaze lost its focus, the city beginning to blur.

Timothy recalled all too vividly the disdain of the guild masters who had attended Nicodemus's conference, not to mention

Romulus's willingness to simply kill Timothy, to end his life. Nicodemus had protected him; the old mage had been his defender and champion, if not his friend. Timothy had friends, of course—Ivar, Sheridan, Edgar, and Leander—but of those, only Leander had a place of respect in this world, and he was a member of the Order of Alhazred.

Not that Timothy questioned Leander's honor or intentions. Not at all. But he worried that if what the Wurm said about Nicodemus was true, his father's old friend might be blinded by his loyalty to the order.

"Hurry back, Leander," Timothy whispered. "Hurry home." His words were stolen away by the breeze that rustled the curtains in the parlor and somehow managed to slip inside the lamp on the table beside him, causing the Hungry Fire within to flicker and dance.

With a squawk that was still tinged with pain from his scorched feathers—now quickly healing—Edgar glided into the room and alighted upon the floor. The black bird hopped several times, coming nearer to him.

"Your tea is ready," his familiar announced.

Timothy smiled and glanced at the rook. "Thank you, Edgar. I'm coming."

The bird cawed, wings fluttering, but instead of flying, he simply turned and left the room on his feet, walking and hopping along ahead of Timothy. The ambient health spells in the house were already at work on Edgar, healing him, but the rook still winced slightly with each hop. Timothy felt badly for him, and for just a moment deeply regretted that he had no magic to heal his friend.

They went down a corridor and a moment later were in a comfortable sitting room. There were chairs and a long, brocaded divan, but Ivar and Verlis had chosen to seat themselves on the intricately woven carpet. There seemed to be an element of ritual to the way they had positioned themselves directly across from each other, yet even with the somber quiet in the room, Timothy was amused by the sight of the two of them—the grim warrior and the monstrous fire-breather—hunched over cups of aromatic mint tea on either side of the low serving table.

"Hukk!" Edgar croaked. "Master of the house! Hukk!"

Ivar and Verlis both rose immediately and turned toward Timothy to bow. This formal courtesy made him extremely uneasy, and there was something more than a little odd about the Wurm bowing to him, but now Tim was the master of the house.

"Please, sit," Timothy said.

The Asura and the Wurm returned to their previous positions, once again arranged almost as though there was purpose to every gesture, to the placement of every finger. Edgar flapped his wings lightly and flew up to stand on the back of a wooden chair that looked as though it had been carved by hand rather than by magic. Timothy did not want his companions to feel awkward, so he joined them on the ground beside the table.

The mint brew smelled wonderful. He took a small sip from the cup Ivar had brought him and closed his eyes, breathing in the steam from the hot drink, letting it pass through his lungs, soothing him. When he opened his eyes, they were all staring at him. A kind of resolution formed within him, and he turned to regard Verlis.

"I'm sorry. I needed a moment to collect my thoughts."

The Wurm's fiery eyes widened, and it dipped its head toward him, horns gleaming in the sunlight that streamed through the window. "I understand. It was necessary for me to gather my own wits. Your father's death has great ramifications beyond the grief of those who cared for him."

Timothy took another sip of mint brew, watching Verlis over the rim of the cup.

"You began to speak of that before," the boy said, glancing at Ivar. "But I know nothing of your people and less of whatever crisis you find yourself in that caused you to seek my father's help."

The Wurm's gaze lingered on Ivar with respect, but also a trace of animosity. Then Verlis turned his savage gaze upon Timothy once more, horns shining gold in the light streaming through the windows. Despite his scaly, plated hide, vicious talons, and the furnace that burned in his chest, superheating the air around him, there was a sadness in Verlis's eyes that made him seem very little like a monster and quite a bit like someone in need.

"Once upon a time the Wurm lived in tribes in the dark, lonely places of this world. We had descended from the Dragons of Old, in the days when Wizards still walked the pathways. Fierce warriors and capable magicians, the Wurm wanted nothing more than to see the human species wiped from existence. Of all the Tribes of People, perhaps our greatest enemy was the Asura."

As he said this last, Verlis glanced at the floor as though burdened by shame. His great bellows churned as he sighed, and fire flickered from his nostrils. Timothy shot a look at Ivar, but the warrior did not even acknowledge him, his focus completely on the Wurm.

"In time, however, we found ourselves with a common enemy," Verlis continued, reaching up to scratch beneath his chin, talons raking his plated flesh with a rasp like footsteps on gravel. "The mages had begun to gather into a terrible union. The Parliament of Mages. It was peace for your kind. But there were enough who hated all those different from themselves that a peace amongst mages could only mean the destruction or elimination of other races."

A chill passed through Timothy, and he wrapped his hands around his cup for warmth. He nodded slowly as he listened to the growl that was the Wurm's voice.

"So the Wurm and the Asura became reluctant allies," Timothy said, at last able to make sense of the formality and ritual between Verlis and Ivar.

"Precisely," Verlis confirmed. "But it was too late. The Asura were warred upon in secret by certain factions within the Parliament and destroyed, all save him." Verlis nodded toward Ivar. "Your father saved him, hid him away.

"The slaughter of the Wurm began shortly after that. With the mages working together around the world, there was nowhere for us to retreat to. Hundreds of thousands were destroyed before Argus Cade rose to secretly thwart the will of those dark and cruel sorcerers who would rid the world of any creatures who were not like themselves. It was, in truth, no less than my species deserved, though we had differences amongst our tribes. My ancestors had lusted for the blood of humans and wanted to decimate their cities. Not all of us were like that, but it was the behavior of the Wurm that allowed the blood-hungry amongst the Parliament of Mages to muster the support to destroy us.

"Yet we were never the threat that Alhazred made us out to be."

Timothy flinched at the name, eyes widening as he stared at Verlis. "Alhazred? The Alhazred? The founder of the order? But my father said he was a great mage. A great man."

The memory seemed to haunt the Wurm, for he hung his head slightly and the fire in his eyes dimmed. "Once, perhaps. So the stories say. But he grew in power, and power corrupted him. It may be that he wore a mask of his old self in front of other mages, but it was only that. A mask. Beneath it, he was the worst of them, whipping up the hatred of our tribes, urging the

Parliament to wage war upon us, when what he really wanted was to leech us."

Timothy frowned, brows knitting. "Leech you? I don't understand."

"Their magic," Ivar said, speaking up for the first time.

Verlis glanced sharply at him, but Ivar was not to be silenced.

"Alhazred captured as many Wurm as he could, and he drained the magic from them. Leeched them. In this way he grew more and more powerful. In the end, the only way your father could save them was to convince the Parliament that instead of destroying the Wurm tribes, they could be banished from this dimension."

Verlis nodded, upper lip curling in disgust. "They were days of blood and fire, of black, ugly magic, and the numbness of death. All that remained for us was to hide, to flee this plane of existence. Against Alhazred's protests, we were banished, and the barrier between dimensions fortified with protection spells to keep us out forever."

Edgar fluttered his wings and then resettled on the back of the chair. "But you got in anyway? How did you manage that?"

The Wurm snorted fire at the bird, who trembled but did not fly away.

"Argus Cade created doors he could use to travel into other dimensions. One such passage led to the world to which we were banished. It was meant only to open from this side, but my tribe forced it open. Alhazred did not steal all of our magic."

Anxious, Timothy glanced at Ivar. "I had no idea Alhazred was so terrible. You'll be glad to know he's dead."

Verlis snorted, eyes narrowing. "Is he? Perhaps so. Perhaps not. Much time has passed since we've had any news of your world. But Nicodemus is no better. He was the Blackheart's most loyal acolyte. I warn you of this because you are the son of Argus

Cade. And now I must go. If there is no aid to be found here, I must return and fight alongside my brethren."

The Wurm rose, its body unfurling with a soft grinding noise as its plated flesh rasped together. Timothy stood up as well, nearly spilling his tea, reaching out toward Verlis.

"Wait. At least tell us why you have come. What troubles you?"

Verlis paused and his faraway gaze seemed haunted by what he had left behind. "In my dimension there is civil war and strife amongst the Wurm tribes. My tribe was decimated by Alhazred's hatred, and we are small in comparison to others. My family is in danger. Argus Cade often visited the realm of the Wurms, though the Parliament prohibited it. He was a peacemaker. I came to ask Argus to broker peace, or, if that proved impossible, to help find a place for the remnants of my tribe to resettle, to escape.

"But Argus is dead."

Timothy felt the heat of anger rise within him. The Wurm were not innocents, but they were no more warlike, it seemed to him, than the mages. Yet Alhazred had wiped them out for his own ends, had slaughtered Ivar's people and manipulated the Parliament. And Nicodemus had been his heir.

My father fought him, fought all of them, he thought, and he wondered how much of this Leander knew.

A jolt of alarm went through him. *Leander!*

"Verlis, I know my father would have helped you," Timothy said, rising to his full height and gazing up at the monstrous Wurm. "My friends and I can do no less. We don't have the magic my father had, but I know we can help. Or at the very least, we can try."

Clearly startled, the Wurm bowed his head in gratitude. "Any aid would be welcome."

Timothy glanced at Ivar, then looked back at Verlis. "First, though, I have another friend I think might be in trouble. My father was mentor to a mage named Leander Maddox. Did you know him?"

"No," Verlis replied, "but I heard Argus speak of him."

"I think Nicodemus has been continuing the traditions of the order. Leander went to see him, to confront him. I'm worried that we haven't heard from him. I have to go back to SkyHaven, to make sure he gets out of there all right. As soon as I know Leander is safe, we'll all go with you and do what we can to help."

Verlis growled low in his chest, the furnace raging and fire spitting from his eyes and flickering in his nostrils. "You offer your aid, son of Argus Cade. Upon my honor, I can do no less than return your kindness.

"We go to SkyHaven."

CHAPTER ELEVEN

Leander awoke with the whistling of the dead in his ears. He inhaled sharply, cold and afraid in a way he had not been since childhood. When he opened his eyes, he expected to find darkness, a dungeon of some sort. Instead he squinted against bright sunlight and raised a surprisingly unbound hand to shield his eyes. It took several moments for his vision to adjust, and when at last he could look around his prison, he was amazed.

The chamber was vast, the ceiling vaulted, and the walls were a single enormous mosaic depicting a scene of ancient combat between Wizards and Dragons in days of old. The Wizards had devilishly cruel features, eyes wild and giddy with violence, faces spattered with the blood of Dragons, who either lay flayed open before them, quivering in fear, or weeping as they cradled their dracunae, their soft, fleshy babies.

It was terrible to behold.

The sunlight that illuminated the chamber entered through a broad, round window in the ceiling. The glass shimmered with the enchantments that had been placed on it to keep him from escaping. The whistling cry of the wraiths continued but, still disoriented, it took Leander several seconds to notice streaks of dark mist in the room, and then one of the wraiths began to draw closer to him.

The feel of their leech mouths draining him was fresh in his memory, and he shuddered and scrambled away from the wraith. Still weak, he nevertheless forced himself to stand, lumbering to his feet and facing off against the gray-mist form that abruptly coalesced, its face becoming recognizable. He knew the woman, a mage of the Drayaidi guild, one of the first to disappear. Her name was Seline Merro, and in another age she had been a pretty but intense blond-haired girl who had sat in the front row as Leander's student at the University of Saint Germain.

"Seline," he whispered.

Massssster Maddoxxx.

The voice rustled like fallen leaves through the room, more in his head than his ears, but what there was of a mouth on the wraith did not move. It cut him deeply to see her face, to remember her as a girl, her bright, attentive eyes turned upward toward him. Seline Merro was dead, her magic stolen from her, body destroyed, likely incinerated, and all that remained was this tainted, poisoned sliver of her soul, enslaved to the horrid Nicodemus.

Yet she knew him. She could still think.

"You are not completely in his thrall, then?" Leander asked, hope and fear doing combat in his heart. Perhaps she was strong enough to thwart Nicodemus.

Wrong, the wraith voice whispered. *You mussst run, Massssster Maddox. You musssst run.*

A shadow of despair blackened his spirit and dashed his hopes. Though she had mustered enough of her self to warn him, she could not help him. "Thank you, Seline," he said. "But I have not the power to run very far."

As he stared at her misty form, trying to see the elegant features of the woman she had been, the gray streaks in the air began to darken. At precisely midday, the sun had streamed straight down into the room, but as the afternoon progressed, the sunlight came in through the ceiling at a different angle, and shadows formed, making the mosaic of the dragon massacre on the walls even more disturbing.

The whistling of the wraiths grew louder, higher, and they became agitated. Their darkness took on greater weight and solidity, and other faces became recognizable. Hissing, the shadow creatures, these poisoned souls of dead mages, began to close in around him again. Where they had clamped their mouths upon him before, he still felt cold and numb, and Leander glanced quickly around, desperate to find some way to defend himself.

He did not hear the door open. Had not, in fact, seen any door at all. Yet when his panic was at its limit, words like claws tore the air.

"Vile things, aren't they?"

The shade of Seline Merro hissed and fluttered away from him, disappearing into the shadows. Leander spun toward the sound of that voice. Nicodemus stood just inside an open door that had not been there moments before, flanked by a quartet of mages. These were not novices or acolytes, but deadly magicians. Not quite so adept as Leander, but he doubted he would ever have a chance to match his magic against theirs.

Nicodemus wore robes of deepest scarlet, scarred with black piping. The wisps of the old man's hair and his long, silver mustache blew in an unseen wind. His grin was twisted, a scowl of disgust and superiority.

The angle of the sunlight in that chamber continued to shift, the shadows deepened, and the mournful wraiths began to move even closer to Leander, caressing him with their misty forms. The professor gritted his teeth and steeled himself against the despair that threatened to claim him. He refused to look at their faces any longer, choosing instead to glare only at the Grandmaster's pink eyes.

"Nicodemus. You will be discovered soon enough. I have been investigating their disappearances for months on behalf of the

Parliament. When I do not make a report, they will assign others."

A prickle of magical power tingled in the palms of Leander's hands but he did not dare attack, not with the Grandmaster and his lackeys and the wraiths all surrounding him.

Nicodemus raised an eyebrow and reached up to stroke his mustache. "They will assign others, will they? Ah, well, I am certain you are correct. But it will be quite some time before they have gathered enough evidence to move against me, and by that time, Professor Maddox, I am afraid there will no longer be a Parliament of Mages. Or, rather, the Parliament will have a new master."

Leander stared, unable to catch his breath as the enormity of Nicodemus's ambitions became clear. "You . . . you cannot be serious."

The Grandmaster ignored him. With a rustle of cloth he brushed back his robes and strode toward Leander. The wraiths flowed from his path and yet deeper shadows, impossible patches of night, gathered around the archmage as he stepped in close and reached out a single long finger and wound it in Leander's beard, tugging it, forcing the larger man to meet his gaze.

"All that remains of the mages you sought are these filthy soul fragments," Nicodemus said, his voice a dry rasp. "Your fate is upon you, Professor Maddox, but it does not have to be *their* fate. You may still save yourself this particular damnation if you will cooperate with my efforts to retrieve the boy. Timothy Cade belongs to me now. He is my plaything, my boy, or he is dead. Save his life. Save your soul. Aid me in bringing him back to SkyHaven."

With each word that spilled from the Grandmaster's lips, Leander found himself growing colder. Yet it was not the chill of fear in him, but of resolve. The wraiths still caressed him, and he still recalled the bone-numbing touch of their hungry mouths, but the memory of his mentor, Argus Cade, and his vow to watch over Timothy, were far more persuasive.

"Trade one damnation for another?" Leander asked, nostrils flaring with contempt. "I rather think not. Instead, Nicodemus, why don't you tell me who it was you were speaking with when I entered your quarters this morning?"

The always pale Nicodemus blanched even whiter and lowered his cadaverous face so that his pink eyes were shadowed by his brow. A low serpentine hiss slid from his lips, and he twitched several times. With excruciating slowness he turned his head toward the mages who had entered with him.

"Go to the boy's workshop. You'll find that metal man hiding there amongst his things. Bring it to me. The freak built himself a toy. I think I'll see what sort of fun can be had with it."

Leander stiffened as two of the mages left the room. He wondered what Nicodemus intended to do with Sheridan and whether or not a mechanical man was capable of feeling pain. He thought that Nicodemus intended to discover the answer to that very question.

Reluctantly Leander glanced around him. Though a circle of early afternoon sunlight still burned at the apex of the chamber, the room had darkened even further. The wraiths were all staring hungrily at him, their eyes bottomless, as though they were not eyes at all, but wells filled with night-black tar. All of their faces seemed to have somehow melted, their personalities absorbed within the sinister control of their master. Even if Seline Merro had been able to help him, he would not have known anymore which one of them she was.

Nowhere to run.

The Grandmaster ran his tongue over his dry lips and a grin spread across his now skeletal features. He reached out to touch

Leander's face, and the leonine mage flinched at the caress of those long, tapered fingers. Sharp nails sliced his cheek, and Leander hissed in pain as blood began to flow.

Then the Grandmaster put one hand upon Leander's chest, and the mage went rigid. Nicodemus's palm and fingers seared Leander's skin even through his robe and tunic. He felt a surge, a flow from his chest, as though he had been torn open, but there was no wound where Nicodemus had placed his hand. No visible wound. The Grandmaster was not draining his blood.

He was drinking Leander's magic.

Steam escaped slowly from the release valve on Sheridan's head. He held it back as best he could, determined not to give himself away. It made the tiniest shushing noise, almost as if the steam itself was urging him to remain silent. In the midst of stacks of crates Timothy had yet to unpack, and behind a table laden with tools and mechanical parts, Sheridan stared at the door to the workshop and waited.

The moment he saw movement at the door, he remembered that his eyes were still illuminated, and with a simple thought, he shut them down. His visual lights faded to black, but the golden afternoon light still streamed in through the window from which Timothy had escaped just before dawn. It had been a very long day. Twice he had avoided discovery.

The metal man doubted he would be so fortunate a third time.

A female mage in emerald green breeches and tunic entered the workshop and paused just inside. She glanced around once, then raised her right hand. Ghostfire blossomed on the skin of her palm and Sheridan froze, the hiss of his steam growing a bit louder.

Ghostfire. Spirit flame. This mage had it at her disposal, at her personal service. This was a sort of magic that Leander had told them was banned by the Parliament. It was dark magic, Master Maddox had said.

Sheridan felt the pressure building in his chest, the steam boiling for release. From his hiding place he watched a second mage enter, this one a tall man in a robe of that same emerald green. His skin was deeply browned and shone in the sunlight like precious metal, and there were ritual symbols carved in his cheeks. The mere sight of him frightened Sheridan, for he could only begin to imagine what such a man might do if he managed to capture Timothy.

Something unfamiliar was born in the mechanical man then, a feeling that stained his circuits and slowed his gears. From the moment when Sheridan had gained awareness—much to his creator's surprise—his mind had been on a journey of evolution. Everything was new, but he quickly learned language and the use of crude tools, then graduated to far more sophisticated functions. Yet those were outward changes. There were others. On Patience he had known only the kindness of the boy who had made him, and the quiet happiness of their friendship. But since he had entered this new world with Timothy, Sheridan had learned to feel a great many other emotions. Anxiety. Fear.

And now fury.

The mages continued to search the room, both of them holding their hands out in front of them, each finger like a wand, tiny sparks spraying from the tip. All of the trepidation was gone from Sheridan now. As he waited, frozen in place, the female mage swiveled her head around and focused on the crates he hid among. Her eyes narrowed. She had sensed something there but was not confident yet that it was her prey. Without alerting her companion, she moved toward the worktable with its array of tools, sparks arcing from her fingers. She moved with caution, but her focus seemed to be more on the tools than on the crates behind the table.

Sheridan felt a strange calm come over him. He waited as she reached the table, passed her hands over it and allowed the tiny tendrils of lightning to caress each tool. As the mechanical man watched, some of those tendrils began to reach toward him. To the mage, the top of his head might look like just another tool, a bucket, perhaps.

She paused, then glanced at the crates, her eyes drawn almost immediately to Sheridan. The mage widened her eyes, and her hands began to reach toward him, sparks jumping at him as she bent over the table.

All along he had been boiling inside. Now he released all the pressure that had built within him. A blast of steam erupted from the valve on the side of his head, the hot, moist air searing her face. The mage cried out and clapped her hands over her eyes. Sheridan's eye-lights popped on, and with one powerful, metal arm, he pushed the mage backward.

The robed man had turned the instant she had cried out, but Sheridan could move more quickly than most would guess, particularly when he had a full head of steam up. Even as the sorcerer pointed his hands at the mechanical man and the sparks on his fingers were replaced by a deep blue light, Sheridan willed one of his chest plates to open, and a nozzle jutted from the hole.

Liquid fire sprayed across the room at the mage. Forced to defend himself, the man forgot his plan of attack. A shield of green magic sprang up in front of him and the fire was harmlessly absorbed into it. But by that time Sheridan was already upon the mage. The defense the man had constructed was meant to dispel fire, not a physical attack. Sheridan barreled into him, metal fist striking the mage with enough force to drop him, unconscious, to the floor.

He did not wait to see if they would be able to pursue him. Sheridan kept going, right out the door, propelled by a determination to prevent Nicodemus from doing any more harm to Timothy. For it was obvious now that the instincts of Sheridan's young friend had been quite perceptive indeed.

The mechanical man fled along the corridor but did not at first encounter any other of Nicodemus's staff. When he came upon a narrow door that had made him curious in past days, he opened it, only to discover a darkened, dusty staircase that he surmised to be a separate passage for the Grandmaster's servants, to keep their industrious comings and goings from the more elegant main stairs.

Sheridan closed the door with a tiny click and disappeared into the servants' back steps, moving more quietly than he ever had before.

They came flying down upon SkyHaven with the sun at their backs. Timothy guided the gyrocraft with Ivar crouched again behind the pilot's seat. Edgar glided silently upon the drafts that swept up from the ocean below. Verlis had gratefully accepted the loan of a golden sword that Timothy took from his father's estate. The metal was precious for a variety of reasons, not the least of which was that it was nearly as resistant to magic as Timothy himself. The Wurm beat his massive, leathery wings, and as he flew, it was clear that the talons on his feet were just as deadly as those upon his hands. The golden sword gleamed in the sunlight as they all descended toward the floating fortress.

The wind whipped past Timothy's ears as he guided the gyro. Far below he saw the shadows of his strange little assault force distorted across the sun-tipped surf. They could have tried to enter through Timothy's workshop window, or even the opening of the aerie underneath the floating citadel, but they could not travel underwater and the sentries would have spotted them too easily in these obvious approaches. Verlis had tried to convince them to wait until nightfall to try to retrieve Leander, but Timothy was not about to wait. His friend might be dead by then. Given the boy's insistence, Ivar had recommended that they make a long circle out to sea and come in from the ocean side of SkyHaven. It made sense. The sentries would be expecting an approach from shore, not from the open ocean. They would also attack from a great height. Even if there were sentries watching the ocean side, they were not likely to expect an attack from directly above.

Or, at least, that was Timothy's hope.

Verlis flew beside the gyro, with Edgar out in front of the craft, black wings like a stain of darkness upon the daylight. They drew nearer, and now Timothy was able to see the turrets and fortress walls of SkyHaven much more clearly. The courtyard lawns and gardens were green and dappled with brightly colored flowers. Several people wandered the grounds. For a place that harbored such sinister industry, it was a picture of peaceful beauty that reminded him never again to judge anything by appearance alone.

Alhazred mages patrolled the external walls and several were perched atop the towers of the central structure. He whispered silent prayers to the spirit of his father and whatever higher power might hear him, hoping that fate would be with them, that the alarm would not be sounded too soon.

Timothy thought about cutting the power to the rotor and propellers, letting the Gyro glide in, but there were too many variables, and silence was only going to carry them so far. He needed the maneuverability the gyro had when its blades were spinning.

Almost the moment this thought had entered his mind, he saw

Edgar dip one wing and reverse direction, black feathers shining as the rook sliced the wind, circled around, and took up a flight position just beneath the gyro. They had worked this signal out beforehand; the bird had reached the outer edges of the magical charms Nicodemus had put in place around SkyHaven. Enchantments that would alert the residents of the floating fortress. Wards that might keep enemies out.

But they would not keep Timothy Cade out. They would not even register his presence. Within him was a null space in the magical matrix. That would not help Verlis and Edgar, but the Wurm had strong magic of his own and felt sure that he could shatter SkyHaven's defenses and lead Edgar in behind him. Timothy did not share his certainty, but they had no other choice. Leander's life was in the balance. If Verlis believed his magic was strong enough, well . . . they were about to find out.

"Ivar, put your hand on my shoulder," he instructed.

The Asura warrior did as he was asked. Timothy felt certain that his null space would extend to Ivar as long as they were in physical contact, just as he was confident that the gyro would not be detected with him at the controls. His touch disrupted magic on contact. And if Ivar was in contact with him . . . well, that was at least a far surer thing than hoping the Wurm could crack SkyHaven's defenses.

Verlis snorted furling black smoke and dove through the air, wings outstretched, falling into place just behind the gyrocraft. Timothy could not see the magical barrier, nor even sense it, so he kept his focus on the towers of SkyHaven below and the sentries that he could see. Those on top of the towers wore dark purple robes, a kind of uniform that marked them as the most elite of the Grandmaster's acolytes.

Timothy narrowed his gaze. Atop a turret toward the back of the fortress—a portion of SkyHaven he had never been allowed to enter—there stood a figure quite out of place: a girl in a long, gauzy green dress with ghostly pale skin and flowing, bright red hair. Almost unconscious of doing so, he tapped the controls of the gyro so that its course would take him down past her.

"We have passed through," Ivar said, the voice close behind Timothy's head, reassuring in his ear.

The un-magician nodded intently. Contact with him had worked. Edgar and Verlis might not be so fortunate. But it was time. A small shred of hesitation lingered in Timothy, but he brushed it away. Leander's life was in peril. And it was too late, in any case. They were in. He refocused on the sentries and pushed the controls of the gyro hard forward, causing it to lose altitude with such speed it was as though it was falling from the sky.

Behind him there came a roar of savage pain.

"What—,"Timothy began. He glanced once over his shoulder and caught sight of Verlis. The Wurm had his black fangs bared and fire was issuing from his mouth along with that bellow of agony. Sparks of magical power danced around his body as though he had been struck by lightning. His wings furled inward and he began to fall.

"Timothy!" Ivar snapped. "Eyes front!"

The boy whipped his head around just in time to pull the controls up. He had been diving too fast, too long. The gyro had built up downward momentum and it shuddered as he forced it out of that descent.

Everything was happening too quickly now. Verlis had been snared by SkyHaven's magical protections. So much for his confidence. Though the Wurm's magical intrusion had caused some sort of disruption in the fortress's defenses, for Edgar had flown close behind Verlis and passed through unaffected.

In his peripheral vision Timothy saw the turrets of the fortress all around him. He had nearly crashed the gyro into one of them, and even now he was lower than the tallest of them, weaving in among them. Several sentries were glancing upward now, searching the sky.

A swarthy mage rushed to the edge of a tower roof and was pointing at Timothy and Ivar in the gyrocraft, shouting something, his face flushed red with alarm. The scowling mage contorted the fingers of his right hand and reached out as though he might claw the air. Bruise-black light formed around his fist and arced out at the gyro, but it dissipated harmlessly even as it touched the flying machine. Ivar still had his hand upon Timothy's shoulder.

"Don't let go of me," Timothy told his friend.

"No," Ivar agreed. "Not yet."

The rest of the sentries were focused on Verlis, and Timothy wanted to turn to look as well, but he did not dare for fear of crashing.

"Verlis will have the power to free himself, or he will not. There is nothing you can do now. Keep your eyes ahead. Stay to the plan," Ivar instructed him, giving his shoulder a squeeze.

Timothy nodded. The plan had been mostly his, after all, and he knew it was a good one. In fact, it was the only one. Not very subtle, but they had not had time for subtlety, not with Leander in jeopardy. Timothy had sent Edgar to fly to Leander's and speak to the man's navigational mage, who had confirmed leaving him off at SkyHaven and not yet having received a summons to return. That was all the confirmation they had needed.

"Caw! Caw!" Edgar cried, and the rook flew out from beneath the gyrocraft and darted upward, toward the red-faced mage who had tried to attack them. The man put up his hands, startled by the sudden, vicious offensive of Timothy's familiar, and Edgar clawed at him, throwing him off balance, keeping him from further magical attack.

As Timothy veered the gyro around the central tower, he saw Edgar beat at the mage with his wings and drive the man off the roof. The mage tumbled end over end, arms waving wildly, a blur of blue light forming around him as he tried to weave a levitation spell to let himself down more gently.

Most of the sentries were still focused on Verlis, and Timothy didn't blame them. The Grandmaster's elite guard were all young enough that they probably had never seen a Wurm before. To them Verlis was a monstrosity. Those leathery wings and the fire pluming from his ferocious maw were a horrifying sight the very first time. Timothy turned the craft around enough that he could see Verlis now, struggling to stay in flight. In that moment, he realized something. The crackling magical lightning that had jolted the Wurm was diminishing.

"He's through!" Timothy cried triumphantly. "Nicodemus's wards hurt him, but he's through!"

The sentries had noticed as well. They knew that at any moment Verlis would have completely shaken off the effects of passing through the magical barrier, and would attack them. They were shouting to one another, preparing to destroy the Wurm. Verlis bent his head and dove, gliding on his massive wings, dipping sideways to fly around the curving wall of a tower so closely that the sentries had to lean out over the edge even to get a glimpse of him.

Edgar swooped down to attack the sentries, drawing their attention away from the Wurm.

But from the tower opposite, Verlis was a clear target. Timothy pressed the control forward slightly, and the Gyro accelerated, practically lunging across the space between turrets. Other sentries had noticed him now, and they were launching magical attacks, but none of them with any more luck than the first. Crackling energy surged up from guards in the courtyard below, and bolts of murderous sorcery flew like arrows from the wall sentinels, but Timothy and Ivar went unscathed.

He pointed the nose of the gyro at the tower ahead. For a moment the two purple-robed sentries stood their ground, but then they dove aside to avoid a collision. At last letting go his grip on Timothy's shoulder, Ivar leaped off the back of the gyro-craft, wielding a short, ironwood fighting staff. The sudden shift in weight on the craft made its nose dip downward, and the main rotor on top of the gyro whined as it sheared off the right arm of the other sentry.

Blood spattered the gyro and Timothy as well, drops of it filming on his goggles. He ripped them off, his stomach convulsing at the sight of the blood and the screams of the injured man. The mage would heal himself, Timothy was sure of that. Somehow he would heal. That was what magic was for, wasn't it?

Yet he could not stop the cold, numb feeling that settled in the pit of his stomach. He had had grand visions of slipping in and snatching Leander and getting out. A grand adventure. But there was nothing simple or innocent about this. Not when he had a man's blood on his face.

He heard Verlis roar again and turned in his seat to see infernal flames belching from the Wurm's gaping maw, liquid fire that engulfed first one, then two more sentries atop a nearby tower. Timothy felt his spine go rigid.

"Caw! Watch out, Tim!" Edgar cried.

The rook cut across his path. Timothy snapped his head around and saw that his familiar was warning him away. Once again only a split second tug on the gyro's controls prevented him from crashing into a wall. As he soared he glanced around, and there she was. The girl was perhaps twenty feet from him, standing at the edge of a low tower. Her green dress whispered as the wind rustled it. She was young, not much older than

Timothy himself, and yet as she cocked her head to one side and regarded him, her cascade of red hair blowing in the wind, she seemed almost ancient. She beckoned to him, gesturing toward a door in the tower.

Who are you? Timothy thought, distracted.

As though he had shouted the words to her, she raised her hand and beckoned to him again. Timothy was piloting the gyrocraft away from her, still under attack. Ivar's voice carried across the sky, and he glanced over to see the Asura warrior leap from a high turret to the fortress wall, where several guards had begun to tear bits of stone from the wall and hurl them at Timothy. He jogged the gyro controls to the left and barely avoided one such attack, but then Ivar landed on the wall, scrambled up it with eerie agility, and began to fight the guards with his bare hands.

Sentries on another turret began to flee as Verlis roared fire at them. One jumped off the fortress and two others quickly dropped down onto the steps that ran around the side of the turret, to a door set into the wall several feet below.

At last Timothy brought the gyro around again, his gaze sweeping the upper reaches of SkyHaven. Only then did he realize that the girl in the green dress was gone. He frowned, slowing the gyro. She had beckoned to him. *Why?*

Then he saw the other set of stairs that went around the outside of that tower, and the door they led to that was still open, only darkness and shadow waiting from within. They had planned to fight off as much resistance as possible and then land, going right through the huge, ornate double doors that led into the main living area of SkyHaven. As long as they stayed together, with their unique attributes, Timothy felt they would have a chance. But now this . . . this new approach . . . had presented itself.

What if it's a trap? he wondered. But then he felt foolish. If the Grandmaster expected them to return, he would not have relied upon a single, mysterious girl gesturing to Timothy from atop SkyHaven.

Nearby, the rook was diving maniacally at another sentry. Edgar clawed at the man, who fell but managed to grab hold of a ledge. The bird left him dangling there and beat his wings against the air, turning to look for more resistance, more prey. Timothy knew that Edgar would be as anxious by now as he was. They were taking too long. They did not want to be up here if Nicodemus made an appearance. There was nowhere to hide.

Then he spotted Verlis. Fire trailed from the Wurm's jaws as he swooped down at several mages who had either fallen or been on the ground to begin with. One of them held his ground, performing a rapid spell that erupted from his hands in silver bolts that were likely to cut the Wurm's scaly hide as easily as they did the air. Verlis brought the golden sword around in front of his body, deflecting the sentry's magic.

The mage who had dared to fight was engulfed in a blaze of magical power, the very spell he had tried to use on Verlis. In moments, he was nothing but ash, as Verlis headed toward the double front doors of SkyHaven's core.

"Caw! Caw! Let's go, Timothy!" Edgar cried as he kept pace with the gyro through every turn and jog the boy's navigation caused.

"No. Let's try that way!" he told the rook, pointing at the stairs on the side of the tower, where the girl had stood. He gestured toward the open door. "Fly down and tell Verlis. We're going in that way."

To his credit, Timothy's familiar did not ask why, did not question this change in plans. The rook simply cawed and darted amid the jutting turrets, diving down toward Verlis.

Timothy swung the gyro around and spotted Ivar clinging to the side of another tower. Atop it was one of the last sentries who had not been driven off or killed. The thin, extremely tall man pointed a single finger down at Ivar, and scarlet light sparked there. He was chanting something—more screaming it than chanting—and Timothy did not have to understand the words to know that Ivar was in serious trouble.

Biting his lip, Timothy pulled up on the controls, causing the gyro to rise up swiftly toward the mage, hurtling toward him. With a jerk to the right he spun the gyro sideways. In his fury and the concentration of his spellcasting, the mage did not look up immediately. When he did, it was just in time for his eyes to go wide as Timothy knocked the gyro into him and sent the man tumbling backward off the wall, cursing as he plunged toward the ocean far below.

"Ivar, come on!" Timothy called.

The Asura leaped out and grabbed hold of the axle that supported the wheels of the gyrocraft. Timothy struggled to compensate for the sudden addition of weight, and in a moment he had them hovering above the turret where he had seen the mysterious girl. Ivar let go, dropping down and rolling out of the way so that Timothy could land. Even as the boy did so, Edgar cawed and alighted upon Ivar's shoulder. Verlis landed with feral, deadly grace, golden sword at the ready, wings folding tightly against his back.

Following a single gesture from a mysterious girl, Timothy at last led them into SkyHaven, intent upon keeping Leander Maddox alive and upon revealing the dark secrets of the Grandmaster.

CHAPTER TWELVE

A numbing cold had enveloped Leander Maddox. His body was like ice, but where Nicodemus touched his chest there was fire. The Grandmaster's touch siphoned the magic right out of Leander, and his life drained along with it. Darkness encroached at the edges of his vision. The wraiths whispered in his ears, some of them still crying in their high, mad voices. Leander felt weakness closing his eyes. He blinked to keep them open but could not. Several times he seemed to drift away to a place of absolute night, only to feel a fresh burst of searing pain in his chest as Nicodemus sucked more power from him. His eyes popped open, and though what little he could still see was out of focus, the old mage's pink, glowing eyes were there, staring at him. The grin that split his face was gleeful.

But it faltered.

In the midst of the fog that tried to drag him back down into darkness, Leander saw a tremor go through the Grandmaster. A look of uncertainty shuddered across Nicodemus's face.

Leander mustered the last of his strength to strain against the grasp of the wraiths that held him. He forced himself to smile. His voice was weak, his throat raw, but he made himself speak.

"What's wrong, *my lord*? You look as though you've just tasted something that didn't agree with you."

Nicodemus seemed not to hear him. The Grandmaster turned away, ignoring the wraiths and his captive. His hand fell away from Leander's chest, and with it the pain began to recede. Though he still ached to his bones and the cold still worked at him, a prickling of fresh sensation went through Leander. The numbness was leaving him. The touch of the wraiths was chilling, but now that Nicodemus had stopped draining the magic from him, he felt as though the fog was lifting from his mind. The room swam into focus once more. He could see the other mages in the room, Nicodemus's acolytes, two of whom stood near the door.

"You!" the Grandmaster snapped, pointing at one of his followers. "Go and find out what has happened. SkyHaven's defenses have been breached. And it isn't one of the other guilds, because I didn't feel them coming through the barriers. They're inside the fortress already! Within these very walls!"

Timothy, Leander thought.

"It's the boy," Nicodemus sneered, shooting a quick, cruel glance at Leander. "I'm sure of that. Doesn't it warm your heart, Professor? He came back for you. What wonderful bait you've made. Now I won't have to go to the trouble of tracking him down."

Adrenaline had given Leander a burst of strength, but now he felt himself flagging once more. The touch of the wraiths seemed to be spilling sorrow into the places inside him left hollow by Nicodemus's leeching. Still, he managed to scowl at the archmage.

"I think you'll find . . . that Timothy Cade . . . is more than you bargained for," he said, voice ragged, words halting.

The Grandmaster did not have to say anything to show how absurd he thought this idea. He sniffed and turned to see that the acolyte he had instructed was still standing by the door, waiting for further commands.

"What are you doing? Go!"

The young mage nodded gravely, turned, and rushed to the door. It opened for him, swinging outward so that Leander could see the corridor beyond, could see freedom waiting for him.

In the corridor a lone figure stood in the shadows. It was strange and awkward, bent slightly and with something jutting from the side of its head. The moment it started to move, Leander knew who lurked there, who it was that had come to his rescue.

As if to announce himself, the release valve on the side of the metal man's head whistled with a spray of steam. The acolyte who had opened the door shouted in alarm and raised both hands, though whether to cast a spell or ward off the mechanical man, Leander could not tell.

Sheridan clanked forward with surprising speed and shot out a metal fist. His blow struck the acolyte on the side of the head and the man toppled to the ground in a splay of limbs. Timothy Cade's greatest invention—and greatest friend—raced past the unconscious man toward the other acolytes who were gathered near the door. Several of them seemed to be too stunned to react immediately, but a female acolyte stepped away from the others and began to mutter a spell, the fingers of her left hand twisting as she drew sigils in the air.

A panel slid open in the mechanical man's chest and a thin tube jutted out. Liquid fire sprayed from the tube and the red-haired woman screamed as it engulfed her left hand. She clutched her hand against her body and tried to smother the flames with her tunic, dropping to the ground and rolling away from the door.

"Idiots!" Nicodemus shouted. "You're sorcerers! It's a thing! An object! Destroy it!"

With the Grandmaster distracted, Leander saw his opportunity. He was still weak and cold, but enough strength had returned to him that he was able to command his muscles again.

He let himself sag against the clutches of the shadow wraiths, then planted his feet firmly on the floor. Though he felt their dreadful darkness filling him where the magic had been drained, he had not been left completely powerless.

Across the room, Sheridan ran at the other acolytes. Steam hissed from the valve in his head and his red eyes glowed fiercely. The young mages had been shocked by his arrival and by his appearance as well—to them, Leander realized, Timothy's creations were their own sort of sorcery—but now they were recovering. Sheridan reached out and grabbed the nearest acolyte and thumped him against the wall. The man slid to the floor, disoriented. A mechanical arm with a buzz saw blade whirred to life as it jutted from his chest, and then another machine appeared from that same hollow in the metal man. This one fired sharp metal projectiles—what Timothy called nails—and two of the acolytes screamed as they were hit.

But there were too many of the Grandmaster's servants in that room. Nicodemus himself stood in the center of the chamber, eyes wide, his long mustache giving him an air of austere severity that only scratched the surface of his cruelty. He pointed a finger at the open door and it swung closed. Sheridan would not be leaving the room.

From across the chamber came several men draped in green, hooded robes, each with the emblem of a green eye woven into the chest. They did not run, but rather flew across the room, levitating. Leander had no idea when they had arrived—in his haze of pain he had not seen them enter—but these were no mere acolytes. They were full-fledged Alhazred sorcerers, like Leander himself. They raised their hands, flesh tinged green like their robes, and spheres of magical power burst to life around their fingers.

"Do not concern yourself, Grandmaster," one of the hooded

mages said, and his voice was a whisper that made Leander shudder to think what faces hid beneath those hoods.

Sheridan fought bravely, but the hooded ones were going to destroy him. They flew at the mechanical man, fists crackling with magic.

"Damn you, no!" Leander roared.

He tore himself away from the wraiths and felt their mouths and fingers ripped from his very soul. A cry of anguish escaped his lips but his pain did not slow his attack. Leander had hoped to attack Nicodemus directly, but with Sheridan in peril he had no choice but to alter that plan. He thrust out his hands and chanted a small string of words. Leander knew he did not have the power to defeat the hooded ones, but he could delay them for a moment.

They froze in midair, paralyzed in time.

But even as Leander stopped the veteran Alhazred sorcerers, the Grandmaster's young acolytes got the better of Sheridan, grabbing hold of him tightly from either side, avoiding the dangerous tools that jutted from his chest.

"Enough!" Nicodemus snapped, and with one long-taloned finger he sent a bolt of black light arcing across the room. The hex touched Sheridan's skull, and a moment later the mechanical man simply fell apart, limbs, trunk, and metal skull clattering to the floor in a heap.

The light went out of Sheridan's eyes.

"No!" Leander shouted, but he was exhausted and fell to his knees in the center of the room.

The Grandmaster turned toward him, sneering once more, and glanced at the wraiths.

"Shall we begin again?"

The wraiths moved in, mouths latching on to his flesh, shadow claws digging into him. The Grandmaster did not hesitate now.

He was no longer in the mood to toy with Leander.

"The boy is here," Lord Nicodemus said. "I believe I am done with you."

As he reached out to touch Leander's chest again, the far wall of the chamber exploded in a torrent of fire. At last something warmed the chill from Leander's flesh.

When Verlis had left his home to seek the aid of Argus Cade, he had never imagined his quest would lead him to the devil Nicodemus himself. But even with his family waiting for him, knowing that he was risking everything, he could not have refused Timothy his aid in this battle. Nicodemus was vile. Had he turned his back on this opportunity, no matter the cost, he would have shamed his entire tribe. Indeed, Verlis was here to help Timothy. But it was hardly a favor, for he would have relished the opportunity no matter what the circumstances.

Timothy knew his way around SkyHaven, and it had been obvious to them all that their destination ought to be the wing of the fortress that had been off limits to the boy while he had lived here. Finding the chamber that was most powerfully protected by the Grandmaster's magic had been simple enough for one with Verlis's sorcerous senses. With the rook flying above him and Ivar running behind, Verlis had led Timothy to the corridor beyond that chamber.

The boy went to the wall—careful to stay clear of Verlis's path—and put both his hands on it, disrupting whatever magical protections Nicodemus had placed there.

With a hiss Verlis spewed a blast of fire from his gullet that incinerated most of the wall, blowing pieces of stone into the room. A blazing brick struck a hooded Alhazred mage in the chest and his robes burst into flame.

Verlis folded his wings tight against his back and stepped into the vaulted chamber. In a sliver of a moment he took in the forces arrayed against them. There were perhaps six young mages, Nicodemus's acolytes, scattered on one side of the room, near the tall double doors. Several others were on the floor, injured or unconscious. The Wurm's entrance had disabled one of the hooded mages, but two remained, far more powerful than the acolytes.

Across the room a man was in the grasp of insidious, flitting shadows, creatures of magic unlike any Verlis had seen before. This, he knew, must be Leander Maddox.

And, of course, there was the Grandmaster himself. The moment Verlis focused his gaze upon Nicodemus, he felt an ancient hatred in his heart, as though the fury of all of his race was welling up within him. The Wurm opened his jaws and hissed at the Grandmaster. Fire flickered and heat bellowed up from his chest.

"Wurm!" Nicodemus shouted. "You dare? Filthy, stupid beast, you dare to enter my home?" The Grandmaster shook his head, shielding his eyes from the bright fire that still roared up from portions of the ruined wall, obscuring his view of Verlis and the corridor beyond. "How? I don't understand. Your kind do not have the magic to—"

"Don't need magic," Verlis growled, wings unfurling, curling his hands into deadly claws. "I'm adept enough, don't you doubt it. But I didn't need magic to get to you."

Verlis enjoyed the confusion in the archmage's eyes and the way his mouth worked as he searched for an answer. In a moment Nicodemus would do what he had always done— destroy the things he did not understand. But he was not going to get that moment.

The Wurm folded his wings again, knowing that his companions would have come up behind him in the chaos of fire and smoke.

When he put his wings down, the Grandmaster sputtered with fury, for Verlis had revealed his secret weapon, the way in which he had been able to break through the spells protecting this room.

Timothy Cade stood at his side, the black-feathered Edgar perched upon his shoulder.

"Boy," Nicodemus said, as though he were scolding the young man. "You have made me very, very angry."

Timothy uttered a soft laugh of amazement. "Good."

Nicodemus raised both hands and a massive wave of sickly yellow energy erupted from them, a hex that shot across the room at Timothy with a thunderous clamor. The two hooded mystics attacked as well, emerald light arcing like daggers from their fingers. Several of the acolytes were unprepared, but the others cast spells of their own. The air shimmered between them and the boy as the various magics collided and merged into a churning storm of malice that should have torn him apart.

The rook took flight, escaping the attack. But the boy did not move.

A rainbow of mist circled Timothy for a moment, and then dispersed. Verlis glanced down to see the boy's smile disappear, and then he started toward Nicodemus. From behind Timothy, the Asura warrior leaped into the room and quickly merged with the colors within. He was no mage, but Ivar was invisible to the acolytes, and with the burning debris and the smoke, he moved like a ghost. Edgar cawed loudly, drawing their attention, and Ivar raced to attack the acolytes.

Verlis turned on the hooded mystics, launching himself into the air in that vast chamber and breathing down a fountain of liquid fire upon them. The mystics defended themselves with magic Verlis himself knew. When they tried to use sorcery against him, he deflected their attacks as well.

And the battle was on.

Edgar shrieked and swooped above them and the mages sent spells searing the air toward him. The rook was far more than a bird, however. After all, he had been the familiar to the greatest mage in the world before serving Timothy and had been in combat hundreds of times.

"Caw! Caw! Run, you amateurs! There's only one way this is going to end!" Edgar cried as the rook darted down and raked his talons across the face of a pale-skinned acolyte.

The Asura warrior stepped behind one of the young mages, staff in hand, and he cracked the length of wood across the back of the man's skull. Before the acolyte had even hit the ground, Ivar had slipped away. Some of them were shouting at the others to find him, to stop the ghost, but they were frantic now and disorganized. In service to Nicodemus they had never imagined having to fight such an unorthodox battle. If it were mage versus mage, they would certainly have been prepared. But they were not prepared for this odd alliance of an Asura warrior, an angry rook, a fire-breathing Wurm, and an un-magician.

One of the acolytes froze, narrowing her eyes as she managed to get a glimpse of Ivar, despite his blending into the colors of the room. She lunged at him, and he easily sidestepped her attack and shot an elbow back into her face. This fight drew the attention of the others. Ivar shoved the woman backward into two of her companions, and then he slipped into a cloud of smoke and disappeared again.

All the while he kept track of his friends. Verlis fought the Alhazred mages valiantly, but neither the Wurm nor his opponents seemed able to get the upper hand. Edgar expertly avoided attack. But Ivar saw the array of metal parts on the floor and knew what had become of Sheridan. The Asura's heart was saddened by this, but there was nothing he could do for Sheridan now. There was, however, another ally who needed his aid. In the middle of the room, Leander Maddox was held captive by dark spirits, their ghostly lips fastened to Leander's flesh, feeding off him.

I must reach Leander Maddox, he thought.

Ivar continued to fight the acolytes, defeating them one by one. He wanted to be sure that Timothy could concentrate on facing Nicodemus. Then he would see what might be done about the dark spirits.

Timothy advanced across the room toward Nicodemus. The man was cruel and cunning and he knew he ought to have been frightened, yet he could not find any fear inside of him. The Grandmaster was a betrayer at best, and at worst . . . Timothy's heart ached when he glanced at Leander and the shadow creatures that were swarming around him. He did not want to know the worst of the things that Nicodemus had been responsible for.

"You've made a grievous error turning against me, boy. I am the only one in the world who can protect you from your enemies," Lord Nicodemus said imperiously. His long silver mustache quivered as he spoke, and he pointed an accusatory finger at Timothy.

"You are my enemy," Timothy replied. "And I can protect myself, thank you."

The Grandmaster's normally pale face grew dark red with fury, and he bared his teeth like an animal. With a grunt he muttered words in an ancient tongue and spread his hands wide. Then he spit at Timothy, but his spittle did not hit the ground. It did not land at all. In the blink of an eye it grew into a large sphere of purplish, oily mucous that passed right over Timothy, surrounding him, trapping him inside this strange bubble.

Or so Nicodemus had intended.

Timothy walked right through the bubble as though it wasn't there, and it burst upon contact with him. He strode up so that he was, at last, face-to-face with the archmage.

"Have I been gone that long?" Timothy asked, glaring at him. "Remember me? I'm the freak. The un-magician. I've come back for my friend. And for you, Nicodemus. I've come back for you."

Poisonous hatred filled the Grandmaster's eyes. Timothy could see Nicodemus weighing his options. The archmage knew he had been trained to fight by an Asura warrior. Nicodemus knew that magic could not harm him. Timothy allowed himself a quick glance around the room and he saw that his friends were doing quite well. The acolytes were all unconscious or moaning on the ground, injured. Two other sorcerers remained, and it appeared that Verlis, Ivar, and Edgar had joined forces against them. It would not be long before Nicodemus and his shadow creatures were the only ones standing against them.

But Nicodemus must have seen this too, for the moment Timothy glanced away, Nicodemus turned and strode to where Leander hung in the midst of the room, suspended several inches off the ground by those black phantoms that preyed upon him. Timothy tried to stop the Grandmaster, but too late.

Nicodemus reached toward Leander. "Another step and I'll kill him."

This time Timothy smiled.

Nearly invisible, Ivar appeared beside the Grandmaster and knocked his hand away from Leander.

Timothy raced at Nicodemus. The Grandmaster tried to strike him but the boy dodged his blow, then struck out with a rigid backhand. His knuckles rapped the Grandmaster's skull and the archmage stumbled to one side. Timothy stepped into a second blow, a flat palm against the Grandmaster's chest, and Nicodemus fell onto the floor. He looked ridiculous sitting there on the ground with wide eyes, trying to catch his breath.

"The spirits, Timothy!" Ivar called.

The un-magician turned and saw that the shadow creatures seemed now to be strangling Leander and sinking their fingers into his flesh, penetrating him without making visible wounds. But one look at how pale Leander's face was, at the despair in his eyes, and Timothy knew that invisible wounds could be infinitely worse.

"Leander!" he shouted, and he ran to the man, his friend and mentor, the only mage in this world who had ever really looked out for him. Timothy threw his arms around Leander and held him in an embrace.

The mage went rigid at Timothy's touch and then abruptly began to sway. Confused and alarmed, he tried to hold Leander up, to keep him from falling. Timothy grabbed hold of him and saw that there was new light in Leander's eyes, a new awareness that was there in spite of the mage's weakness.

Then Timothy saw pale, misty figures flitting about above him and around Leander. His breath caught in his throat as he realized that the shadow creatures were gone. *But no,* he thought. *Not gone. Just free. Free from Nicodemus.*

Leander crumbled to his knees and then slid to the floor. Timothy tried to hold him up but the burly mage was simply too huge. Still there was a thin, exhausted smile on Leander's face as he looked up at Timothy.

"Tim," the mage said.

"I don't understand. What happened?"

"They were all . . . draining me. Attached to me," Leander explained, eyelids fluttering, on the verge of unconsciousness. "Grandmaster . . . leeched their magic out, fed off it for himself. Murdered them, but kept their shades as slaves."

Timothy glanced around at the wispy white silhouettes that flitted up toward the ceiling, drifting out through the walls.

Leander coughed, and when he spoke his voice was a rasp. "When you touched me, whatever it is in you that cancels out magic . . . it freed them . . . freed their spirits from Nicodemus's control."

Timothy shook his head in horror. *Stolen magic,* he thought. *Nicodemus survived on stolen magic, kept himself young, made himself powerful. But that kind of power doesn't mean anything to me.* Carefully he touched Leander's face, frowning, so many questions on his mind.

Yet in spite of his horror, he was also elated. He was an abomination to the mages of this world. Without magic, they thought of him as useless at best. A freak at worst. But un-magic could be a useful power of its own. *I did it!* The thought raced through his mind, over and over. *I did it! I saved Leander. And all of those poor mages . . . I stopped Nicodemus.*

Guess I'm not so useless after all.

He smiled, feeling better than he ever had since leaving the Island of Patience. Then he heard Ivar shout his name.

Timothy spun in time to see Nicodemus crouched over Sheridan's shattered remains. The pieces of the mechanical man were scattered on the floor. He had seen this when he entered the room and his heart had ached at the sight, but he had tried to tell himself that Sheridan might be rebuilt, that Leander was the one in danger at the moment.

Now the Grandmaster reached into the pile of metal parts and shot to his feet, clutching one of the tools that Timothy had built into Sheridan's chest cavity. It was a metal prong, and upon its end was a razor-sharp circular saw. Nicodemus smiled, his weathered, papery skin wrinkling hideously as he started toward Timothy.

It wasn't over yet.

Ivar raced across the room, his footfalls silent upon the floor. His skin coloring shifted to try to match his surroundings, but he called out Timothy's name again, and he drew Nicodemus's attention. The archmage raised an arm and with an effortless flick of his wrist he struck the Asura warrior with a hex that sent him spinning across the chamber to crash into the wall.

Edgar cawed and swooped down at him, but the Grandmaster used magic to lift some of the still-smoldering stones from the floor and throw them at the rook. Timothy's familiar was caught in the left wing by a piece of smoking debris, and it singed his feathers, causing him to crash to the ground with a panicked caw.

"Timothy!" Verlis roared. But the Wurm could do nothing. One of the hooded mystics was still standing, and it was all Verlis could do to shield himself from the mage's magical attacks on the other side of the room. His wings were folded tight against his back and he vomited fire at the mage, whose robe and hood had been scorched and whose face was charred and blistered. Yet the mage battled on.

Timothy faced Nicodemus alone.

"You think because magic cannot harm you that you cannot be harmed?" the Grandmaster snarled, marching toward him. "This won't be the first time I have killed with my bare hands, boy. And I'll wager it won't be the last."

Timothy waited for Nicodemus to reach him. "I'll take that wager," he said.

The saw blade glinted in the chamber light. The Grandmaster lunged. But Timothy had been trained for combat by Ivar, and without magic Nicodemus was nothing but a vicious old man. Tim did not dodge out of the way. Instead he simply turned his body to one side and grabbed hold of Nicodemus's wrist. The

Grandmaster fought against his grip, and Timothy grasped the other wrist as well.

Lord Nicodemus gasped, his eyes wide, and his lips peeled back from his teeth. His jaws gaped and he began to shudder. Timothy tried to pull his hands away, to draw back, but he could not. He could only stare into the horrifying grimace on the Grandmaster's face as a sudden fountain of silver light erupted from inside the archmage.

"What . . . what is it?" Timothy whispered.

But even before the words were out of his mouth he knew the answer. It was magic. All the magic that Nicodemus had leeched from other mages. Just as his touch had disrupted the control that the Grandmaster had over those poor shadow creatures, it had now shut down the old man's power over the magic he had stolen.

The blast of silver light blew a massive hole in the ceiling of the chamber. Cracks spiderwebbed along the walls, and fissures opened in the floor with a thunderous tumult.

"No . . . no, it's mine," the archmage whispered, eyes sinking into his skull, voice becoming little more than a whisper.

Then Lord Nicodemus, the Grandmaster of the Order of Alhazred, withered away to dry, papery skin and brittle bones, and then even those crumbled to ash.

It was true after all.

Without magic he was nothing.

EPILOGUE

Alastor slunk through the inky darkness of SkyHaven's lower levels, ever so careful not to be seen. *They* were searching for him, and he was not about to allow himself to be discovered. The familiar missed the fine meals provided by the Grandmaster, but would make do with the simple pleasures of SkyHaven's vermin population.

The cat moved deeper into the bowels of the fortress, darting from one pool of darkness to the next, and soon arrived at the enormous engines that thrummed with the magical energies that kept the castle in the sky afloat. The space behind the engines was cramped, but well hidden, and the magic emanating from them would make it difficult for any spell to locate him here. During the day he rested, but after dark he emerged to prowl the empty halls.

Outside the sun was rising. Alastor slid into his place behind the engines, surrounded by the bones of vermin he had caught. He did not know how long his life would be this way, how long he would need to remain hidden, but he was not concerned. The cat closed his eyes, content in the knowledge that he would know when it was time. He would wait patiently for a sign that would bring him out of the shadows, and then he would exact horrible vengeance upon those who had wronged his master.

Alastor began to purr as he drifted off to sleep.

It is only a matter of time.

Timothy wanted to go home. He would have felt far more comfortable at his father's estate—*his* estate, now—and with the portal his father had created he could go back and forth to the Island of Patience. That was what he felt he needed now more than anything else, a few days on the island, beneath the warm sun. The way it used to be, just Timothy, Ivar, and Sheridan. And now Edgar.

But it wasn't to be. Not yet.

It had been four days since the Grandmaster's evil had been discovered, four days since Timothy had faced Nicodemus and destroyed him. Chaos had prevailed in that time. The Parliament of Mages was investigating, of course, and Leander was still among its agents. The Order of Alhazred was being controlled, for the moment, by a tribunal of other guild masters, whose responsibility was to root out those who had been aware of Nicodemus's crimes, even taken part in them. Those loyal to the Parliament and to the order, but not part of the Grandmaster's inner circle, were being restructured as a new ruling body for the Alhazred guild.

It was a time-consuming process. Timothy was bored with politics, but as SkyHaven was the site for the tribunal and the investigation, and Leander had to remain on the floating fortress, Timothy had decided to remain with him. When Leander could leave, they would leave together.

Though he had bragged to Nicodemus that he could take care of himself, and he knew it was mostly true, Timothy wanted to keep his friends around him. A simple spell from a healing mage had repaired Edgar's burnt wing. Though Ivar still had to deal with disdain and shabby treatment from most of the mages he met, he had his own room right beside Timothy's now. Leander had insisted.

Yet there was another reason why Timothy had wanted to

remain at SkyHaven for the time being. His workshop was there.

The sun shone brightly outside the windows and bathed the workshop in the warm golden glow of late afternoon. A cool breeze rushed through the room and the sound of the surf far below was a comfort to Timothy as he bent over one of his worktables, intent upon his task. Despite all the other things he had created, he had never been so consumed by his work.

Timothy let out a long breath and wiped his face with a rag. Before him on the table lay the silent, unmoving form of Sheridan. For days Timothy had been repairing him, rebuilding him, using both original and new parts. In some ways he had been improving Sheridan. The new gyros in his legs and lower torso would give him better balance and reduce the noise he made. His upper body would be stronger now. The steam engine inside him would pump more smoothly.

The only thing Timothy had left untouched was Sheridan's head. He had not even attempted to start the mechanical man's steam pump. Timothy knew that it was possible, even likely, that Sheridan had suffered enough damage that he would have lost all of his memory, all of his personality. For days he had pushed such thoughts away and continued at his work.

When Sheridan was done, when Timothy had finished with his repairs and upgrades, only then would he turn the steam pump on and wait to see if the light would go on in Sheridan's eyes.

He took a long drink from a glass of water and glanced out the window at the ocean and the distant shore. Then he picked up the last of the new gyros he had to install and bent to fit it into place.

There was a knock at the door.

Timothy turned around quickly, the events of previous days still fresh in his mind. It would be some time before he was willing to give his trust to strangers again.

"Yes," he called.

The door opened and Leander stepped into the room, his massive frame filling the doorway.

"Still at work?" the burly mage asked, nodding his great head toward the worktable.

"Until he's done." Timothy smiled tiredly. "I know, I know, you want me to rest. And I will. He's almost ready."

Leander cast a sad glance at Sheridan's still form and walked farther into the workshop. He rested one huge hand on the mechanical man's chest and turned to Timothy.

"He saved my life, Tim. I hope you can save his."

Timothy gave a curt nod but he did not want to discuss it, so he changed the subject. "What's happening upstairs? Have they sorted things out at last, disbanded the tribunal?"

A grave expression passed across Leander's face. "They aren't going to disband the tribunal. Not for a while. The Order of Alhazred has its new Grandmaster, but the tribunal will still be overseeing our Guild for some time, just to make certain there aren't any other schemes that Nicodemus set in motion before he . . . before his evil was discovered."

Timothy let his gaze drop, but only for a moment. "You said they chose a new Grandmaster?" he asked, looking up. "Who is it?"

Leander raised a hand and pushed his fingers through his shaggy red beard, gaze shifting around the room as though the question made him uncomfortable. Timothy understood immediately. He grinned and poked the big man in the stomach.

"It's you, isn't it? That's wonderful, Leander. That's . . . wait a moment." His smile faded. They had made plans, and now those plans were being dismantled. "It means you can't come back and live at the house, doesn't it?"

Leander nodded slowly. "The Parliament and the tribunal have decided it would be best for the Grandmaster to continue to oversee the guild from SkyHaven. If there are still those who are loyal to Nicodemus, any schemes they have planned would likely originate here. There are dozens of hidden rooms and passages. We've only begun to unearth the secrets of this place. So, yes, I'm afraid I have to stay."

Timothy felt a tiny ache in his heart as he thought of his father's house and of the Island of Patience. He would visit them both, and soon, but for now . . .

"Then I will stay with you. We all will."

The new Grandmaster smiled. "I'm pleased. I will worry about you less if you're close by."

"Don't forget, though," Timothy said. "I promised Verlis I would return to his world with him, that I'd help him save his family."

Leander nodded. "And I know you will honor that promise. I will offer you what help I can. When will you leave?"

Timothy glanced down at Sheridan's lifeless form. "Just as soon as I can. The day after tomorrow, perhaps. Or the next day at the latest."

Several moments of silence passed between them as Timothy and his friend considered all of the changes that were taking place in their lives. Then Timothy frowned.

"Has the investigation turned up anything about Nicodemus's master?"

"Nothing yet," Leander said gravely. "I know I heard him speaking to someone, someone to whom he deferred. That is one of the main reasons why the Parliament wants me to remain at SkyHaven. With all of its secrets, it's possible that whoever was giving Nicodemus orders may still be here somewhere." His brow furrowed with concern. "There may be certain dangers for you here, Timothy, but I've given it a great deal of thought. I don't think you'd be any safer at home. At least here, we're all together."

Timothy nodded slowly in agreement.

"And what of your own search?" Leander went on. "Any sign of the mysterious girl in the green dress?"

Timothy felt himself flush a little and he smiled. "Nothing yet. But I saw her, Leander. I did. If she hadn't guided us, shown me where to land, we never would have reached you in time."

"The tribunal has kept track of all the comings and goings at SkyHaven, and there's been no report of a girl fitting the description you gave. The guards and groundskeepers and mages have all been spoken to, and no one remembers her."

"But they would," Timothy said firmly. "She was remarkable. It's possible she lived in a part of the fortress that was hidden away, but Ivar has been searching for days and has found no trace of her. It's almost as though she was a ghost."

"Or a very powerful mage in her own right, to hide her trail from an Asura warrior," Leander suggested.

Timothy nodded, remembering the girl's sad, green eyes. "True, but not in league with Nicodemus. I don't think so, at any rate. There was just something about her."

Leander smiled knowingly. "I'm sure there was. Now then, I've got things to attend to. I'll see you at supper?"

"Yes. I'll be there."

The red-haired mage—the Grandmaster of the Order of Alhazred—turned and left the room, pulling the door shut behind him. Timothy watched him go and then returned his attention to the metal man on the worktable. Unmoving. Silent as though dead.

And suddenly Timothy could not wait anymore. Sheridan was not completely repaired, but he had to know. His chest felt tight and he gnawed his lower lip as he set aside the final gyro he had been about to install. The steam engine was ready to go. There was water in place. There was chaktury coal, which would burn for years if properly ventilated. All he needed was a match..

Timothy reached for the lamp on the table and opened it, Hungry Fire flickering brightly in the ocean breeze. He lit the tip of a small piece of kindling, then lowered it and slid the burning tip carefully inside Sheridan's chest cavity. He touched it to the chaktury coal, and the small stone began to burn.

He shook out the match and quickly closed the engine, snapping the furnace into place and then closing the chest cavity as well. There were noises inside Sheridan's metal body as the coal heated the water and the steam pump slowly began to come to life. Timothy held his breath and waited. There was a rattle and a hiss and he could hear the whir of the pump as it started up. He stared expectantly at Sheridan's face.

A full minute went by and his heart sank.

Timothy lowered his eyes and let out a shuddering breath.

And a gasp of steam answered in reply.

He looked up to see that the red lights of Sheridan's eyes were looking at him.

"Timothy . . . what happened?" the mechanical man asked. "Was I sleeping?"

"Yes," Timothy said. "Yes, Sheridan, you were sleeping. Time to wake up now."

OutCast

DRAGON SECRETS

by Christopher Golden & Thomas E. Sniegoski

THERE'S A NEW EVIL IN TOWN

After fighting for his survival in the city of Arcanum, Timothy must repay a debt and help his friend Verlis's clan, the Wurm. Though the Wurm are known as bloodthirsty, child-eating dragons, Timothy has agreed to help bring peace to their war-torn world because he knows all too well that appearances can be fatally deceptive—and history can be riddled with lies.

But before Timothy can travel to the Wurm world, ruthless Constable Grimshaw imprisons Verlis deep under the sea. Now Grimshaw is on a manhunt to destroy Timothy and his friends. Timothy has no choice but to do the impossible: outrun Grimshaw and free Verlis. For the fate of the Wurm rests on his shoulders. . . .

CHRISTOPHER GOLDEN is an award-winning, best-selling novelist. He has written dozens of books, including many works of horror and fantasy for both teens and adults. Christopher has also written dozens of comics, including titles based on such famous characters as Batman and Spider-Man. He lives with his family in Bradford, Massachusetts. His Web site is www.christophergolden.com.

THOMAS E. SNIEGOSKI is a novelist, comic-book writer, and pop culture journalist. Tom has been working in the comic-book field for ten years, for companies such as Marvel and DC. He lives with his wife, LeeAnne, and loyal retriever, Mulder, in Stoughton, Massachusetts. His Web site is www.sniegoski.com.